Flight

6

David Henry

New Alaska Library
Published by David Henry Books, a division of
Hawaii Vacation Group (USA) Inc.

Grateful acknowledgement is made to
Encompass Multimedia Film Works (USA), Inc.

Set in Times New Roman

Cover design by
Duehmig Imagery LLC (USA), Inc.

PUBLISHER'S NOTE
This is a work of fiction. Names, characters, places, and the incidents either are the product of
the author's imagination or are used fictitiously, and any resemblance to actual persons, living
or dead, business establishments, events, or locales is entirely coincidental.
The publisher does not have any control over and does not assume any responsibility for
the author or third party Web sites or their content.

Visit us at:
Davidhenrybooks.net

In Memory of

Captain Doug Lampe

&

First Officer Mathew Bell

To my father Joseph,

In all my worldly travels,

you remain the greatest man

I have ever met

AUTHOR'S NOTE

The story that follows is a novel based on true events both in the aviation community and in the world of the terrorists, the associated timeline and association with one another is just that; a story.

Raine Airways is a fictitious airline but the loss of Flight 6 in Dubai is true. At this book's release, the full cause of what started the intense fire onboard the jet resulting in the crash has yet to be disclosed.

All of the characters and their names are fictitious. I speculate that the events, such as the demise of Anwar al-Awlaki unfolded somewhat like presented here, though I am unable to give full justice to the real men and women that perform the drone aircraft operations due the secrecy of their work.

I have attempted to portray the countries that surround the story as realistic as possible, including the cities of Dubai, Sana'a, and Radda. Each town and village mentioned throughout the book is real and I hope that they are portrayed as accurate as I remember.

For the city of Dubai, it is a paradise on the seashore and I encourage anyone to take time and visit. The people are wonderful and their culture truly inspiring.

It's a semi-true story

Believe it or not

I made up a few things

And there's some I forgot,

--Jimmy Buffett

List of Characters

Scott James	747 Captain
Margaret (Maggie) Hurley	NTSB Inspector
Don Lambert	Captain of Flight 6
Mike Barrett	F/O of Flight 6
Mark Mitchell	CIA Agent
Greg Cochran	Raine Airways F/O
Da'ud (David) Hassen	UAE's Investigator
Jafar Khah Hamdard	Pakistani Worker
Agib Khah Hamdard	Jafar's son
Ibrahim al-Asiri	Terrorist
Karim al-Asiri	Ibrahim's brother
Hadid al-Otaibi	Friend of Ibrahim
Atash	Ibrahim's cousin
Anwar al-Awlaki	Main Terrorist
Samir Khan	#2 Terrorist

Faria	al-Awlaki's first wife
Saadia	al-Awlaki's second wife
Suha	al-Awlaki's daughter
Jim Prescott	Margaret's boss
Josh Barad	Dubai Police
Jenny Christine	Secretary at Raine
John Fenton	Raine Airways
Lamar Wallace	Drone pilot
Olivia Rose	Drone Sentry
Derek Johnson	FBI Agent
Shauna Marshall	Homeland Security
Rob Morris	MI5 Agent
Dahi Knalfan	Dubai Police
Andy Owen	Raine Airways IRO
Ethan Hurley	Margaret's dead husband

Part I

SETUP

RADDA

Ibrahim al-Asiri sat, a rifle across his knees, among the six men who had gathered on the second floor of a four-story house built of gray-red stone and mud bricks on the southern edge of Radda, a small village just south of the capital of the Al Bayda Governorate of Yemen. Their leader—an imam, wearing a gold-colored bisht and a white kufi skullcap—sat on one of the many large pillows that lay on the dusty wooden floor of the room, all dimly lit by a single light bulb suspended from a chipping stucco ceiling. The curtains had been drawn tightly closed, and the air was thick with smoke from the hookah that was being passed among the six men. A small, noisy fan in the corner oscillated back and forth. The room was scattered with AK-47 rifles, small arms, and several rocket-propelled grenades. This was a dangerous land, ruled by the gun and controlled by these leaders of al-Qaeda.

Ibrahim and the others, all in traditional Arabic garb, had

just come from evening prayers at the Amerya Mosque, an Islamic school where the imam preached. This imam was in hiding from the authorities, and he now kept his public exposure to a minimum. He had just preached a sermon on the topic of jihad against the US and Israel in which he had called on his followers, and all Muslims, to take up arms against the *Kuffar*. Ibrahim—and his brother, now far away in Cologne, Germany—were ones who had answered that call.

The imam was a young looking man with a dark, unkempt beard and never seen without his wire-rimmed glasses. He spoke with authority to his men, but always kept a kind smile.

The congregation of followers gathered around him was relatively small, yet strongly devoted. The imam's second in command was named Samir Khan. He sat on a pillow on the far side of the room with a rifle across his legs, wearing a dirty thawb. The reading glasses suspended on the end of his nose were broken, held together with a small wire. Kahn, like the imam, held dual citizenship in the US and Pakistan, and he also spoke fluent English. He was editor and publisher of the online jihadist magazine *INSPIRE*, and he was the imam's most loyal follower.

Ibrahim often thought of himself as more of a disciple to the imam than a mere follower. He was a Saudi-born terrorist whose specialty was explosives and was now the principal designer and builder of 90 percent of all the bombs that came in or out of the Arab peninsula. Ibrahim knew that despite his talents in this area, his collogues didn't trust him; they thought of him as the most volatile member of their group, with a destructive personality and a somewhat lower IQ. But he knew they needed him. They needed his expertise with explosives and his creative ability for their bombs construction. He smiled; one day he would prove to them just how intelligent he was, how much more he could do in service to their cause.

The plan Ibrahim and the others had gathered tonight to

complete was simple. They would ship pre-made bombs to their counterparts, the sleeper cells that lay in wait in Chicago, New York, and Cologne. The trial shipments sent over a month ago had successfully reached their destinations, and now the bombs were ready. Each had been cleverly designed and hidden inside name-brand cartridges of printer ink, each of which contained one pound of the high explosive pentaerythritol tetra nitrate, *PETN*: ten times the amount needed to level a house. The shipment to Cologne contained two cartridges—over two pounds of PETN—and each was equipped with cell phone circuitry for remote detonation.

Their target in Cologne would be the giant Christian cathedral called Kölner Dom. The cathedral was one of the largest in the world, playing host to thousands of visitors each day, making it the perfect target for the imam and his band of terrorists. Construction of this massive Catholic church started in 1248 and was officially completed 632 years later in 1880. Ibrahim gloated to think of it: the grand building had survived the onslaught bombing of the Allies during World War II, but it would not survive the bomb Ibrahim had designed.

The bomb material was a plastic explosive undetectable to x-ray screening or trained sniffer dogs, the type needed to get through the tight security imposed on all cargo that entered Western nations. The quantity and quality of the explosives was weapons grade, a type normally available only to large governments. The imam's political connections and the financial support he had developed throughout the Middle East had made it possible to obtain his needed equipment.

The imam had spent the last three years working out the details of this plot. Each sleeper cell was coordinated by one of the men in this room tonight. Ibrahim worked the Cologne operation, Samir Khan had Chicago, and the imam himself had New York. Suicide bombers had been recruited and were in place for each assignment.

Now, the imam motioned for the other men to sit. The quiet conversations throughout the room came to a stop and each man took a seat around his leader.

"Welcome, my friends and brothers," the imam began. "We gather tonight, the last night before we send our weapons of death into the belly of the infidels."

Smiles and restrained cheers went up. Ibrahim bowed toward the imam as he sat on his pillow, while Samir and those closer to the imam reached for his hand. Most of the men were chewing khat, the green plant leaf with an amphetamine-like stimulant that many Yemenis indulged in. The imam abstained from the practice.

He allowed himself a satisfied smile as he glanced at Ibrahim, who had placed the final items in the boxes that were now ready to be sealed shut. The innocuous-looking packages contained music CDs, clothes, and books printed in English, as well as the printer cartridges with the explosives. Ibrahim was proud of the work he had done: The planning to reach this night had been long and hard, and he shared in the great level of achievement everyone felt now that each package was complete.

It was Ibrahim's brother Karim who would carry the bomb to its demise in Cologne. Ibrahim and his brother had worked closely with the imam since they had arrived in Yemen from their home country of Saudi Arabia. Both brothers had been orphaned as children and had attended the Imam College of Islamic Law in Saudi Arabia, an orphanage for lost boys. Their radical Islamic teachings had begun at an early age, and now, as young adults, their entire lives were steeped in the fog of jihad and martyrdom. Ibrahim had even been sent to Iran to learn the fine art of explosives and bomb construction, where he had developed a small network of finance and support for his cause.

The packages would leave no trace back to the imam and

his group. The imam had instructed his third wife, Aminah, to steal the identification cards from two female visitors during a women's afternoon tafrutas earlier in the week.

Aminah and the imam's daughter Suha would deliver the packages to shipping centers in central Sana'a, their faces cloaked behind the black veils worn by most Yemeni women. Between the full veils, the stolen national identification cards, and the false return addresses on each of the packages, no questions would be asked, and there would be no way to trace the packages back to the senders.

Suddenly the room was quiet. The electricity in the building had been lost; the bulb hanging from the ceiling went dark, and the fan ceased its noisy comfort. No one was surprised; rolling blackouts plagued this area of the Yemeni nation. No one ever knew when the power would come back on. No one ever assumed that it would, and if it did, it would last only several hours at a time before failing again. *Yet another reason to hate the rich and powerful West and their allies*, Ibrahim thought as he and the others sat and finished their work, huddled together on the floor in a room now lit only by candles and oil lamps that barely cut through the lingering hookah smoke.

There were bigger things that might go wrong with this operation than a blackout, however; Ibrahim was aware of that. But he also knew that the imam was not one to operate without a backup plan. In the event that the explosive packages were found before they made it to their destinations across the globe, the imam and his followers would build and ship them again, but this time, they would place them aboard westbound cargo aircraft themselves.

Ibrahim, with a connection in Dubai, was working that exact angle. They had no operatives at the airport in Dubai at this date in time, but they did have intensive persuasive recruitment procedures. One way or another, he knew, the imam would carry forth his jihad, and he was proud that the imam trusted him to play such a large role in it. The imam that sat before Ibrahim and this group of jihadists was Anwar al-Awlaki.

Anwar al-Awlaki was a US citizen, born in New Mexico in 1971 to Yemeni parents and held dual citizenships. His father, Nasser al-Awlaki, had been a Fulbright scholar, earning his master's degree in agricultural economics at New Mexico State University and his doctorate at the University of Nebraska. After working at the University of Minnesota, Nasser had returned to Yemen with his family when Anwar was seven years old, where he had served as agriculture minister and then as the president of Sana'a University.

Anwar had returned to the United States in 1991 to attend college, earning a BS in civil engineering at Colorado State University and a master's in education at San Diego State University. As a young man, he had spent time in a Yemeni prison for petty theft. It was there that he became enthralled with the radical Muslim movement and jihad training. After a visit to Afghanistan in the aftermath of the Soviet Occupation, a hatred for all things Western began to develop within him. He had witnessed the destruction of Islamic villages and mosques and the killing of innocent civilians by the atheist communists. Here he had met a young Arab fighter, a Saudi named Osama bin Laden who inspired Anwar to continue the war against the West, to carry forth the jihad that these al-Qaeda fighters had begun.

Since Anwar spoke fluent English and Arabic, al-Qaeda considered him a valuable asset, and he was the main translator of their message of jihad for the benefit of non-Arabic speaking Muslims around the world. His name had continued to surface in numerous terrorist plots inside the US, UK, and Canada: Many of al-Awlaki's recorded radical preaching's had been discovered on personal CDs and laptop computers belonging to terror suspects. Rumors abounded that the imam had been a principal player in the September 11, 2001 attacks in the US.

On the night of this meeting in Radda, al-Awlaki stood as the ranking member of al-Qaeda in the Arab Peninsula— AQAP, in NATO talk—and he was on the United States' targeted killing order. And soon—if his plan succeeded, he knew—he would be in the crosshairs as one of the most wanted men in the world.

Ibrahim sealed the final package with tape and secured the address labels on the top of each box. He felt a great sense of accomplishment at having his latest creations ready, almost in the hands of his brother and the other soon-so-be martyrs. Within days the infidels would be brought to their knees as a result of his hard work and dedication. This was one of his proudest moments.

ALASKA

The window alongside his desk was open, a slight breeze into the den mixed the aroma of blooming cottonwood trees with the smell of fresh brewed coffee from Scott's cup. His house had a magnificent view of Turn Again Arm and Cook Inlet, the bay stretching out from Anchorage into the Gulf of Alaska. The sun reflected off the snow-capped peaks of three active volcanoes that lay across the bay. They would be sun kissed for hours.

It was the peak of Alaska summer, and the northern sky had been nearly daylight the entire night. The weather, typical for Anchorage at this time of year, was sixty-eight degrees with bright sunshine: sunset at eleven in the evening, the sun merely dropping and staying just below the horizon, soon to rise and bring the morning sunshine back over the Chugach Mountains by three a.m.

Scott James had watched the sun's slow ascent over the mountains while he sat at his desk, putting the final touches on a book that he was writing. He could hear the seagulls play and squawk at each other flying up the mountainside from the coastline below. They had a keen eye for anything that looked eatable and would swoop down at anything that looked like food. Scott always offered them what he had in the way of food scraps, so the gulls and magpies did a daily fly-by to pick at anything he'd left on his porch rail. *If I ever get tired of looking at this*, he thought, *it's time to move south.* But he knew that wouldn't happen. He had no desire to move back to the lower forty-eight with its insane traffic, scorching hot summers, and fishing that could never match Alaska's. He had found his home.

Scott was forty-seven years old, six feet one, medium build, and hoping to hang on to the last of his blond hair. He had grown up an Ohio farm boy, one destined to be a farmer himself had he not flown that Cessna while in high school. That flight had changed everything for Scott, and he was soon off to college with the hope of becoming an airline pilot. Scott had attended Ohio State University, where he earned a degree in Aviation. He'd started his career flying small airplanes right out of school: night flights, mostly, where he moved cancelled checks, auto parts, iced down transplant organs, almost anything they could fit in the back seat to cities around the Eastern U.S. *Those were the days* he thought. *No money and living with your parents. Now that was a tough gig.*

But he had made it to bigger airplanes and better flying. He was now a Boeing 747 captain for Raine Airways. The *seven-four*, in pilot-speak, was his favorite of all the jets he had flown over the years, and he hoped, if at all possible, to fly it until he retired. He enjoyed his trips starting from Anchorage and flying to the Far and Middle East, with stops in Asia and Europe. Soon Australia would be added to his list of destinations. Scott had yet to visit Australia, and he was looking forward to a new continent, as well as a few new red pins stuck in the large world map that he kept hung on his den wall to display his worldwide destinations.

Scott finished the last of his coffee, saved his file and

turned off the computer then called his dog. They were off to the airport to pickup Maggie, his girlfriend coming on from Washington DC. The drive was short and Scott was soon waiting in his spacious GMC Yukon at the Anchorage International Airport. He had purchased the large SUV before moving to Alaska, and now that he found himself living in the North, he considered it a perfect match. From where he sat, he could see the Chugach Mountains rising to over eight thousand feet on the eastern side of the city, and he noted that the winter snow had almost vanished.

He was by himself, save for his dog Bair, asleep in the back seat. His longhaired black lab looked like a small black bear, so his name—spelled after Scott's mother's maiden name—came fairly easy. But except for Bair—and except for Maggie, whose flight, he reminded himself, should be approaching at any minute—it seemed as if he'd always been by himself since he had moved to Alaska six summers ago. Typically clad in flip-flops, shorts, and a cotton Hawaiian shirt, he knew he fit more the beach bum ideal than the Alaska outdoorsman. He sat contemplating his life and how he had arrived so far north when he was more of a sunshine and warm water type of guy. But the view that lay out his window, he knew, made up for most of the cool weather.

As he waited, the bush pilots took off from Lake Hood Seaport just to the east, one after another transporting their would-be salmon slayers to all parts of Alaska in hopes of the best fishing of their lives. He watched, hoping to see his close friend and long-time bush pilot Ron Hulse take off in his de Havilland Beaver, carrying his latest passengers into the remote parts of Alaska. Scott's mind wandered to those wild streams, some of them rarely touched by humans at least— before the last several years. He and Ron had spent many memorable seasons fishing together in streams all over Alaska. But some salmon runs seemed to be depleting from many of the trustworthy steams, pushing many anglers further out into normally pristine areas in their quest for the ever-elusive sockeye salmon, the red gold of Alaska. He couldn't wait to be back at it himself, and he made a mental note to call his friend in the evening for an updated fishing report. Fishing in Alaska was Scott's passion, his constant endeavor. It was fishing that had been his real motivation moving to Alaska.

Scott watched the lone security officer slowly walk her beat back and forth as cars came and went, having picked up their newly arrived quests. Security always seemed a little lighter at the Anchorage airport compared to the other airports Scott operated in and out of around the world. Anchorage liked to put on a different front, much more relaxed, friendlier, almost like the Caribbean Islands. Scott found that part of Alaska ironic: For such a large state, many of the local mindsets reminded him of "island time." *Manana*, Scott would say, quoting one of his favorite Jimmy Buffet songs.

Maggie could not be here soon enough, he thought. Margaret Hurley—Maggie, to Scott—was his steady girl, or as steady as they could manage at three thousand miles apart.

Scott had been happily married once, but his divorce had been a long time coming, and when it finally came, the financial cost was higher than he had expected. His colleagues that had gone through this *Aviation Induced Divorce* had all made it through and were doing well. Scott did too. His life was the best it had ever been—busy schedule, many outdoor adventures—and after six years, he was still enjoying life as a single man again.

And then, while on assignment for his airline at a National Transportation Safety Board meetings in Washington DC, Scott met Maggie. Scott's airline, Raine Airways, had lost an airliner, a DC-8 in Greensboro, North Carolina to an onboard fire. There'd been no loss of life, but the aircraft was destroyed. The fire had started in flight, and the crew had done an exceptional job of getting the plane on the ground, but the fire was intense and the resulting heat and meltdown had eliminated any evidence of the ignition source. Although what started the fire was never positively identified, many factors pointed to lithium batteries as the possible cause. This prompted the gathering of airline executives and leaders of the battery industry to address concerns about shipping lithium batteries on commercial aircraft.

The meetings had seemed unproductive to Scott. Almost everyone involved understood that it would be impossible to stop shipping lithium batteries on the airlines. The batteries, along with all the modern electronic devices they powered, were among the most common goods shipped; to stop the air transportation of lithium batteries would shut down a huge portion of the overnight air shipping business. That left industry leaders debating about the safest shipping methods, and the meetings ended without any real change to the status quo. But Scott remembers the meetings as extremely worthwhile; they had brought Maggie into his life.

Maggie had been a keynote speaker, having been one of the principal investigators into the loss of Raine Airways' aircraft. She was younger than Scott by six years, but they'd seemed to connect from the moment they met. After several dinner dates in Washington and a rendezvous in Chicago a month later, they were now together whenever their schedules would permit. He thought back to one of their phone conversation. *"I'll be on United Flight 235 this Saturday morning at eleven-thirty a.m.,"* she'd said to him earlier that week. "Do you know anyone who could pick me up?"

"I'm not sure," he'd said, trying to sound somewhat serious. *"I'll call around and see if anybody has a free moment. You'll have two whole weeks here, right?"*

"I'm all yours for two weeks, baby!"

Scott knew, or at least felt, that Maggie wanted something more from their relationship, something more long term. That thought scared Scott a little. He loved Maggie and could not imagine his world without her in it, but marriage was not something he felt ready for. Why complicate something that was working so well? Maybe someday he'd be up for the big commitment.

His phone gave its usual ding. There was a text message: *got bags headed out!*
I'm at door 3, he texted back.

He saw her walk through the doorway marked with a large black three, and he jumped from the driver's seat to greet her. Their long-awaited time together was about to begin.

SANA'A

The morning sun was already beginning its on slot of earth baking heat and it hadn't even cleared the small hills on the Eastern edge of the small village of Radda, in central Yemen. A light breeze had begun bringing with it the aroma of the stable just outside the living area of their home. Aminah smelled the offensive odor and closed the back door to the kitchen.

Aminah was beginning her day as always, baking bread for the day's meals while preparing breakfast for her family. Hot coals in the tenour were just becoming the correct temperature as she stuck the large, round flat dough onto the inside walls of the oven. Soon, the dough would become kudom bread that she would serve to her family for their morning meal, along with sweet tea and omelets with goat meat. This morning she cooked extra food to take on the all-day journey that lay before her and her daughter Suha.

My daughter, Faria told herself, watching Aminah work. *I bore her, to my husband of fifteen years*. Sometimes it was hard to remember this; Suha enjoyed her new stepmother Aminah. She was fascinated by her Western appeal and followed her lead whenever possible. Sometimes Faria felt she had lost her daughter, just as she had lost her husband she was now forced to share with Aminah.

Faria was the first to wed her husband. It was young love, with the world before them and all the dreams and aspirations of any new couple. The life they shared early on in their relationship was wonderful, full of hopes and plans for a bright future. But it soon became apparent to Faria that life in an Arab marriage can be somewhat one-sided as far as the wife is concerned. They were no longer the loving couple she had hoped they would always remain, and they hadn't been for years. Her husband's goals and aspirations had soon changed, and she became a token, a trophy in his life. Soon Anwar began searching for his second wife.

Faria was never the same person after that. Never again the happy, inspirational force she had been as a young woman. Now she was bitter, feeling betrayed, used, and unloved. She had given her husband three wonderful children and the finest years of her life. Now he was no longer hers. Aminah was her husband's newest wife. She was from the West: young, blonde, and with radical ideals that seemed to match her husband's ever-expanding principles of Islam. Faria was much shorter that Aminah with dark hair and having grown large over her mid years with children and food as a passion, she felt overwhelmingly out of Aminah's league. Anwar spent his free time with his newest bride, and he laid with her every night since their marriage, never visiting Faria, never reminding her why they had married so many years ago. She lay awake at night plotting, planning a way to get her husband back. Back to her, where she was his favorite, his soul mate once again.

Her husband, Anwar al-Awlaki was preoccupied this morning more than usual. A man had delivered a new cell phone to their home before sunrise, and he was making a call to someone Faria did not know. The CIA could easily track cellphones and new ones had to be obtained on a regular basis. She was aware that many al-Qaeda leaders had been found and murdered by the West after being tracked using a cellphone one too many times. Today, Faria supposed, was an exception and calls would need to be chanced.

Their family was one of few who had luxuries such as a cellphone or a computer with Internet service. Aminah and the children had regular access to the computer, but with the rolling blackouts that lasted as much as sixteen hours and power back on in the middle of the night, it was usually Anwar who sat at the computer when the electricity was available. They had just acquired a small portable generator capable of operating the computer. Now Anwar's wives and children were beginning to enjoy daily access to the outside world through the Internet.

Anwar finally ended his call and returned to the cooking area. "Are you nearly ready to go?" he asked Aminah. He barely looked in Faria's direction.

Today, Aminah and Suha would be traveling by car into Sana'a after the morning meal. This day they would be helping directly with the jihad, and Aminah was more than eager to assist in her husband's plans. She longed to be an important part of her husband's life and his quest to destroy the West. She longed for that in a way Faria never had.

Aminah had been born in Croatia as Irena Horak, a blond, thirty-two year-old Islamic convert who had been raised Catholic in her hometown of Zagreb. She had started a long distance relationship with a Muslim man who introduced her to Islam, but she soon became disenchanted with their relationship due to his rather lax devotion to her newfound religion. She had soon sought a more fulfilling and rewarding position in her Islamic faith.

Unknown to her, Anwar had requested a more Western

bride be found for him. His friend, colleague, and fellow jihadist Murad Mitchell had discovered Aminah through Facebook and had set up the distant meeting between the two through videotapes. Aminah felt that her life had been an act of God, leading her to the important role as the wife of this radical jihadist. Inshallah, *Allah will help us,* was her response to al-Awlaki's request for marriage. Soon enough, Aminah had come to Yemen willingly, joining Anwar in his life of Islam and whatever that might bring—and disrupting Faria's entire world.

Faria had come to despise her husband's friend Mitchell. *Why had he been so involved in finding Anwar a new bride, a Western trophy to disrupt her and her children's lives?* It had always seemed to her that Mitchell had more than Anwar's best interest in mind, some alternative motive in sending this woman to Yemen.

But whatever Mitchell's real goals may have been, he had succeeded in replacing Faria in Anwar's affections. Now Aminah, renamed for the mother of the prophet Muhammad, and her husband worked side-by-side in their quest for jihad, and Aminah was eager to help Anwar send their holy war to the West.

Faria had borne Anwar's first three children, and she had once been deeply in love with Anwar. But that love had faltered over the years due to Anwar's single focus on his jihad—and on his newfound Western bride, Faria reminded herself. Faria now kept mostly to herself, helping with the children when necessary. She would do so now, she thought as she left the kitchen for the bedrooms to make sure that Suha was up and ready to risk her life for her husband's holy war. But she found her daughter still asleep.

"Suha, you should be awake," Faria said, gently shaking her shoulder. "What is wrong, young one?"

"I am so sorry mother," Suha replied with a soft moaning

sound. "I think I am sick,"

"Oh, my dear." Faria felt her forehead. "You have quite a fever. Lay back, I will get you some aspirin and water."

She returned to the cooking room, where they kept a large plastic bin full of medicine and first aid supplies. She found a new bottle of Tylenol and dispensed two tablets into her hand.

"Is there something wrong?" Anwar asked, seeing Faria with the first aid box out.

"Suha has a high fever," she replied, not looking in his direction.

Anwar walked to Suha's bedroom, Faria following with the tablets and water. "What is the matter with you, daughter?" Anwar asked with a soft fatherly tone.

"I do not know, father," she said. "I feel sick and weak, and I think I am going to vomit."

Anwar felt her forehead. She was very hot. Suha sat up to take the medicine and water, and then she quickly lay back down. Anwar left the room. He paced the long dark hallway several times. Faria could feel his displeasure throughout the house.

Clearly, Aminah could feel it as well.

"What is wrong, Anwar?" she asked as she walked from the cooking room.

"Suha is sick with a high fever," Anwar said. "Who can we find to replace her at this last moment?"

"I will go," Faria replied from the bedroom doorway, almost before thinking about it. Both Anwar and Aminah stared at her. "What does it matter?" she asked. "I look as much like the person on the ID card as Suha. Besides, why send a young girl to do this dirty work?" She walked down the hall passing them both. No other words were spoken.

Anwar stood there for a moment, frowning in thought. She guessed what he was thinking: he was trying to find any reason not to trust her, his wife of many years, to deliver the result of his years of work. She sat facing him, not letting her face show any expression.

"Why would you want to go?" he finally asked.

Faria didn't give her real answer to this question, the one that was slowly coming to her.

"To help you with your work," she said. "And so that a sick little girl does not have to be involved. Is it not enough that I wish to help you?"

Anwar was a man never short of words. He had an answer of profound magnitude for any question that was directed toward him. Yet at the moment, he was lost for words. The women were to depart for Sana'a immediately, and he must have two women to deliver the packages. Faria knew that her husband could see no other option.

"Very well. You may go in place of Suha," he said. "Be prepared to leave." He looked at her with a hint of suspicion, and then he turned and walked to the small room that held his computer.

*

The sun now reached above the horizon, and the temperature inside their home began to rise. They were living in a large portion of a two-story, brown, mud-baked brick building. From outside, the building looked somewhat stylish, with traditional Yemen round arched windows in a Loggia design, decorative stone work on the flat roof line, and a satellite dish on the roof that pointed toward the sky.

The inside remained traditional Yemeni style, with no furniture other than several small tables. His computer sat on one in a small alcove off the main hall that separated many of the rooms. Numerous rugs and large pillows lay across the dining area. The curtains were pulled tightly shut, making the daylight appear an off-green hue as it filtered through the fabric. A small fan oscillated back and forth moving the warm air. One picture hung on the wall of the largest room on the first floor, a portrait of Osama bin Laden.

Anwar had been on the run and in hiding with Faria, Aminah, and their three children for over two years. He was on the U.S. and Yemen governments' most wanted list for his ties with al-Qaeda in Yemen, possible connections to the Christmas Day Underwear bomber over Detroit, and the Fort Hood, Texas shootings. This home had been their shelter for several weeks as Anwar and his men had planned and prepared the final stages of the bombs to be shipped from Sana'a to New York, Chicago, and Cologne. Today was the day they would send their boxes of jihad to their brethren abroad. *Soon the Kuffar would suffer again by Anwar al-Awlaki's hands*, he thought with a smile

The trip was too dangerous for Anwar himself to make. His image was well known throughout Yemen, and if anything went wrong, the authorities were sure to recognize him in Sana'a. A car had been delivered earlier that morning which would be used to drive the women. The bomb expert of Anwar's—Ibrahim al-Asiri, Faria remembered—would be doing the driving.

Yemeni postal service was as reliable as its electricity. The only reasonable solution, Anwar had argued, was to ship the packages through freight forwarders in the Yemen capital Sana'a. Two facilities had been chosen: the UPS Store, also doubling as the Sun Tours and Travel Company, on Damascus Street in the Haddah area, and the DHL office just three miles north on Zubairy Street. The trial shipments, made weeks ago, had been sent from the same facilities to slightly different addresses in the exact same cities, so as not to show a pattern. The shipping companies would not necessarily be the carriers for the entire route, and the packages would most likely be transferred through several shipping mediums prior to their final destination. Anwar had no way of knowing what company would complete the final delivery—nor did he care, as long as they made it safely to their destination.

The sun was now in its full glory above the hills to the east. Faria squinted her eyes, shading her face with her hand as she watched a motorcycle approach through the window. It was Ibrahim, arriving on time.

"Good morning my friend," she heard Anwar say, and he helped hold the motorcycle up as Ibrahim stepped off.

"Good morning my brother," Ibrahim replied. "It is a great day in our quest."

"Yes it is, I wish I was to be going with you."

"We will miss your leadership," Ibrahim said. "However, we will be unbeaten in our struggle."

Yes, you will miss him when I have him back, and this jihad is no longer Anwar's quest, Faria thought giving him an evil look through the window.

"The auto is here. Let us load our shipments. The women will be ready when we are done," Anwar said with a smile. Hearing this, Faria made haste to get ready, checking on Suha again. Her daughter was now fast asleep. Her fever felt much lower, and she had kept the fluids down. She would be fine until they returned from Sana'a.

The distance from Radda to central Sana'a was only one hundred and fifty kilometers, but with the poor road conditions on a large portion of their travels and heavy traffic in Sana'a, the trip would take most of the day. Aminah and Faria emerged through the front door of the house and walked towards the waiting vehicle. Anwar explained that they would both ride in the back seat of the black Suzuki Vitara, a small four wheel drive SUV with a vinyl top and plastic windows on the sides.

As the women sat down in the back of the auto, Anwar handed Aminah the federal Yemen identification cards that she had stolen just days prior, as well as eighty-five thousand Riyal, or *YER,* equivalent to four hundred US dollars. It was enough to ship all three packages. They would need both of the ID cards, as well. The plan was to use Aminah with one ID to ship the first package and Suha—now, Faria—to use the other for shipment of the last two packages. The ID verification was one of the few security checks in place for shipping out of Yemen. Anwar was sure that the packages would be x-rayed prior to being placed on board an aircraft, but the explosives would not be detectable. He was confident that all potential problems had been covered and planned for. The packages would make it to their final destination.

Faria looked around the seats. There were no safety belts to be found. She could only hope that the SUV had a working air conditioner.

Anwar shook Ibrahim's hand and wished him luck. He turned and reached for Aminah's hand. He patted her shoulder and smiled at both of his delivery girls. Faria tried to remember the last time he had smiled at her in that way. She smiled back, through her black silk veil.

"May Allah guide you and protect you in your travels, my dears," Anwar said.

"He will, Anwar, and we will return soon," Aminah replied with a smile behind her veil.

As the small SUV started down the street, they tried to get comfortable in the small back seat. It would be a long day for both of them. But both women took a sigh of relief as they felt the cool air from the air conditioning begin to reach the back seats.

The SUV hit a rather large bump; Faria bounced from her seat, hitting the vinyl roof above them.

"You should slow down, Ibrahim!" Aminah yelled to the front of the vehicle. Her relationship with Ibrahim, Faria knew, was one of mutual tolerance. Ibrahim treated her like all other Yemen women: lower class then men, subservient, with no opinions permitted in his world. He had never approved of Anwar marrying a Western woman and felt that she was just a distraction to their cause. But Aminah still kept that Western edge of female disobedience and never allowed Arab men to demean her. Sometimes Faria envied that. Ibrahim did not reply, but she felt the vehicle slow down.

"I am surprised that you join us on this important quest," Aminah said quietly to Faria.

"Why should you be surprised? You are not the only one who can assist Anwar with his calling," she replied, attempting to keep her disdain for this woman well hidden.

"Yes, but you have never seemed interested before."

"I have kept busy with my children and our home," Faria said. "I've never had the luxury of your worldly games."

"This is no game, Faria," said Aminah. "This is Allah's work we do, and if you insist on helping, you should at least understand your important role today."

"I understand my role, Aminah," Faria replied. "Don't you worry yourself."

They reached the edge of Radda. The city where they had come to hide, Faria knew, was an al-Qaeda stronghold. Men and boys ruled the streets riding small motorcycles and beat-up Toyota pick-up trucks, all carrying AK-47s or some kind of firearm handed down from the last political or social unrest in the Middle East. Many stopped and stared, seeming to know the destination and purpose of the small SUV's travels. They were allowed to pass by without being harassed.

They drove between sand colored buildings that sat jumbled together, each appearing to reach higher than its neighbor, all of them erected on a large rock outcropping three and sometimes four stories high. The buildings all had the same basic design: rounded-top windows aligned on each of the upper floors with little or no color change from building to building. From afar, this gave the city itself an appearance of being one large building, almost a single color from light to a dark brown with an occasional white structure or freshly painted mosque in the midst. No one stopped or interfered as they passed between the ancient buildings, and soon they were soon out of the city.

The drive was long. The road was normally hard packed clay inundated with potholes that were sometimes half the size as the SUV itself, a path that was nothing more than a wide camel trail. Occasionally a strip of asphalt would appear for several kilometers, and Ibrahim would quicken their pace.

"We'll have to endure these poor road conditions until we reach the main highway that leads into Sana'a," Aminah explained. "Suha and I traveled the same route when shipping the first trial packages. I made a map, if you would like to see it."

She drew the map out of her colorful dress. Many of her Western ideas had not disappeared, Faria knew, and fashion was one of them. She had shed her all-black burka style dresses for the bright and colorful traditional dress of Yemeni women called the Radi Curtain. The soft cotton cloth was worn over her head and draped to her feet. It was adorned with black and red geometric designs and accented with white lines like a curtain that would have hung in a Western style home around the turn of the twentieth century. Her black silk veil was garnished with gold beads. This, along with her dress, covered her blond hair, leaving only her eyes and fingertips exposed for anyone to see.

It made Faria feel inadequate. She knew that Aminah, as a Western woman, had been educated far beyond that of many of her counterparts, including herself. The SUV hit another large bump, and Faria let out a small scream as she reached for a handhold, feeling she would be ejected from the vehicle. The road seemed to smooth out again and she relaxed her grip. She wondered what she was doing here, why she had obeyed her sudden impulse to come on this journey.

The SUV traveled along the road marked as N6 between Radda and Dhamar. The weather and surrounding landscape was that of a desert. The rolling hills were barren of green vegetation except for the occasional scrub bush, palm, or the dragon trees that dotted the land. The dragon seemed to be from another world, shaped like a funnel or a giant mushroom with its dense round green leaved canopy supported by large white branches. It had been named for its blood-red sap that was still used by the local tribes for dyes and medical potions. As they passed a dragon tree, Faria could see a baboon swinging from one the branches, enjoying what little shade was available as the morning sun baked the arid ground.

Ibrahim turned off of N6 onto an even rougher road, a bypass around the city of Dhamar, and both passengers held tightly to the plastic handgrips on each side of the SUV. They soon turned onto a more modern highway marked N1, which led into the Yemen capital of Sana'a, and the women began to relax again. This road was mostly smooth, and the traffic picked up as they neared the city. This was a large city compared to where they had been spending most of the last year in hiding, and many Western cars and pickup trucks filled the city streets. Toyota and some Russian style vehicles appeared to have the majority of the market, Faria thought as Ibrahim navigated through the ever-narrowing streets.

Finally, Ibrahim parked on the street a block before the UPS building. He would not be going with the women. It was the women's hidden faces and the false identification cards that would help protect the leaders of this plot.

Aminah and Faria crawled from the back of the SUV and took the package that was to be sent with this shipper. It was a short walk in the heat, their veils helping to filter the fine sand that seemed always present in the air. Faria was excited and scared at the same time. She knew she carried a package of death, a shipment of jihad that would further the cause her husband had willingly undertaken. She felt part of something much bigger than herself, and the apprehension within her built as they walked along the side of the street.

Faria hated the thought of more deaths and terror in the world. She was tired of living in hiding, moving her children from house to house, strange men showing up at their home at all hours of the day and night, her husband so pre-occupied. She hated the life she had, and this jihad she was now assisting in was the major cause of her unhappiness, the reason she had lost her husband's affections to this new woman. Her eyes filled with tears behind the veil. She still did not know how to get out of her dismal situation, how to stop this insanity and return her life to the way it had been years ago. She took a deep breath and pulled herself from the self-pity that at times could overwhelm her.

"We shouldn't need to say anything, just complete the shipping form they hand us like I explained in the car. He will ask for my identification card. We will use yours at the next stop. Understand?" Aminah asked quietly through her veil.

"Yes, I understand," Faria said. "I will have no problems."

The women ceased speaking altogether as they neared the front entrance to the store. The sign printed in Arabic read *Sun Tours and Travel*, with *Send Site UPS* written nearby in English. They entered the store, Aminah carrying the single package addressed to Cologne, Germany. A small bell over the door announced their arrival. The store was one large room with plastered walls that had been recently painted. The paint odor hung strong and sour in the air. The walls were adorned with posters of alluring world vacation destinations. A long counter sat at the far end of the room where a plastic palm tree stood in the corner. The wood floor creaked as the women walked across the room.

A male clerk stood behind the counter. He looked at his latest customers, offering no outward acknowledgement of the women. Aminah laid the box she carried on the counter. Her hands were sweating, Faria noticed, though whether from the heat or the excitement she was not sure. The shipping address was clearly marked on the label, along with the false return address. The clerk handed her a shipping form, which Faria completed in Arabic. For some reason, her eyes kept returning to the tracking numbers that would follow the packages all the way to their destinations.

I could stop this now, Faria thought. *I could tell this man what death this package contains, how he is in danger just handling it. But they would arrest me and I would never see Anwar again. They would hang me for this or worse, stone me in the street. I must think of another way.*

"I must see your identification card," the man said as Faria returned him the form.

Aminah pulled her stolen card from the pocket sown inside her curtain dress and laid it on the counter. The clerk looked over the stolen card and filled in the necessary information remaining on the shipping form. He then slid the card towards her, picked up the form, and placed the box on the scale behind him.

"Thirty YER," the clerk said, turning back to the counter. He meant thirty thousand Riyals, about one hundred and thirty US dollars.

Aminah counted out the money and handed it to the clerk.

"Thank you," she said in Arabic, the clerk merely grunting an acknowledgment. He handed the carbon copy of the shipping label back to the women. Quickly, Faria folded it and placed it in her pocket. The women turned and left the store, turning left out the door toward the waiting SUV. Faria's heart beat was still racing at a sprinter's pace.

"A great weapon in our holy war is on its way to our

brethren in Germany," Aminah said reverently. Faria did not reply.

The next shipment of bombs at the DHL store went just as smoothly, without questions or problems, the second stolen identification card working just as well as the first had. Now it was merely a long drive back to their temporary home outside Radda. It would be after dark before they arrived, Faria thought as she watched Aminah open the sack of food she had prepared that morning. She handed some forward to Ibrahim, who took it without saying a word. Faria still had the shipping receipts. Neither Ibrahim nor Aminah had thought to ask for them, she realized. And the women adjusted their seating as the SUV hit the first of many bumps to come.

DUBAI

The morning started out like most on the edge of the Saudi desert with its all-consuming, stifling heat. After two years in Dubai, Jafar still had not adjusted to the temperature. The only reprieve from the daunting, sweltering inferno that tormented his skin and lungs was inside the building, yet here he stood, outside along with his fellow workers.

Jafar wore Western style jeans and leatherwork boots bought from a second hand store near where he lived. His button-style shirt was clean and white, and he wore his black hair medium length with a beard cropped short and neatly trimmed. Jafar prided himself on looking clean and professional. He listened closely for his name to be called, watching, as the construction workers were, one by one, assigned their fates. Those whose names were called moved to the assigned foreman's area.

Today, Jafar's pockets contained thirty-two dirhams, a cell phone, and a small business card that he turned over and over as he waited to see whether he would retain his employment for another day.

Jafar Khah Hamdard had lived in Loralai, Pakistan, for most of his life. His family was from the Andar tribe, who had fled Afghanistan to escape the Soviet invasion in 1979. Jafar's father and older brother had been killed when Soviet tanks shelled the city of Kandahar, leaving Jafar, his mother, and her elderly brother to flee to Pakistan. By the time the Soviets withdrew in 1989, Jafar's small family unit had established a new home, and they never returned to Afghanistan.

Loralai was a moderate size village in the northern section of Pakistan, seated almost five thousand feet above sea level on a plateau that jutted down from the Sulaiman mountain range. Life was improving in the district, but for the vast majority of its people, life consisted of cattle, sheep, and goat herding, none of which Jafar had a taste for. He had tried mining in the Chamalang coalmines, but the work was long and hard, extremely dangerous, with minimal pay.

After the Soviets had left their homeland, a power vacuum ensued, and an intense civil war began. Jafar's hometown of Kandahar fell to the Taliban. After the American invasion into Afghanistan in 2001, the Taliban had been pushed out, and many of them had found their way to Pakistan and close to the Loralai area. It was more important than ever before, he thought, to find a better life for himself and his family outside the small city.

The lack of higher paying jobs had driven many of the town's young men to find work outside the country and Jafar intended to join the exodus. He had hoped to make enough money in Dubai to build a real home in Pakistan. He dreamed of a wonderful, warm house for his wife and family, a house with a solid roof and a wooden floor, one that kept the winter draft from sweeping in through cracks and holes. He would send money home each week so that his wife and son could eat well and have the small luxuries that Loralai could provide: modern kitchen utensils, kerosene heaters, soaps and perfumes, and most of all, schooling for his son Agib.

The death of Alia, Jafar's beautiful, loving wife, had changed all that. She had developed cancer in her breast. By the time it was discovered, it was too late for any effective treatment. She lived through the summer, Jafar and Agib caring for her every need, but nothing could stop the death that grew inside her body, and by early fall she was gone. Jafar had buried her in the family plot next to his mother's grave, next to where Jafar had planned to be laid upon his own demise.

After Alia's death, Jafar wanted nothing more than to leave Loralai, but now he would have to travel with his son. He had no close family with whom he could leave Agib with while he went away working in some foreign city. His uncle was much too old and did not do well with children. And he knew that leaving Agib with friends or distant relatives might place his son into the hands of the Taliban. The Taliban were always on the fringes and looking for young recruits. Jafar could not take that chance. *Better a delay in his schooling than the schooling of the Taliban,* he thought, and he signed paperwork to bring himself and his son to the UAE, to work.

*

The numbers of jobs available in Dubai were now a fraction of those at the peak construction frenzy that had brought Jafar and thousands of foreign laborers from all over Asia—Pakistan, India, Burma, and more; almost every Asian nation was represented—looking for work. The United Arab Emirates, knowing that its vast oil wealth would someday dry up as the black gold under the sand became depleted, was planning for its future. Its destiny, the leaders thought, was to become a world banking and tourist destination, and the city of Dubai would be the crown jewel. Dubai now had the world's tallest building, Burj Khalifa, the Palm Island, Burj Al Arab, and the magnificent Atlantis Hotel. It had built an indoor downhill ski slope, where the desert people could feel and play in the snow for the first time in their lives, all while spending their dirhams in one of the most modern Western-style shopping malls in the world. The city of Dubai offered visitors and residents every possible way to spend their money and to do so in the most luxurious fashion.

The city of sand had roared into its modern existence seemingly overnight, with vast oil wealth driving its expansion. No expense had been spared, and elaborate artwork of stone, steel, and glass had transformed a magnificent skyline on the edge of the Persian Gulf. It was a city that boasted each of life's excesses and at the same time demanded some of the restrictions of a predominantly Muslim society.

Jafar's employer was the Obaid Al Jassim Construction Company, who provided the finishing workers to complete the office spaces inside Burj Khalifa. The building was more than just the tallest; its design and construction, Jafar felt, made it one of the most beautiful structures in the world. That was his impression each time he walked through the side construction entrance. Rarely did he get to see the massive entrance and its enormous saltwater aquarium that greeted the building's patrons and clients. But during his time in Dubai, he had been through most of the building and knew its backstage workings, the skeletal body of this behemoth that stood against the Dubai skyline on the edge of the Arabian dessert.

Burj Khalifa was said to be eight hundred twenty eight meters tall, over two thousand seven hundred feet, but its true height seemed to be an ongoing debate among the countries that had lost the bid for title as home to the world's tallest building. There were one hundred sixty floors, many of which Jafar had personally been involved in finishing. He was an apprentice finisher, working with anything: plaster, ceramic tile, cabinetry, and his favorite, fine wood trim. He had found that he had a steady hand and a keen eye when it came to woodworking, and his foreman had assigned him ever-increasing challenges. His talents had greatly improved since his arrival in Dubai.

His finest work came when he had been given the task of finishing the mahogany railing that rose from the grand ballroom up and around the viewing deck that spanned the entire perimeter of the one hundred and fiftieth floor. The view was spectacular. Forests of glass-tinted skyscrapers mushroomed from the desert in Dubai, and here one could witness the entire city with its five hundred and seventy completed high-rises. More than seven hundred were either under construction or planned for the future, the Persian Gulf in its grandest scheme. Powerboats, cruise ships, and dozens of marinas lined the coast. Jafar loved his work and the panoramic view it offered. Burj al Arab, a building shaped like the sail of a boat, could be seen on the skyline along with Palm Island, the enormous man-made oasis of sand that jetted out into the Persian Gulf.

Burj Khalifa was officially completed and opened to the public in January, but many of the floors remained unfinished. Interior completion of some of the final floors would now continue at a much slower pace. Often, Jafar was tasked with wood trim and plaster conditioning. *Final Conditioning*, his shift leader liked to call it. Jafar called it "fixing all the mistakes." The large plaster crews and finish workers moved through each floor at a rapid pace, making many small blemishes and mistakes that could not be overlooked. Jafar was tasked with repairing all of these errors. It was an easy job, and for most of the day, he was left to himself to complete his work among the smell of new carpet and paint. As he worked, he enjoyed the finest office settings and high-rise views money could buy, knowing he would never indulge in these luxuries after the contract was up.

He had expected the work on Burj Khalifa to last until he had saved the money he needed. But the world economic slump had recently hit Dubai with a vengeance. Suddenly there was a glut of unrented space, and construction on many of the buildings the UAE leaders had planned for their world-banking metropolis had slowed or stopped. Each week brought more and more layoffs and desperate situations for hundreds of the men who were building this modern city. Most contractors had not provided the workers they hired with arrangements for return travel to their home countries, and some workers had not saved enough money for return passage by the time the work began to stop. Many were now abandoned in a foreign land. Jafar told himself, fingering the card, that he would not let this happen to him, or to his son.

While in Dubai, Jafar had been saving every bit of his earnings that was not absorbed by his rent, food, or his son Agib's schoolbooks. The home they now shared would be considered a slum in many parts of the world: cement block buildings stacked together on the edge of the desert sand, a quick-built housing unit for the thousands of workers relocated to the UAE to build the Arab's city of Oz. Their home was a one-room dirt floor flat with a single table and overhead light. They shared a communal toilet and shower room several doors from their flat. His only luxury was the cell phone he had purchased to help look for additional work.

He needed at least one more year of work, he knew, to afford Agib's schooling and make a down payment on a house. He would need to work even longer to pay for the ship and bus travel expenses that would return him and his son to Loralai. But far sooner, he realized, his construction work would run out.

He knew that his foreman at Burj Khalifa liked him, liked

the fact that Jafar worked hard without complaining. He liked the fact that Jafar had not become involved in the demonstrations that many of the workers had taken part in over the past several months in an attempt to change the poor wages and appalling living conditions that most of the foreign workers had found when arriving in Dubai. Jafar had kept to himself and spent what little free time he had with his son. This might keep him on the payroll for a few extra days, he thought.

Jafar did not want to return yet. Not until he was complete, learned, able, successful. Not wealthy—he knew that would never be possible with his wages—but it was steady income, no matter how small. And unlike so many of his brethren working beside him, he did not have to send his money home to needy family members. Agib was his only family since his wife had died.

The thought of his wife always brought a tear to his eyes. Even after three years, he felt so alone without her. So much had changed in that time, more than ever before in his thirty-two-year life. His world had changed completely. Life was now all about securing a safe future for Agib, and he knew that this meant returning to his homeland soon. Agib must be enrolled in a finer school such as the Government Primary School, Shin Gul Shah. This was where Jafar had attended, and he hoped his son would someday as well.

There was no real schooling here among the masses of workers in this forsaken desert. His mind played opposites when thinking of Dubai; one day he admired the vast beauty of the city and all it had to offer, the next he hated its mere existence. He often felt trapped in a foreign land.

He continued to flip the card over in his hand while listening for his name to be called. Two weeks ago, when he had learned that work on the Burj Khalifa would not last as long as he had expected, Jafar had applied for a job at the airport. He remembered standing next to the processing table as a technician demonstrated where to place the palm of his hand for scanning. The plate of glass turned a bright green color as it made a quiet hum. The early morning sun radiated through the full-length windows lining the south wall of the small room, causing Jafar to shield his eyes. The technician turned and drew down large plastic blinds that blocked most of the sun's rays.

"Next palm," the technician said in Arabic.

Jafar didn't speak fluent Arabic. His native language of Pashto shared the same alphabet as Arabic, but the two languages were not related. He had learned enough of this new language to get through his day, but he enjoyed practicing his English whenever he could. Almost everyone here seemed to speak some English, at least enough to communicate with all the foreigners.

He placed his left hand down flat on the glass, and again the machine turned green and hummed. The sun was already beginning to heat the small room, and he could hear the air conditioner kick on, blowing cool air in through the ceiling vent.

Jafar had applied for the only job he could find, a tug driver position responsible for towing trailers of cargo to and from aircraft all around the Dubai International Airport. The electronic fingerprinting had been the last step in the background check process. Dubai Airport took its security seriously and would hire only employees with no criminal background and no links to terrorist organizations. Jafar had neither of these, and he felt he would have no problems getting the job.

"Thank you," the technician had said in an almost robotic fashion, as if he had done this single task thousands of times.

"How long does the process take?" Jafar remembered asking.

"One to two weeks if there are no problems," the technician had told him as he handed Jafar a business card. "In ten days, call the number on the card and ask for Mr. Sarraf. He will tell you if you are to have an interview."

"Please exit through that door," the technician said, pointing to the obvious. Jafar turned and walked through the door that led back to the main entrance of the airport employment office and back into the heat, just like today's heat. The sun had risen above the horizon, and he began to sweat the moment he left the air-conditioned cocoon of the building. Workers were beginning to file into the airport. Jafar hoped he could become one of them before his construction job came to an end.

He had looked at the card every day since. One side was printed in Arabic, the other in English. It read: *Danwwar Sarraf, Manager of Loading Operations*. Every day, as he listened for his name to be called, he resisted the urge to dial Mr. Sarraf's number, to end the waiting, to put the uncertainty to rest, to give his life the smallest feeling of order.

The job, he knew, would pay about the same as he made now, but it offered fewer hours each week, which meant Jafar would be even longer saving money for his return home—and what was more, most of his time would be spent outdoors in the relentless desert heat. He had not come to Dubai to operate a tug at an airport. But the situation had changed, and neither he nor Agib could afford for him to go a single day without work. If he could get the job at the airport, he thought, fingering the card in his pocket, he would have options.

And suddenly, he heard his name called. Quickly, he gathered with the group of workers who were still employed. *I am still needed, for today at least*, he thought, as he stood waiting for the call to be completed and for his foreman to send them to their day's tasks.

"Let's get to work," the director yelled to the men who had

been called.

The remaining workers would be out of a job. He felt sorry for them, and at the same time thankful that he was still working. But he knew it was just a matter of time before he walked away one morning with the other jobless souls. His only hope now, he knew, was Mr. Sarraf, and the card in his pocket.

HEROES

Captain Donald Lambert had gone for a short jog from the crew hotel on the sidewalk along 308th Road. Don, like most international pilots, attempted to keep the effects of the numerous time changes on his body to a minimum. It may have been early afternoon in Dubai, but for Don and his circadian rhythm, it was four a.m. A daily run was the best way he had found to stay ahead of the fatigue.

But the intense heat of the mid-day sun had cut his morning exercise short. He felt tired more than invigorated as he entered the luxurious thirty-four-story Fairmont Hotel. The sight of smiling, always-attentive employees reminded him that this was one of the finest hotels he had ever stayed in. His next flight was Cologne, Germany, due to depart in three hours, which would give him time to wash up, enjoy a quiet meal, and do some reading on his latest spy novel, *The KGB Alive and Well*.

Don had been an airline pilot now for over twenty-five

years, a University of South Dakota graduate who had worked his way to the top of the aviation ladder. He was a 747–400 captain flying to destinations all across the globe for Raine Airways. His current routing had him away from home for over two weeks. *Two weeks too long*, he thought, with a new baby daughter at home, his first and the joy of his life. He and Susan, his wife of nine years, had decided it was time to make an addition to their family. His wife's career was successful and stable, and she was able to take off as needed whenever Don was flying. Their daughter, Lily Louise Lambert, was now eleven months old and after today's flight to Cologne, he had just one more flight scheduled to Louisville, Kentucky, a major hub for Raine Airways and the home of the Lambert family. Don couldn't wait to make it back home. He knew he would have his work cut out for him, sharing baby time with Lily's grandparents.

Children had seemed to be the central theme to Don's conversation with his first officer and co-pilot, Mike Barrett, over the past days of flying together. Mike Barrett had been a pilot for almost twenty years, having flown for Raine the past four. His experience had come from the military, a Naval Academy grad with close to eight years flying the F-18 Hornet and then a short stint flying for a commuter in the New England area before coming to Raine. This was Mike's first four-engine, heavy jet.

Although younger than Don, Mike had started his family expansion earlier in life, and his kids were now nine and twelve. His family lived in Racine, Wisconsin, and Mike was eager to be home with his family. His son Drew was starting seventh grade football, and Mike didn't want to miss a moment of his training. His daughter Rachel was starting her piano lessons this very day. So many important events, Don and Mike agreed, occur in a family's life while a pilot is far away in a foreign city; flying around the world and making stops at exotic ports had their moments, but those times grow old when your own world lies on the other side of the globe from you.

It was now late afternoon in Dubai, but it was breakfast time for Don, who was trying to ignore the time difference of over twelve hours from home. His first meal of the day would be a light one, he thought, the waiter pulling the chair out and motioning Don to have a seat. An American breakfast menu was hard to come by in the afternoon, so he chose the Café Sushi. It was a small, slightly hidden away dining experience on the fifteenth floor, overlooking the city of Dubai where it unrolled its streets into the endless sands of the Arabian Desert.

He could see the hotel pool area several stories below. *Not many takers in this heat,* he thought to himself as he glanced over the menu. Hummus with pita bread caught his eye, and he ordered his meal. *Nobody can make hummus like the Arabs.* His cell phone rang. "Hello, this is Don."

"Hi Don, this is Amy in Crew Scheduling. How are you this evening?"

"Doing well, Amy. How are things in Anchorage?"

"Same old, same old. But I have a small change to your schedule. Your departure time has been pushed back by one hour due to late arriving inbound. New departure time will be fifteen zero five Zulu, that's nineteen zero five local this evening, a delay of one hour. We have notified your ground transportation of the change. Pick-up is now seventeen hundred local."

Don quickly wrote down the times on a cocktail napkin and repeated them back to the scheduler. *Welcome to aviation,* he thought. "Okay, Amy, thanks, we'll be there," he replied. "Have you contacted Mike yet?"

"He's my next call, Don. Have a safe flight," Amy replied, and the call ended.

Always something, Don thought as he set his phone back down on the table. As soon as he got back to his room he would call Mike to make sure he had received the schedule change and follow-up on their transportation change.

He enjoyed his quiet meal, the waiters always so attentive. He looked through the daily Dubai newspaper that had been delivered to his room early this morning. Dubai had always seemed like a mixture of two vastly different cultures, and the written articles seemed to highlight all of the contradictions he'd observed here. On one hand, Dubai was a modern desert city that flourished on oil money gained from Western nations' addiction to the black gold that lay beneath its sand; it was a desert city that hosted the tallest building in the world, showcasing hundreds of extravagant high-rises and enormous man-made islands jetting out into the Persian Gulf. A city that boasted all of life's lavishness and many of its vices.

On the other hand, Dubai was the centerpiece of the United Arab Emirates, a nation that was not only ruled by an Arab Muslim prince, but that also sat in the center of the Middle East, surrounded by ultraconservative Muslim nations. Don smiled: *What happens in Dubai stays in Dubai*. He felt the Las Vegas slogan fit well with this city, finding the clash of two vastly different cultures the perfect hypocrisy. *Maybe Western ideals will someday win the day*, he thought.

He finished his meal, paid his bill with his American Express card, and headed for his room on the thirty-first floor. He was to depart the hotel in two hours.

*

Don and Mike met in the hotel lobby at exactly four fifty-five p.m. Their airport shuttle was waiting outside the front entrance of the hotel.

"Good morning, Don," Mike said with a smile, even

though it was now early evening here in Dubai.

"Morning, Mike. Did you get some sleep?"

"Some," replied Mike. "It was too damn hot to venture outside." Mike preferred cold weather, Don knew.

"I got out for a short jog," replied Don.

"I just stayed inside most of the day, that heat was too much," Mike said. "I didn't sleep too well last night, so I worked out in the gym."

"The gym is okay," Don said. "I just don't care for treadmills."

The bellman approached, dressed in a traditional white Arab thawb and the summer ghutrah with a black ogal. "Your car has arrived, gentlemen," he said, assisting the pilots with their luggage and then escorting them to the front of the lobby. Don could feel the heat and humidity rise as they walked through the grand revolving entranceway.

Waiting outside was a black Cadillac limousine with the air conditioning running on high. Mike sat down in the back seat, which was equipped with a full cocktail bar.

"Look at this, Don," Mike said pointing to the extravagant mini bar in the limo, "why do we always get this great service on the way to work and not on the way to the hotel?"

"Doesn't seem fair, does it?" Don laughed. "Somebody must have told them about your taste for fine Kentucky bourbon."

The ride from the hotel to the Dubai International Airport was less than thirty minutes through the center of the city. The limo drove past masses of workers filing home at the end of their day. Skyscrapers lined the streets as their car ventured eastward, the buildings slowly receding into elaborate single-story whitewashed stucco structures, most of which lay beyond a gated concrete wall of the same color. Don figured these were homes of the more prominent city residents.

The airport, as new looking as the majority of the city, had a small terminal by modern standards, but its elaborate design and artwork made it an attractive entry point for foreign visitors. Both pilots tipped their driver and walked quickly through the automatic sliding doors, eager to make their way as fast as they could from the limousine to the air-conditioning inside the terminal.

Even after considerable time spent in the Middle East, Don still found the Arab dress fascinating. All male airport personnel seemed to wear the same uniform: brilliant white cotton thawb with matching white ghutrah headscarf and black ogal band. Many Arab businessmen wore the western suit and tie. Don figured the choice between thawb and suit depended directly on whomever they were going to do business with that day.

Women's attire spanned the entire worldwide range of clothing. Some wore high heels with mini-skirts and low-riding tank tops. Blue jeans and tennis shoes seemed popular today, and Mike's eye was caught for a moment by a woman in jeans and a plaid shirt wrapped with a white and gold streaked veil who passed on his left.

"I'm liking the mystery behind the veils," Mike said quietly.

"Exquisite," Don agreed. "I'd prefer the fad stays over here, though."

The terminal's main walkway was lined with full-grown palm trees adorned with white lights wrapped up the trunks and into the branches. It reminded Don of Christmas in the tropics.

Both pilots cleared customs and security through the main terminal. As they continued their walk, they were surrounded by masses of people, all of whom seemed headed in a mad rush for departing flights or the baggage claim. Don always enjoyed the underlying sense of urgency at large airports; everyone seemed to be trying to get somewhere as fast as possible. Fresh coffee brewed from almost every eatery and the small deli, and the strong smell of spices was making him hungry.

"We always have wonderful catering out of Dubai, and that's a good thing, 'cause I'm getting hungry," Don said, more to himself than to Mike.

The flight crew's journey through the airport terminal ended with a small wait at the far end of the building next to glass doors that allowed access to the cargo ramp. There, they waited for the airport official who would escort them to their airplane.

Don stepped into the men's room. There were no urinals, just walled stalls equipped with a garden hose and a nozzle. No toilet paper to be found. The hose water overspray, which covered not only the entire toilet but also the walls and ceiling, made him laugh out loud, and he walked out without even considering the possibility of using the facilities.

"I sure appreciate toilet paper," he said to Mike.

"Makes you long for home even more, doesn't it?" replied his copilot.

Their escort arrived. Don and Mike were on their own for transferring their bags, which they loaded into the small white utility van. The driver headed towards the Raine Airways jet, which was parked across the terminal with all the international long haul aircraft. They drove past a United Arab Emirates A380, the largest commercial airliner in the world: a wide body, double deck aircraft that stood over eighty feet tall at the tail, with a wingspan of over two hundred sixty feet and four engines capable of carrying it airborne with over eight hundred passengers.

But the most popular long haul, worldwide airliner, Don thought, remained the Boeing 747–400. At the far end of the ramp, along a row that contained dozens of this commercial jetliner, sat Don and Mike's 747, tail number N571RA. It was an exact copy of the passenger 747, but it had been outfitted for cargo pallets instead of passenger seats.

Standard procedure at Raine Airways left the interior pre-flight and most of the cockpit set-up up to the co-pilot. The captain of the flight's responsibility was to perform the exterior pre-flight, or *walk-a-round,* as the flight crews referred to it. Maintenance had attached a large external air-conditioning cart that pumped the flight deck area with cool, comfortable air, making Mike's pre-flight much more comfortable than Don's. Don began his rather heat-filled task as soon as he arrived at the jet.

"If you are not up in fifteen minutes, I'll send a camel to recue you from the heat," Mike joked as he climbed the stairs to the cooler air of the cockpit that sat three stories above the heat of the concrete tarmac.

Both crews performing their assigned duties could have the jet ready for engine start and taxi with-in thirty minutes, but to prevent anyone from rushing and missing something important, the crew had over sixty minutes to ready Flight 6.

Don liked having a short flight number for a change. The flight number used is decided by the airline using their own set of standards, but like most flight crew members, he preferred one or two digit flight numbers to help prevent any miscommunication with air traffic controllers. Most scheduled carriers operate using a call sign other than their company name over the radio. Raine Airways' was Speed Flight: Speed Flight 6.

Cargo was still being loaded through the large cargo door on the left side of the aft fuselage as Don made his way around the tail of the plane. He stepped aside as a tug pulled another five-trailer convoy of wheeled dollies towards the loader. Each dolly held a container or pallet full of cargo bound for Europe. A retractable cargo pallet loader called a K-loader rose from the ground to the main deck of the plane. It would lift two containers at a time to the cargo door and maneuver the individual cargo pallets on board using small conveyor belts. Once inside the plane, the containers were positioned using rubber wheels mounted in the floor of the aircraft's cargo area. Only one person was needed to operate the K-loader, but it took at least two workers to push the pallet onto the loader and two workers to handle the pallet once it had been conveyed onto the plane. It was a relatively quick process, and experienced ground crews could load the entire 747 in about an hour.

Don knew the main deck held thirty-three pallets, and with the line-up of tugs and dollies still on the ramp, he surmised that his plane was about half loaded. He completed his inspection of the exterior and headed up the crew stairs. They would be ready to go as soon as the plane was loaded.

He had worked up quite a sweat by the time he reached the top of the internal ladder that led him to the flight deck area, but cooled off quickly stepping inside the cockpit. "It all looks good outside," he remarked to Mike, who was busy preparing the navigation computer. "Ready for some coffee?"

"Absolutely. I'll need a whole pot of it to get to Cologne," Mike replied.

Don poured two cups of coffee from pot Mike had brewed in the small crew galley and glanced through the catering that Mike had already stored away. "Fantastic," he said, noticing the hummus and flat bread that he had ordered. He loved the hummus from this caterer. He stepped into the cockpit, handed Mike his coffee with one cream and one sugar, and maneuvered himself into the captain's seat, careful not to spill his cup.

"Weather looks good until we reach Germany," Mike relayed to Don. "Rainy and cold up north."

"Always seems to be raining when I'm in Cologne," Don replied. "What's with that? I think I like this heat better than the cold and wet."

"I've had all of this heat I can stand for a while," remarked Mike.

After twenty minutes Don had finished his review of the flight plan, weather briefing and aircraft performance numbers, and he'd completed his portion of the cockpit setup, checking all of Mike's work. Mike checked Don's work as well.

"You all set up over there?" Don asked.

"Yes sir, ready to go," Mike replied, finishing the last of his coffee.

"We've flown together over the past two weeks," Don said. "All the standard procedures and callouts we've previously briefed remain the same. Any questions?"

"No questions here," replied Mike.

"It's your leg, your brief," Don instructed. Although each crew had their standard tasks to complete on every flight, flying duties normally alternated between pilot and co-pilot, which kept each crewmember current and proficient at the controls. This was Mike's flight leg.

"Then this will be a right seat, eight hundred seventy one thousand pound, max thrust takeoff on runway three zero right. Our initial clearance is runway heading to five thousand. No engine out procedure, and we have fifty-five minutes of fuel dump time. Transition level is fifteen thousand. Any questions or additions?"

"No questions. Let's do the Before Start Checklist," Don instructed.

The atmosphere in the cockpit now took on a more serious tone. Standard procedure at Raine Airways required that at the start of the first checklist, crew conversation had to remain limited only to what was necessary for the flight. From this point forward, all communication had to be precise, and standard terminology was key until the flight had reached flight level one-eight zero—18,000 feet.

The jet was ready, as far as the flight crew was concerned. Now it was just a matter of the loading. A colored monitor on the center instrument panel displayed the position of all the doors in the aircraft. The last of the cargo doors, Don noted, had been closed.

Moments later, the load supervisor, a young Arab man in his late twenties, entered the cockpit wearing a baseball cap and writing on a metal clipboard. His bright yellow t-shirt said *The Beetles.*

"Hello, gentlemen," he announced with a British accent, not looking up from his paper work. He sat in the jump seat behind the captain's seat and finished his writing.

"How's your day going, young man?" Don asked.

"Jolly well so far," said the supervisor, "and it's almost quitting time. Here's your weight and balance." He handed the paperwork to Don.

Each pallet had been weighed as it was pulled from the cargo building, its number and weight then sent to the weight and balance office. A load planner sitting at a computer shuffled the pallets' positions to ensure the proper aircraft loading and sent the information via radio to the load supervisor at the aircraft, who had confirmed the positioning of each container as it was loaded on board the plane.

Don looked over the numbers and read the aircraft's zero fuel weight to Mike, who entered it into the flight management computer. The computer calculated the takeoff gross weight to be 853,000 pounds. Don checked this against the paperwork and signed the weight and balance before escorting the load supervisor out and down the yellow ladder-like stairs.

"Thanks for your help," he said to the load supervisor as he closed and sealed the entry door.

Once back in his seat, Don fastened his seat belt and put on his headset.

"Cockpit to ground," Don said into his mic to the mechanic who was plugged into the audio system at the nose gear wheel well just below the cockpit.

"Hello, sir," replied the mechanic in a heavy Arab accent.

"Good evening. Door lights are out and the parking brake is set. You are cleared to pull the chocks and stairs."

"Roger. May we pull external power?" the mechanic asked.

Don looked at his overhead panel to confirm that the auxiliary power unit was running and providing the necessary electrical power to the plane. The APU light was on. "You are cleared to remove external," Don replied. "Confirm the pitot covers and gear pins are removed."

"Gear pins and pitot covers are removed," said the mechanic. "You are cleared to pressurize hydraulics."

"Below-the-line," Don said to Mike indicating that they were cleared to turn on the hydraulic pumps and complete their checklist items.

The dialog between Don and the mechanic was standard and precise, as were all their cockpit communications: designed to be same each time so that nothing was omitted and anything abnormal caught everyone's attention.

"Cockpit to ground," Don said. "We will be using runway three zero right."

"Roger, Captain," the mechanic announced. "Release the parking brake, and we will start your push to face south."

"Parking brake is released."

"Roger, sir, you are cleared to start all engines."

With that, the crew of Flight 6 started all four of the General Electric CF6 engines, cleared the mechanic off the headset, and called Dubai ground control for a taxi clearance. Don and Mike's pre-flight and taxi to the active runway was smooth and by the book. The weather was clear, and there were no major issues with the jet other than a momentary trip-off of one of the ship's air conditioning control units called a PACK. Mike completed the abnormal checklist, attempting to restore its operation. He was able to turn the PACK back on, and it appeared to be functioning correctly. They approached the takeoff end of the runway, in line behind several other aircraft waiting for takeoff. Don set the parking brake.

They sat facing southeast. The sky was now nearly dark, the sun sitting just below the western horizon behind the lights of the Dubai skyline. Don could still see the last of the day's sunlight looking out the right side cockpit window. Flight 6 was now next in line for takeoff at the Dubai International Airport. In a matter of minutes, they would be airborne.

VACATION

Maggie caught sight of Scott parked under the overhang that stuck out four cars deep and ran the entire length of the arrival area of the airport terminal. Even at the height of summer in Anchorage, it was cool in the shade, and she found it downright cold relative to where she'd been.

As she walked towards him, she imagined him looking at her from his truck. She was a beautiful sight to see, she thought. She had dark Italian hair, golden skin and a fabulous figure with the cutest toes Scott said he had ever seen. She was almost as tall as Scott was, and she knew he liked the idea of kissing a girl without having to bend over. Today, she was wearing a tight fitting cotton top that showed off a hint of her attractive cleavage. Her jeans fit well, and she'd worn open toed sandals to show off her toes. She knew Scott would love that. Margaret was in love with Scott, and she was confident of his love and affection towards her, but she had her hopes up for a stronger commitment from him during this time together. What exactly that was she still wasn't sure.

Margaret had grown up along the East Coast halfway between Annapolis, Maryland and Norfolk, Virginia. *Because Norfolk is where I have to be and Annapolis is where I want to be*, her father always said. Her father had been in the Navy and spent most of his time stationed at the naval shipyards in Norfolk when he wasn't at sea. As a child, she saw little of her father. He was protecting the country, her mother would always tell her. When he was home, however, they had a wonderful time together. Both she and her younger brother Reggie admired their father and cherished their time with him. When he finally retired, the family moved to Annapolis on the Chesapeake Bay and into her father's dream house with his sailboat parked within walking distance from his lawn chair. Just in time for Margaret to move off to college.

Margaret had attended MIT, earning her masters in chemical engineering. (Scott liked to tell her she was a whole lot smarter than he was.) She had worked for British Petroleum out of college, but she had always hoped to work with the National Transportation Safety Board. Finally, fourteen years ago, she had landed an accident investigator position and never looked back. She had become an outstanding investigative scientist, one of the best in the business. She loved her work, career, and life, but she loved her vacation time with Scott even more.

"Hi, beautiful," he said to her with a smile, arms stretched wide for the hug they both had been daydreaming about since their last time together.

"Hi baby," Margaret replied almost in a yell as she wrapped her arms around Scott. It was a long, tight, loving embrace, followed by a passionate kiss that drew the attention of several bystanders. Margaret realized she had missed him more than she expected. She could tell he felt it too; the smile that they shared said it all.

"How was your flight, baby?" Scott asked.

"Too long and too bumpy!" she replied. "How do you stand those long flights all the time?"

"It helps to have a front window seat," Scott replied with a smile. "Are you hungry?"

"Starving; the food on that flight was atrocious. And they called it first class seating!"

"I know of a great place to take you. It had a four star review on the Travel Channel."

"Really, are we eating walrus?" she said with a smirk.

"If that's what you want," he said, laughing. "But they serve a salmon BLT that's out of this world." He lifted her bags into the truck.

"As long as we can get into the sun," she said. "Wow, it's cold under here."

Scott, always attempting to be the gentleman, opened her door and held her hand as she stepped up in his SUV.

"We are off for a full week of fun and fishing," he exclaimed as they drove out of the airport overhang. "Hope you brought your waders."

"You have my waders," she ribbed him, "and my fishing pole."

"As a matter of fact, I do," he said. "It's about time you got back here. I've been missing you!"

"Oh, and I missed you, sweetie—and Bair. Where is he?"

"I thought we would have dinner downtown before we headed home," Scott said, "so I left him at the house."

They drove toward the center of Anchorage headed to Scott's favorite restaurant in Alaska, the Glacier Brew House. There were many fine places to eat all over Anchorage with most packed full of tourists at this time of year. Scott had made reservations for six-thirty, and it looked as if their timing would be perfect.

Margaret held Scott's hand as she gazed out the truck window at the beautiful scenery. She hadn't come with an ultimatum;

at least, she continued to tell herself that. She knew Scott was not ready for marriage—his last had left such a bitter taste in his life. But she did have hopes for something more, something closer maybe.

But how could we ever make that happen, she thought, distracted by the vast beauty of the mountains. Their careers were so far apart. She had to live in Washington D.C., home to the NTSB headquarters. A commute from Alaska for her was not even thinkable. But what about Scott? Did he really have to live in Alaska? Many pilots lived far away from their base, or *domicile,* as Scott called it. Could Scott move from Alaska? Would he ever want to? All of these questions had been raised before with no real answers, or at least not the answers she wanted to hear. How could this long distance relationship survive? Did she want it to survive?

Of course she did, she told herself. Scott was the best she had discovered since her husband Ethan had died in the accident five years ago. Scott had been the only real relationship she had been in since, not including the odd dates she had endured. Each of those men had seemed like boys looking for a new mother in the form of a smart, strong, professional woman to take care of them. Not Scott. He was almost the polar opposite of those men. Scott was extremely independent, reliable, adventurous, and romantic. No, she decided, she would let it play out for the near future. No reason to add turmoil to their short time together. She would keep her feelings to herself for now.

As Scott had predicted, the meal was wonderful. Margaret settled for a salad and had a taste of Scott's sandwich as they shared a bottle of Marietta Armé. The company and conversation relaxed her, and they soon wandered from the restaurant, walking along the downtown streets. Flower baskets filled with bright arrays of yellow marigolds and dark blue lobelia hung from each tall green lamppost. Large flowerpots lined each street with bright red geraniums and tall green dracaenas, all of them growing to exceptional size due to the almost constant daylight. The city looked like one large flower garden. A small sign at the visitors' center claimed that over thirteen hundred flower arrangements decorated downtown Anchorage.

The next stop was the Millennium Hotel for a walk through their lobby. Scott had taken her here on her first visit, and she enjoyed seeing all the Alaska memorabilia, so they always stopped for a quick tour. An extensive display of the animals and fish that could be seen in the wilds of Alaska was there, stuffed and mounted on the walls. A ten-foot grizzly bear stood on his back feet, a realistic reminder that humans were not at the top of the food chain in Alaska. A bright white polar bear seemed to be walking behind a glass wall that the hotel had put in place to prevent tourists from petting him. Moose and caribou adorned the walls, and each species of salmon was on display, all at record size. A four hundred pound halibut covered an entire wall next to the staircase, and the largest Artic grayling Scott had ever seen was on exhibit next to a colorful rainbow trout.

They walked around the lobby, stopping in the Fancy Moose Pub and ordering Alaska Ambers to enjoy on the outside patio that overlooked Lake Spenard and the floatplanes that landed one after another, most returning from a day's fishing. The Alaska Range, its peaks covered with snow year-round, offered a perfect Yukon setting as backdrop.

"What an incredible place this is," Margaret said for what was probably the fifth time today.

"I never get tired of looking at it," Scott replied. "We have another great view waiting for us at the house. What do you say we take this party to the hot tub on my deck and watch the mountains from there?"

She gave his hand a tight squeeze. "I'm ready as soon as

you are, baby," she said.

They finished their beers and headed for Scott's house, which sat at almost one thousand feet above sea level along the Chugach Mountain hillside in South Anchorage. The drive was short, and soon they were in the warm waters of Scott's spa that sat on an upper deck. The view was spectacular, looking out over the waters of Cook Inlet and Turn-Again Arm. From their vantage point they could see the entire Alaska Mountain Rage on the western horizon: all white-capped peaks, including the three quiet but still active volcanoes that extended north to Denali, the tallest mountain in the United States.

The evening was grand, peaceful, and romantic, and as they both agreed, too long in coming. They both cherished the moment, looking forward to repeating this evening's events over the next two weeks. *And what comes after that*, Margaret thought, *what happens to us after the next two weeks?* But she made herself forget it for now.

DEMISE

"**S**peed Flight 6, line up and wait runway three zero right," instructed the British accented tower controller.

"Roger. Line-up and wait, runway three zero right, Speed Flight 6," replied Mike as Don turned on the plane's strobe lights, released the parking brake, and began to spool the motors. At this heavy takeoff weight, the airplane needed extra breakaway thrust to start moving forward. Don advanced all four throttles until the engines reached forty percent N1, and the jet began to move. As the aircraft's speed reached seven knots, he reduced the engine thrust almost to idle. The huge plane maintained its forward momentum as Don taxied onto the runway. Smoothly, he lined up the jet with the nose gear directly over the centerline, using the minimal amount of runway length to do it. *Runway behind you and altitude above you are two things that do a pilot no good*, he thought.

As Don pulled the throttles to idle, he announced: "Parking brake is not set, Mike. It's your jet, and I've got the radios." Tonight, with Mike flying, Don would be responsible for all the radio calls.

"Roger, I have the jet," replied Mike, indicating a positive transfer of the aircraft's control.

Over the flight crew's headsets came the clearance. "Speed Flight 6 Dubai tower, winds are two seven five at four knots, runway three zero right, cleared for takeoff."

"Roger, cleared for takeoff runway three zero right, Speed Flight 6," Don replied as he turned the last of the plane's exterior lights on.

Mike advanced the throttles forward to seventy percent, engaged the auto-throttle switch, and called, "Set takeoff thrust."

Don placed his hand back on the throttles as the levers moved forward automatically to the takeoff setting. He verified the final power setting and responded with "Thrust set" as the powerful engines pushed the crew back into their seats, accelerating the lumbering aircraft down the fourteen thousand foot runway at the Dubai International Airport.

"Eighty knots," announced Don.

"Checks," was Mike's response.

At one hundred and sixty-five knots, Don called, "Rotate."

Mike pulled firmly on the control yoke, and the giant bird slowly took to the skies.

"Positive rate," announced Don, indicating that the plane was climbing as indicated on both the barometric and radar altimeters.

"Gear up," was Mike's response, and Don raised the landing gear handle.

It was a perfect day for flying, calm winds and clear skies forecast through most of the flight. Raine Airways Flight 6—bound for Cologne, Germany, and filled with almost 200,000 pounds of freight—was airborne on a routine flight. The routing would take them over the Persian Gulf, west along the northern edge of Saudi Arabia, across Jordan and over Turkey into Eastern Europe, and then on into Germany. Flight time was scheduled for six hours twenty-three minutes.

"Speed Flight 6, contact Dubai departure one twenty-six point two, goodnight," the tower controller instructed.

"Roger, Speed Flight 6 switching, good night," was Don's reply.

"Dubai departure, Speed Flight 6 passing one-thousand six hundred for five thousand, good evening," Don announced over the pre-set frequency through his Telex headset.

"Speed Flight 6 Dubai departure radar contact, climb and maintain one-one thousand, eleven thousand. Good evening," came the reply from an Arab accented controller.

"Roger, climb maintain one-one thousand, Speed Flight 6," Don responded as he dialed the newly assigned altitude into the altitude window on the glare shield. Mike responded by pointing at the new altitude and continued the climb.

The flight was smooth. Don scanned the skyline and looked down at the shoreline of Dubai. The sun had now passed well below the horizon, and the lights of the desert city shone bright in stark contrast of the dark sea and the barren desert that sandwiched this rich metropolis. The flight would be in the dark, following the sun around the globe, but never catching up and slowly losing the chase. It would be late evening when they arrived in Cologne. *A great way to see the world*, Mike thought as they continued to climb out and away from the Dubai terminal area. All the city lights would be visible as they headed along the coast of the Persian Gulf. He hoped the sky would be clear over Jerusalem.

As the 747 approached eleven thousand feet, the crew was handed off to Emirates Center and cleared to flight level three six zero. Don and Mike continued their climb through calm air. The radio chatter was filled with dozens of carriers that a pilot only heard in this part of the world. Air Arabia, Bahrain Air, Kuwait Airlines, Oman Air—the list was too long for

Don to contemplate.

The worldwide-approved language for aviation communications was English, and each pilot and controller was required to speak it fluently. *It doesn't help if you can't understand them through that accent*, Don thought as he heard an Air India pilot respond to a controller's request. The language barrier was what Don and most pilots found the most difficult about international flying. *Sometimes British controllers are the hardest to understand, and we share a common language,* Don smiled.

Only the Chinese had held out against using English as the common aviation language. They spoke English with Western carriers, but all transmission with Chinese carriers was spoken in Mandarin. That left surrounding pilots unable to determine what the Chinese carriers were doing, which had led to serious safety issues in the past. After years of petitioning the Chinese Aviation Authority for a change to English as the official aviation language, the Chinese had recently announced that they would adopt English into their air traffic control system. It would take several years to see real change, Don knew.

But his drifting reflections stopped abruptly as they passed through flight level three one zero. He could smell smoke.

Adrenaline spiking, he glanced over to Mike for a moment. Mike looked back at Don with the same expression. A moment later, the Main Cabin Fire Warning light illuminated, along with the Master Warning light, and a loud warning bell sounded.

Don pressed the warning light to silence the bell. Both crewmembers immediately pulled the oxygen masks from the small compartments that sat below their cockpit windows, removing their headsets and donning the masks over their faces.

"Captains up," Don announced over the cockpit speakers using the microphone switch on the control yoke.

"I'm up," Mike responded.

"Mike, I think this is real," Don said, forcing himself to sound more in command than he felt. "I smelled smoke right before we went on O2. Let's level off here." He reached for the MAIN DECK CARGO FIRE checklist in the quick reference checklist booklet stored just to his left, and then he began transmitting to Emirates Center. "MAYDAY MAYDAY MAYDAY, this is Speed Flight 6. We are leveling at three two zero with a cargo fire. Requesting immediate vectors back to Dubai, over."

Mike had already begun to level the jet. When he heard Don's request with Emirates Center, he started an immediate right hand turn back towards Dubai.

"Roger, Speed Flight 6, we copy your emergency," said the controller at Emirates Center. "Turn right heading one zero zero, descend and maintain five thousand on Dubai altimeter one-zero one-seven, speed at your discretion. When able, state fuel and souls on board."

"Roger, right turn to one zero zero, descend five thousand. Two souls with eight hours fuel, Speed Flight 6," Don replied back as he turned the compass bug to the assigned heading and dialed down the altitude window to five thousand feet. He waited for Mike to respond with his acknowledgement of the ATC instructions, watching the turn and the descent to begin.

Flight 6 was now 110 miles from the field, departing flight level three two zero—32,000 feet—speed Mach point 85.

Don's mental state had just entered a small, confined space. Adrenaline pumped hard thru his veins, and his heart rate was at a sprinter's pace. He knew Mike felt the same. The worst possible situation for any flight crew was an onboard fire, an emergency condition with an outcome so uncertain that no crewmember would ever want to face it in flight. The history of onboard fires had shown that the pilots had less than twenty minutes to get safely on the ground before losing control of the jet. It was a worse case scenario that all crewmembers practiced during training to survive. Don and Mike were facing the real thing and both knew exactly what was unfolding all around them.

The first items on the checklist had already been accomplished; the flight crew had donned their oxygen masks and established communications between them. The next procedure was a serious step. On any modern airliner, the incoming conditioned air used for pressurization and passenger comfort was controlled using a PACK system: pressure air conditioning kit. The 747–400 operated with three independent PACK systems. The checklist directed Don to turn off two of the three PACKs and open the outflow valves, depressurizing the aircraft in an attempt to starve the onboard fire of any usable oxygen and, in theory, extinguish the fire. With one of the three PACKs remaining on, a limited amount of airflow would be ducted into the cockpit, which would keep smoke from entering and obscuring the crew's visibility.

As soon as Don pressed the cargo fire switch, the aircraft depressurized. It began almost immediately. He felt his ears pop from the depressurization, and he saw smoke flow into the cockpit. *That's not supposed to happen*, he thought as he and Mike put on their smoke goggles to shield their eyes. In a matter of moments, the entire flight deck was filled with smoke. His mind flashed back to the moments before takeoff: one of the PACKs, he recalled, had briefly failed.

Flight 6 was now 75 miles from the field, descending through flight level two four zero—24,000 feet—speed 345 knots.

Don completed the last items on the checklist and then turned his attention to Mike, helping him to get the jet on the ground. He loaded the approach for runway one two left into the flight management computer. These preset instructions— the instrument landing system, ILS—would allow the autopilot to fly the approach and land on the runway automatically. This was the same runway they had taken off from, and Don's plan was to head straight back to it. But as he began to load the aircraft's approach speeds into the computer, the visibility through the smoke began to worsen; he could no longer see the screen. He looked over at Mike through the dense smoke; Mike was flying with his face as close to the flight instruments as he could get.

"Speed Flight 6, contact Dubai approach on one two seven decimal niner, they are aware of your emergency," Don heard over the speakers. He was unable to see the audio panel to change to the new frequency. The smoke was now so thick that he couldn't even see Mike.

"Negative center, we have smoke in the cockpit, and we cannot see our instruments. We are unable to change frequencies. Request remain with you, over," Don responded with his best attempt at a calm voice.

"Roger Speed Flight 6, understand. Stand by."

Mike struggled to see the outline of his instruments. The thick smoke came in waves, and his flight instruments looked as if someone was turning them on then off. With the autopilot and auto throttles engaged, his plan was to level off at 5,000 and then to slow the jet for the final descent and landing. He could see his altimeter for only moments at a time through small breaks in the dense, black smoke.

Flight 6 was now 44 miles from the field, descending through 11,000 feet, speed 330 knots.

Don reached to the overhead panel, feeling for the storm light switch that would turn on all the cockpit lights. He moved the warning light switch to BRIGHT. Neither helped their visibility.

"Speed Flight 6, Speed Flight 6, this is UPS one four," said a new voice over the radio. "Dubai approach requests that you descend to two thousand feet. We will be relaying their instructions on guard, over." Flight 6 had descended out of range for the radio frequency they were tuned to, and Dubai Approach had asked an over-flying aircraft to relay their messages. Guard was the emergency frequency of 121.5 megahertz that all aircraft monitored for this type of emergency.

Mike reached up and dialed the altitude window down, the instrument that allowed the autopilot to descend to the selected altitude. He could barely read the numbers and selected what looked like two thousand feet.

Don could not see his audio panel through the smoke to switch his microphone to guard. He was unable to respond to the assisting aircraft. Again, he could smell smoke. He suddenly realized that it was all he was breathing, and he began to cough and choke from the fumes. He yanked his mask off.

"I'm out of oxygen," he coughed out. "I'm going to grab us the portable bottles." He got up from his seat and leaving the cockpit, headed for the emergency oxygen supply tanks mounted in the aft flight deck area.

"Roger that," Mike responded over the cockpit speakers. "Get back fast; I can't see shit!"

Mike could not see Don get up from his seat through the smoke, even though the captain was only inches away. He tried hard to focus on the instruments, putting his face and smoke goggles as close to them as he could, but he saw nothing but black. He put his hand up to his smoke goggles and saw only the skin of his fingers as they touched the glass. His feet hurt—no, his entire legs hurt, a sharp pain rising up through them. He suddenly realized that the metal floor beneath the small layer of carpet was scorching hot. He lifted his feet and propped them on the footrests mounted on the forward instrument panel. Now he could feel the heat with his hands.

The plane started to level off, and he could hear the engines' thrust increase. He was sure that the jet had leveled at two thousand feet, but how far was Dubai? How much time had passed since they had turned around and headed back? How long had it been since Don had left the cockpit? It felt as if someone was asking him these questions from far away. His mind raced, trying to think of a way to clear the smoke he was trapped in.

Voices over the radio pulled his mind from this smoke filled world.

"Speed Flight 6, Dubai approach requests that you descend on the approach. You are cleared to land, any runway."

"Roger," was all Mike could think to say as he sat there, engulfed in a sea of smoke. He could not see the glare shield panel that was right in front of him. He felt the instrument panel, feeling for what he thought was the APPROACH button that would allow the autopilot to capture the localizer and glideslope for runway one two left and pushed it. The smoke was so thick that he had no way of knowing if they were even close to the assigned heading and altitude. He began to cough, thinking of his daughter's first piano lesson. *I'm going to be late to my son's football game.* He heard the engines throttle back and felt the jet nose-over into a gentle descent. It was the last thing Mike would ever feel.

NEWS

Daylight had been sneaking in around the curtain's edge that wrapped the inside of Scott's camper for hours. His home away from home was a Lance ten-foot slide out style complete with a toilet, shower, and a small kitchen equipped with a refrigerator, stove, and microwave. Summer days in Alaska are light for almost twenty-four hours, and outfitting a camper for a dark night of sleep is always a challenge, no matter how ideal the sleeping quarters. But Scott knew that the mild temperatures and sound of rushing water from a nearby stream made for a peaceful sleep, even if it never got dark.

It was early morning, the first full day of Maggie's vacation in the Great North. She laid there smiling across the bed from him, both of them at the start of two weeks of fun and adventure in Alaska. She turned over and kissed Scott good morning.

"Coffee?" she asked.

"Oh yeah, baby, that sounds wonderful," he replied sleepily. Bair, lying under the small camper's table, rolled over on his back and yawned.

"Looks like a beautiful sunny day out there," Maggie announced.

"Every day is beautiful in Alaska," Scott corrected.

"Oh yeah, I've heard of some beauties," she said. "Like twenty below zero and blowing snow. Now that's a beautiful day."

"*This* beautiful day is not going by without some fish in the boat," Scott said, sliding into his socks and jeans. "While that coffee brews, I'll load up the raft." He kissed Maggie on the cheek, reached for his toothbrush, and stepped out of the camper.

They had driven several hours south of Anchorage to the Kenai Peninsula. They would be camping and rafting along the Kenai River, one of Alaska's prime destinations and a salmon fishing extravaganza. The aqua blue, glacier-fed river was close to Anchorage and accessible by road, making it attractive to hundreds of people, tourists and locals alike. Scott called the road-accessible areas combat fishing zones: dozens of fishermen and women would line the shore, shoulder-to-shoulder, setting up a monofilament gauntlet against the sockeye salmon swimming upstream.

Scott usually avoided the massive group of fishing insanity by floating down the river in an inflatable raft. With his air-filled boat, he and Maggie could find quiet, remote areas to fish without coming close to locking fishing line with a would-be salmon slayer. Scott was able to stake out his own fishing hole.

Today, the large red raft was loaded with more gear than they needed, but they had the room on board since it would just be Scott, Maggie, and Bair. The raft was capable of comfortably seating five large men, and Scott had removed two seats for added space and comfort. He loaded his fishing tackle, a dry bag with spare clothes, camera, binoculars, plenty of food, and his bear gun. It was good to be prepared for any situation—a river full of fish, he knew, could attract more than just human fishermen.

Maggie stepped out of the camper with a fresh cup of coffee and toast, which she handed to Scott.

"Thank you. Almost ready here," he smiled.

"I have to get my boots and jacket, and I'll be ready to go," Maggie replied, heading back inside the camper.

Scott retracted the camper's stabilizer bars and attached the raft's trailer to the truck. With all their gear loaded and the fish on ice, they broke camp and headed out with all their equipment neatly packed in their modern-day covered wagon. It was a short drive, and soon Scott was backing the raft down the large boat ramp next to the bridge in Cooper Landing, at the start of the Kenai River.

Kenai Lake spanned over twenty miles from just north of Seward, Alaska to its transformation into the Kenai River. The lake, over five hundred feet deep and fed from several glacial tributaries, gave the lake and the river their signature sapphire blue hue: a soft, almost clear teal, like a bright blue sky with a hint of thin white clouds.

Scott launched the raft and all its gear into the slow moving headwaters. The raft was the workhorse for Alaska outdoor adventures, capable of being stowed in a small airplane and flown deep into the wilderness, yet able to safely carry over a ton of gear and hunted game. It was an extremely safe mode of transportation even in heavy rapids and was able to handle almost any Alaska river. Today's float would be extremely safe; there would be no white water rapids—just the way Scott liked it. *The water is too damn cold to be swimming in*, he always said.

Bair's leash was tied to the raft and he looked official in his bright orange life jacket with his tail wagging and his paws on the bow. The river was mostly smooth, but it would quickly pick up speed when they floated out of the headwaters. Several years ago Scott had watched as someone's dog was swept down the river, no one able to save him. He was not about to let Bair suffer the same fate in this river. All of Scott's passengers, including his dog, donned life jackets.

Maggie tied the bowline around a nearby rock and watched over the raft while Scott drove the truck and its now-empty trailer to the adjacent parking lot. Here it would be picked up and delivered downstream to the take-out point by a group of drivers who did nothing but shuttle these rigs all summer long.

Scott walked at a quick pace back to the river; excited to be starting another adventure with the girl he loved. He was going to have to marry this girl someday if he wanted to keep her, he knew. *Wow, why does that thought give me the chills? And how can I ever get her to move to Alaska? I don't want to move to D.C.* He had asked himself these things at least a hundred times. For now, he let the thoughts float away from his mind.

It was still mid-morning, and the sun had just climbed above the Chugach Mountains that lay to the east. Not a cloud in the sky. The slight westerly breeze brought with it the sweet aroma of cottonwood and spruce pollens. As Scott neared the river, he saw Maggie with field glasses spying on a bald eagle who sat atop the tallest spruce tree along the northern edge of the water.

"Bet he's looking for his lunch," Scott said, announcing his return.

"He's beautiful," she said.

"So are you!" Scott said kissing her cheek. "I love your perfume—is that essence of *OFF?*"

"It's a French mosquito spray," she said with a big smile.

"It goes well with your fishing jacket. What do you think? Are you ready to get this outfit moving?"

"I'd love to. Let's launch this ship."

Attire for the day was state of the art chest waders and matching fishing jackets. Scott sported a Smith and Wesson forty-four magnum on his belt, and Maggie was suited with a canister of Alaska bear pepper spray. They both looked as if they had stepped from the pages of an Eddie Bauer catalog, Scott thought.

Bair barked with excitement as Scott stepped into the raft. Sitting in the center rower's seat, he slid the twelve-foot oars into the oarlocks. Maggie untied the bow and pushed the raft into deeper water, climbing aboard like a pro. Scott began rowing toward the center of the river. Two hundred yards wide at its source, the first mile of the river was relatively slow-moving, requiring Scott to row downstream. Soon the river would narrow, drop in elevation, and pick up speed. All Scott would have to do is steer, keeping the raft toward the middle of the river while avoiding any large protruding rocks and enjoying the scenery.

After an hour on the water, three bald eagles, and one black bear sighting later, Scott rowed to shore along a sharp bend he hoped would be a productive fishing hole. Bair was out of the raft as soon as he felt the bump of hard soil. Maggie jumped from the raft and tied off the bow as Scott stowed the oars.

Once ashore, Scott unhooked Bair from the leash that was keeping him near the raft. He took off running full speed along the water's edge. Scott learned early on that his dog, with his long black hair, looked too much like a small black bear to be running around alone in bear country, another reason for the bright orange life jacket. Even on hikes around the city of Anchorage, his dog had been mistaken for a small black bear several times, and he now sported a red bandana around his neck anywhere they went. *Wouldn't want some dumbass with a gun thinking he is a bear*, Scott thought as he watched his dog run into the bushes and disappear.

"He'll come back, right?" Maggie asked, concerned.

"He doesn't go far, Maggie," Scott said. "As soon as we catch a fish, he will be back at our feet."

He got his fishing pole ready while Maggie took off her life jacket and relaxed on the raft seat, rolling up her sleeves to catch some sunshine. Scott could see that he would probably be fishing alone at this stop.

Two rafts full of tourists floated past, and Scott gave them a *Welcome to Alaska* wave. He walked to the river's edge and cast a line upstream, letting the current pull his orange Russian River fly downstream, a lead weight keeping it along the river's rocky bottom.

Unlike all the other species of salmon who returned to the rivers to spawn, the sockeye salmon no longer ate once they reached fresh water. Their normal diet of small shrimp, seaweed, and the orange-colored krill that gave the fish its deep red flesh were not available in fresh water. Because they were no longer eating, catching them could be tricky. But Scott knew that the salmon tended to swim close to the riverbed, where the current is slightly slower. His goal was to present a bright fuzzy fly wrapped around a sharp hook in front of the fish in hopes of hooking the fish in the mouth—or better yet, annoying the fish so that it would strike the hook.

Whatever the chain of events that occurred under the milky, opal blue depths of the river, they worked well enough, and Scott quickly latched onto a bright silver-gray salmon. The fish jumped through the water's surface, thrashing its body in a desperate attempt to free itself from whatever had seized its jaw. The fish tried several more fleeting attempts to rid itself of the hook by jumping high above the water and then power-diving below.

His adrenaline flowing, Scott slowed his actions and enjoyed the fight. This was his passion. He had caught hundreds of these wonderful fish in Alaska's rivers, and he was well rehearsed in landing a ten-pound sockeye with little effort and few mistakes. He wouldn't lose this fish to the river. He wished the fight could last longer, but in less than a minute, he had the fish close to shore, its energy spent after having fought both the pull of the line and the relentless flow of the current. He landed his prey with a quick twist of his wrist and a steady pull on his G-Loomis nine-weight fly rod. All the splashing had caught Bair's attention from his adventures, and he came barking to Scott's rescue. He ran and barked at the flopping fish, making half attempts to bite what he saw as *his* catch. Using a small club, Scott quickly put the flopping fish out of its struggle with a sharp blow to the top of its head. He turned and gave Bair a job-well-done pat, and then he pulled the hook from the fish and held his prey high for Maggie to see.

"Nice job, honey," Maggie said with a smile.

"Thanks! Nice looking fish, huh?"

"Yes, and what a beautiful day for a float," she replied.

Scott smiled back. He knew that Maggie enjoyed fishing, but she loved the float, the water, the scenery, and the relaxation far more than dealing with slimy fish.

There was a bark—a serious, defensive bark. Scott turned around quickly to see Bair standing at the edge of the alder trees, the hair on his back standing straight up. He began backing up, still barking furiously.

"Bair," Maggie called, now standing in the raft. Bair paid no attention.

Scott hoped it was just a moose or a porcupine that had his dog's attention, but he reacted, preparing for the worst. He threw his fish in the bow of the raft.

"Let's push off now, Maggie," he said.

"What about Bair?" she exclaimed.

"We won't leave him," Scott said. "Let's just be ready to

get out of here."

Still visibly nervous, Maggie stepped from the raft, just as the bruin stepped from the trees. Its nose was high in the air, and it was walking straight towards the raft, ignoring Bair's snarling defense.

Maggie yelled for Bair.

"He's a big one," Scott said calmly, attempting to ease her fears while staring at the biggest grizzly he had ever seen on this river.

Bair continued to bark non-stop. He backed toward the raft as the bear advanced closer, keeping a safe but aggressive distance from the oncoming menace. Scott tried to remain calm. The bear was in search of fish, he deduced, and the splashing caused by Scott's catch was sure to have caught his attention.

Scott and Maggie pushed the raft into the current, Scott holding the bowline to prevent the raft from floating downstream. He called Bair, hoping to get him close enough so that he could grab his life jacket and pull him into the raft. But Bair kept barking relentlessly, paying no attention to his master. His only thought was to fend off this giant intruder.

"Scott, what are we going to do?" Maggie yelled. She had her pepper spray pointed at the bear as he continued his slow march toward them.

"I guess we'll have to give him what he wants," Scott said. He didn't want to admit that this bear was about to steal his newly caught fish.

He unsnapped his pistol strap and then reached into the raft. Keeping one eye on the oncoming bear, now standing less than thirty feet away, he picked up his fish. He knew that the bear was only interested in fish, and that the bear was unlikely to follow them into the stream. What he didn't know, he thought, heart racing, was how far the bear was willing to go to get the fish before they could escape.

"Maggie, hold the raft," he said. "I am going to try to grab Bair after I throw the fish."

"He's closer to me," said Maggie, her voice suddenly calm. "I can get him."

"Okay, let's see what this bear does," Scott said. He held the fish up, trying to get the bear's attention. Scott wasn't sure if the bear could see the fish, but he knew he could smell it. He tried to judge his trajectory. Bair, still barking as loud as he could, took several steps to the left and closer to the raft, leaving a straight path for Scott to toss the fish. It landed with a thump several feet in front of the bear.

Maggie ran to Bair and grabbed him by his life jacket, turning back to the raft half carrying, half dragging the dog with her. She reached the raft and with a pull, yanked Bair from the water's edge and tossed him into the raft. She then stepped up and fell into the raft just as Scott pushed off, and the raft began its quiet, frictionless glide down the river. The bear was standing over Scott's fish, oblivious to the fleeing raft and its occupants.

Bair had finally stopped barking and Maggie pulled herself up into the seat in the raft's stern, her heart pounding and her hands shaking.

"Dang it, I hate losing a fish like that," Scott said.

"I could see it," Maggie said in a quiet and quivering voice. "His huge claw swiping across my back. He w-would have knocked me down and eaten me like a fish." She began to cry, her whole body shaking and cold. Scott realized immediately that the fish was the least of his concerns.

As a bend in the river approached, he rowed the raft to the edge of the slow moving water and pulled onto shore. Stepping to the back of the raft, he wrapped his arms around Maggie. She had stopped crying almost as soon as she started. *A tough girl,* he thought as he hugged her tight.

"You did great, sweetheart," he said. "Thanks for saving

Bair."

"I really thought that he was going to eat me," Maggie said keeping an eye on the line of trees and brush for another bear to coming running out.

"I would never have let him get you," Scott said. "I would have shot him dead in his tracks if he had taken one step past that fish."

He could tell that she wanted to get away from shore and the chance of another bear, so he hugged her tight again, kissed her forehead, and said, "Let's get away from this area. I know a place where there are no bears around."

Scott helped her move to the bow of the boat, where he could keep his eyes on her and not have to turn around to talk. It was obvious that the fun had left this raft trip for Maggie, and chances were that she wouldn't want to leave the raft for the rest of the journey. Scott knew of a sure fishing hole about a mile ahead where he could get his three fish and then head for the take-out. The daily limit on this river was three fish per person, and Scott felt certain that since he'd had to share one of his fish with the grizzly, he wasn't required to count it.

The day's weather remained perfect for Alaska, clear skies with little wind and temperature close to seventy, and after a short time, Maggie was back to being herself. Scott docked the raft along a large island with few trees where he knew there would be no bears. It turned out to be a great place to fish, and after Scott had landed his second salmon, Maggie was in the water trying her luck.

Overall, the float had been one of the best Scott could remember in recent summers. The weather had been perfect, and the fishing was grand, Scott having caught his three fish without spending hours slapping water. Even Maggie had landed two nice nine-pounders. Bair played hard in the river, and all three were looking forward to a relaxing evening around the campfire.

The pullout was just ahead at Jim's Landing. Scott had no idea how it got its name, it was really no more than a small gravel boat launch with an even smaller parking lot, just an outcropping where the Kenai River meandered back close to the Sterling Highway on its journey across the peninsula on its way to the sea. As Maggie tied off the raft, Scott headed towards the cluster of parked vehicles in search of his camper and trailer, leaving Maggie to begin the task of unloading some of the supplies she knew they needed out of the raft before they set off down the road. When he came back, Maggie was scrambling through the clothes and gear in the dry box. From inside, her phone was ringing.

"I can't believe we have cell phone coverage clear out here," she said as she pulled it out.

"A damn shame," Scott said with a frown.

Maggie answered the phone. "Hello, this is Margaret," she said with some trepidation. Then: "Hi, Jim. I don't know how I'm doing; you tell me."

Jim Prescott was her boss and the deputy inspector at the National Transportation Safety Board. He was a brilliant scientist and Maggie said she enjoyed working for him, but she also hated his habit of calling during her leisure time. Scott hoped this call was just routine.

But it wasn't; he knew it the moment Maggie turned and looked at him. Her eyes said it all.

"Raine had a crash," she whispered to Scott.

They had been out of civilization now for one day. Cellphone coverage was spotty at best, and there was no real media coverage of any kind. Scott dug through the dry box for his iPhone. He had several voicemails and text messages. Quickly, he googled *747 plane crash*. Slowly, numerous hits appeared on the screen.

747 Cargo Plane Crashes in Dubai, Crew Lost, the headline read. *Raine Airways 747 lost in Dubai Crash*, read the next. Scott slumped down, sitting on the edge of the trailer.

"What do we know so far?" Maggie was asking her boss on the phone. Moments passed with nothing said while Scott read the news stories. According to the media, the flight had been airborne only twenty-three minutes when the crew reported an onboard fire and smoke in the cockpit. Only twenty-three minutes, he thought, amazed—it had to have been quite a fire to bring down a 747 in such a short time. He watched Maggie; he knew her mind was compiling all of the logistical problems she and her team would be faced with during an investigation this large in a foreign country.

"The UAE will head the investigation on this and you know it," she said to Jim, indignantly. "We will be nothing but a puppet for their conclusions."

There was a long pause, and Scott imagined what her boss might be telling her: the UAE, as far as he knew, wouldn't have expertise to investigate an accident like this. It might be terrorism. The White House might become involved. He tried to imagine which of the Raine pilots it might have been. Was Don Lambert flying that line lately? Didn't he have a new baby?

"Count me in," Maggie said finally, looking at Scott. "But I'd like to travel through D.C. on my way."

After another minute, she hung up the phone and turned toward Scott. "Jim gave the Dubai government two to three days for set-up," she said. "I have to be there, with the full team, in two days. There's a direct flight to Dubai out of Dulles every afternoon. Can we make it to the Anchorage airport by tomorrow morning?"

"Yeah, we can make that happen. Did he mention any crew names?" Scott's mind was going through the pilot list, trying to remember who was flying out of Dubai this week.

"No. I doubt any information has been released yet. I'm sorry, Scott," she said, putting her arm around him. "I know they are all family."

"I'll try to make some calls on the drive back to Anchorage," Scott said. "Let's get this party wrapped up and you headed south. This has to be the worst way to end days of fun and fish." *Who could have been flying that jet?* he asked himself again.

Part II

INTRIGUE

WORK

"That is all!" the foreman yelled in English. He repeated the phrase in several languages as the group of men began to divide up into those who stayed and those who did not. Jafar's name had not been called. His mind was racing as he walked quickly up to the foreman.

"Are you sure my name is not on the list?" Jafar asked.

The foreman began to turn away and Jafar reached out to hold the man back by grabbing his shoulder.

"Get your hand off me, asshole!" the foreman shouted, all his earlier friendliness toward Jafar suddenly gone. "If I didn't call your name, then it's not on the list! Turn your ID badge in at the table." He turned and walked away. Afar did the same, dejected, and walked towards the line forming at the small table.

Jafar stood in the line and moved quickly to the front as the men before him turned in their ID cards and left the job site. He followed the group out. As often happened, many were talking about the upcoming protests and what they could do to get back at the system that had left them stranded in this foreign country without a job. But Jafar had no time for that. He had a young son to support whose future depended on an education. Steady work was the only thing that mattered to Jafar. At this moment in time, his only hope was the tug driver job at the airport.

Damn this situation, damn this country, damn this heat, he thought as he left the construction site.

He walked to the side of a large concrete lamppost, shading himself from the morning sun, and he flipped open his cell phone. The number to the airport loading manager was already programmed in. He had called the number on the tenth day as instructed, but according to Mr. Sarraf, his security check had not been completed, and they could not give Jafar any information.

He could feel his heart pounding and his hands began to sweat. He had to have a job. What would he do if this next step fell through? There were no jobs available here for men like him. Jafar had come as a carpenter, a builder, and a skilled laborer. Now he stood among hundreds of tall buildings, each filled with offices that he had helped to build. Now they were filled with bankers and lawyers and what else, Jafar did not know. He just knew that those offices held no hope of a job for him.

He hit send on his phone, and soon he heard it ring.

"Hello, Mr. Sarraf's office," the voice said in Arabic.

"May I speak to Mr. Sarraf, please?" Jafar asked in the best Arabic he could conjure.

"What is your name and business with Mr. Sarraf?"

This was more Arabic than Jafar could respond to. He was forced to speak English, hoping the man would understand. "My name is Jafar Hamdard. I completed an application for a driver two weeks ago, and I am calling to ask for the job."

"Very well, please wait a moment," the man replied in

perfect English.

Jafar braced himself for a long wait, but the man quickly returned to the phone. "Mr. Hamdard, you have passed your security check. Mr. Sarraf will meet with you this afternoon. When are you available?"

"Anytime," Jafar said, trying not to sound desperate. "At this moment, even."

"Mr. Sarraf has a slot at nine thirty this morning," the man said. "Are you available?"

"Yes, yes, I am on my way," Jafar replied. He turned toward the adjacent street, already packed with morning traffic, and hailed a cab. "Airport Road," he told the cabbie as he sat back and enjoyed the slight air conditioning the small car had to offer.

The traffic was thick, bumper-to-bumper, and the ride would take less than an hour during this time of day, but he knew he would arrive with time to spare. Most of the cars on the road were taxis, mixed together with trucks of varying sizes and shapes, all seeming to be overloaded with some stack of goods. The remaining autos where those of the wealthy: Maybach 57Ss, Pagani Zonda roadsters, Saleen S7s, and Lamborghinis. Ah yes, the Lamborghinis were on every street, Gallardos, Murcielagos, and Countachs, all of Jafar's favorites. He liked the fast cars and envied the rich playboys with their oil money. Dubai was the Las Vegas of the Middle East and the Muslim world; here almost anything went for those with the money. What happens in Dubai stays in Dubai, and Jafar knew that many were here for that reason alone.

But Jafar didn't mind taking the taxis. Taxicabs in Dubai were not the high cost luxury travel option they were in Jafar's hometown of Loralai. The taxi service in Dubai is subsidized by the government, and at this moment in time the major means of transportation in the city. Some buses flowed, and soon Dubai Metro, a fully automatic, high speed, driverless train system, would transport over 200,000 passengers a day. The Red Line was already partially open and was Jafar's best means to and from work—his former work, he reminded himself. When the Red and Green Lines were both up and running by the end of this summer, many of the thousands of taxis and their drivers would be out of work as well.

"Take this next right," Jafar commanded the cabby.

They had turned onto Quad Avenue, which would take them to the entrance of terminal two and the offices of Al-kunaiby Cargo. The road was crowded with traffic, and people were walking along the sides of the road in every direction, many dressed in white HAZMAT suits. A large airplane had crashed the day before, and Jafar guessed that they were close to the site. He had not seen the smoke or fire from his apartment, but he had seen it on the front page of the paper, and it had been the focal point of conversation wherever he went. He was thankful that no one on the ground had been killed.

He pointed to the gate entrance, and the taxi pulled up next to the security building attached to the chain-link fence that marked the edge of the airport property. The meter read twenty-one dirhams, about five and one half U.S. dollars. Jafar paid the man and stepped from the cab. A strong odor of jet fuel filled the air. He wondered if it was from the crash scene.

He was back in the desert heat, and the sweat was beginning to seep from every pore on his body. The thought of working outside in this heat caused him to swallow hard and he wrung his wet hands. It would be even less appealing if it always smelled as it did today. But he had to have work, and he would deal with all the difficulties until he found something better—provided they hired him. He opened the glass door leading to the offices. Once inside, the cool air surrounded him, and he began to feel more at ease with each passing moment.

"I am here to speak with Dawwar Sarraf," Jafar said to the desk clerk. "My name is Jafar Hamdard. I spoke with a man here about an hour ago. I have an appointment."

"Wait one moment," said the clerk, the phone receiver already in his hand. He spoke in Arabic on the phone, and Jafar could only pick out a few of the words, but he was sure the clerk was speaking with Mr. Sarraf. He hung-up the receiver and looked at Jafar. "Mr. Sarraf will see you. Please follow me."

The interview was short and sweet, and Jafar found himself with a stack of paperwork to complete. He was to start work first thing in the morning. A small class would be presented, covering the operation of all equipment and safety procedures on the cargo ramp.

His picture was taken, and Jafar was issued an ID badge to be worn at all times while on airport grounds. A fellow employee, Aban, was assigned to give Jafar a tour of the facility. The first portion of the tour took them onto the cargo ramp, where Jafar was introduced to what looked like controlled madness. Dozens of small tugs were pulling six and seven square wagons at the same time in every direction, all of them loaded with large square pallets. Dollies and cans, they were called, Aban informed him. *I have much to learn*, Jafar thought.

The ramp was full of large jet airplanes, and Jafar felt inspired as he walked under the wing of a 747. *Oh, how life had turned around*, he thought with a smile. *Life did work out sometimes for good people*. He was extremely proud of himself, and he couldn't wait to tell Agib about their good fortune. He was happier than he had been in weeks as he was escorted back out through the security checkpoint, where he was instructed to return at eight a.m. the next morning. Jafar shook Aban's hand, thanked him for the informative tour, and left the building.

It was less than a block to the Red Line Metro station from the entrance to the airport. It would be an easy commute, Jafar thought while looking at his new ID card with pride. Not watching where he was walking, he bumped head-on into a man who had been standing just outside the airport entranceway. The man looked at Jafar, but said nothing. Jafar smiled and said excuse me in Arabic then, he suddenly recognized the man; he had been standing there when Jafar had entered the building almost three hours before.

As Jafar continued his stride towards the Metro station, the man turned and followed.

Jafar didn't look back, but he could feel the man walking behind him. He wasn't concerned. *The man must be going to the station like all these other people*, Jafar reassured himself, glancing around at other commuters. This was a public place, and he was safe. *Besides, what would some stranger want with me? I have no money.*

He scanned his NOL card, walked through the turnstile of the Rashidiya Metro Station, and stepped onto the boarding platform for the Red Line just as the train arrived, slowing to a smooth, almost silent stop. He glanced around, looking for the man he had bumped into. The man was standing several people back, staring straight at Jafar. It sent a chill down his spine.

He entered the car and sat in an empty seat. The man followed him onto the train, passed behind him, and stood riding as a straphanger. *This man is just a rider*, Jafar reminded himself, sitting back and trying to relax in the comfort of the cool air.

This was the start of the Red Line, traveling from the airport on the eastern edge of Dubai to the western edge of the city some thirty-five miles away. The train he rode in had that new car look and smell, and the side windows were full length, offering a grand view of the passing scenery as it accelerated westbound through the late morning sun. Jafar was excited to share the good news with Agib, who would be home with his studies. Jafar had been home schooling him as much as possible, assigning reading and mathematics work for Agib to complete each day and then reviewing and adding to his studies each evening. But today, he would call for a break in Agib's studies, and they would go together to the Chinese diner that served the pot stickers they had both come to enjoy since their arrival in Dubai. Today would be a small celebration.

Jafar watched at each stop, waiting for the man behind him to disembark from the train, but as each stop came and went, the man remained standing there. Jafar turned his head to look at the man. He was staring out the window, his hand holding tight to the strap from the ceiling. He was wearing a dirty ghutrah that sat askew on his head and a once white thawb with food stains down the front. His scraggily beard was long and unkempt, and his hands were black with dirt. At that moment he turned and stared directly at Jafar. It startled him, and he looked away.

Jafar's stop was number eleven, the Al Jafiliya Station. The high-speed rail made short order of the ride, and he arrived less than thirty minutes from the time he had boarded. As he stood to leave the train, the man that had followed him on board turned and left the train, staying close behind.

Jafar quickened his pace, almost running down the escalator of the elevated train station. He turned right and walked across the open lot of hard sand toward the Zabeel bicycle path that led to his small apartment. When he reached the asphalt path that circled the large Zabeel Park, he turned behind to see the man walking in the same direction. His pulse began to race. *Why is this man following me?* The question kept running through his mind. He continued his fast pace, making his way around the park and onto the elevated walkway that crossed over the busy Sheikh Rashid Road. He was now less than a block from his apartment.

He looked back again as he walked down the stairs of the walkway. The man was gone. Jafar stopped, staring back at the path he had just followed, looking for the stranger, but he saw no signs of him. He began to relax, took a deep breath, and continued his walk home, now feeling somewhat foolish for having thought that a strange man had chased him, his mind turned to Agib and the dumplings they would share tonight. He had not seen the man cross the road under the walkway, where he stood watching as Jafar walk into his apartment building

*

Faria had finally devised a plan she was sure would stop the madness and return Anwar to his family, return him to her without his ever knowing who had betrayed his jihad. All she needed was the family computer. She had little computer experience, but knew Aminah had been teaching Suha the basics of searching the web and sending emails. The morning after she and Aminah had mailed the packages, she persuaded Suha to teach her what she needed to know

Now, she had to wait for the house to be empty of her family before she dare send this email. If she could stop his jihad, maybe stop the packages of death and destruction from arriving, then maybe Anwar would give up and come back to his family. Back to her, like it had been so long ago. The children were outside playing. Aminah had gone to the small town market. Anwar had simply left. Electrical power had been on for the entire morning, and Anwar had even left the computer turned on. This would be her chance.

Faria was mortally nervous sitting down in front of the screen. She clicked the mouse, and the computer came to life, its color screen waking up. She went over the plan she had thought through again and again ever since getting the packing slips. Of course she had to return the copies of the packing slips to her husband—Anwar was too careful to forget that detail. But before doing so, she had made time to copy them. She had the tracking number of all three shipments.

Even if she mistrusted Anwar's jihad, she still felt she could not trust the West with her information; they had been in hiding for years, and she feared repercussion. But Saudi Arabia was a large ally of Arab Muslims. They would be able to stop the bomb shipment without backlash to her or her husband, she was certain. Besides, she would not sign the email. They would not even know who sent the information.

Faria clicked on Google and typed in *Saudi Arabia police.* Numerous news events came up on the screen. She had just clicked on the link for *Riyadh Police Department Ministry of Interior* when she heard the door to the cooking room open.

Her heart raced. She quickly turned off the monitor and stood in front of the small aluminum desk. Two of her children were laughing as the cooking room door slammed closed, and then she heard the sound of them pouring glasses of water from the pitcher. She waited, hoping they would quickly return to the outdoors. In a moment, the door opened and she heard them run from the house to resume their play in the yard. She turned the monitor back on and sat again in front of the screen.

She quickly scanned the web page and found an icon that read *Contact Us.* To her surprise, it opened when she clicked on it, just like the email page she was familiar with. She listened for any signs of someone entering the house. A car motor was off in the distance and seemed to be getting closer. On the page, the cursor was flashing in the Subject field.

She could hear the car approaching quickly as she worked. After a moment, she had typed the following message on the screen:

> 3 boxes Are sending from sanaa to aMerica and germany.
> they have bombs in them. THE box numBers are
> D457389200-11 D457389300-12 and UPS436298026345

She placed the cursor on the return address to delete it, but it would not go away. Her heart raced. The car had pulled up just outside the front of her home. She tried to delete the address again, with no results. A car door slammed, somewhere close by. Her hands were sweating, and she felt herself begin to panic. It was Anwar's voice just outside the door talking with someone.

She had no way of removing the address from her email. They would know who had sent it. She read the address—it was just numbers. It didn't have her family's name on it. *Maybe they won't know*, she told herself in a panic. *You must send this,* she told herself. *It's the only way to return Anwar and stop this insanity.* Again she attempted to remove the return address with no success. *Hit Send,* her voice inside her heard screamed, *Hit Send!*

The front door of the house opened. She moved the mouse pointer over the Send button and clicked. The email flashed from the screen, replaced by the message:

Your Email has been sent

"Faria," Anwar called from the front room.

She quickly closed the Google window and turned the monitor off. Standing from the chair, she walked into the cooking room to greet her husband.

DISCOVERY

An anonymous tip is sometimes the key to blowing a terrorist plot investigation wide open, and the FBI was happy to have received the call. This time, the clue had come from a highly unlikely source: Prince Mohammed bin Nayef, Saudi Arabia's deputy minister in charge of counterterrorism. Someone with inside knowledge of Anwar al-Awlaki's plans to deliver homemade bombs targeting US and European sites had provided Saudi Arabia with a critical piece of information: the tracking numbers of the packages containing the bombs en route to the Western cities. The Prince was not at liberty to share how he had received his information, nor could he offer any ideas as to who had sent the bombs. But he had supplied the FBI with just what they needed to find and seize the explosives before they entered the US to be picked up by waiting terrorists.

Information on the packages came relatively quickly. Both shipping companies provided the FBI with full cooperation, and it wasn't difficult to follow the shipments. Three boxes that had been shipped from Sana'a, Yemen. One package was bound for Chicago, one for New York, and one for Cologne, Germany. The tracking numbers showed that two packages had been shipped through DHL and flown from Sana'a, Yemen, to Dubai International Airport, where they had sat for two days waiting on the next available flight. They had then been transferred to a FedEx 777 that was currently in route to London's Heathrow Airport in the UK. The package shipped through UPS had been flown to Dubai and immediately transferred to a Raine Airways 747 scheduled to Cologne. Prince Nayef's tip had come too late for the crew of Raine Airways Flight 6.

Working with the FBI and MI5, Britain's Air Traffic Control informed the crew of the FedEx plane shortly before they landed at London Heathrow that a possible explosive package was on board their aircraft. The crew followed standard operating procedures for such an event, landing safely and taxiing to an isolated area on the airport. After an emergency evacuation by the flight crew, authorities seized the plane, unloaded the cargo container holding both packages from Yemen, and secured each package in a bombproof container for transport to their lab in London.

BBC reporters were present as the plane was sequestered to the far side of the airfield, and a news helicopter fed live footage of the event to the nation's televisions. The suspicion of bombs was highlighted on all the main news agencies worldwide throughout the day, as was speculation about the crash of Flight 6. The Western world waited for confirmation from the authorities that bombs had indeed been found on board this US-bound FedEx aircraft.

While the media speculated, MI5 worked to disarm the bombs. At first, the packages appeared to be harmless. Each box had contained souvenirs, clothes, CDs, and several books written in English, along with the HP LaserJet printer cartridges. Each item was closely examined, but all attention soon focused on the printer cartridges. When the cartridges were disassembled, the experts found a sophisticated, expertly constructed bomb hidden inside. Chemical analysis of the bombs showed that the printer toner had been replaced with a military grade plastic explosive known as PETN, an odorless white powder and one of the most powerful known explosives. Each cartridge contained enough explosive material to easily bring down an airliner or level a large building.

One of the FBI agents, who had been investigating the 2009 Christmas Day bombing attempt, recognized the PETN as the exact same material found on Umar the underwear bomber. Was it the same network? The same instigator?

The shipping company had supplied the destination addresses for the packages. The address in New York had been an empty office building owned by a Jewish senior center next door. In Chicago, the address was an inactive Orthodox synagogue. Each location was being watched, and each morning, as the shipping company made their deliveries, a disguised FBI agent would deliver identical packages to the addresses in hopes of nabbing co-conspirators. But so far, no arrests had been made.

The latest Sharing of Information Act had opened the doors for US agency cross communications and had even resulted in better country-to-country intelligence sharing. It was beginning to show real results in the hunt for terrorists worldwide. Now, the FBI began to compare notes with the CIA, focusing on the one fact neither agency could ignore. The bombs had been shipped from Sana'a. Now they had a positive connection with Yemen.

Yemen had recently become the CIA's latest operations area for al-Qaeda in the Arab Peninsula, or AQAP, in NATO lingo. Its operative and newly labeled leader was an imam named Anwar al-Awlaki. The CIA had been looking for al-

Awlaki for almost three years with the hopes of eliminating him before he instigated a terrorist plot. It was discovered that al-Awlaki had been in contact via email with Nidal Hasan, the assassin who had killed thirteen and wounded twenty-nine at Fort Hood, Texas, in November 2009. al-Awlaki's name also continued to surface in the investigation of the underwear bomber. Although al-Awlaki had not yet been linked directly to either of these plots, the plastic explosives gave authorities the evidence they needed to conclude that he was the driving force behind each plot and could probably be tied to the loss of Flight 6. This top leader of al-Qaeda had just become the CIA's primary suspect.

The CIA agent assigned to find and take-out Anwar al-Awlaki was named Mark Mitchell. Standing six feet, four inches and weighting in at two hundred forty pounds, Mark towered over most Middle Eastern men, but with dark hair and eyes and a full beard, he blended into the population. He had spent seven years as a Navy Seal, signing up right out of high school, studying politics in college while earning a BA in Middle East studies from George Washington University and his masters' in public policy from Harvard Kennedy. His mother, who was born in Afghanistan, had taught Mark the language while he had grown up just outside of Philadelphia.

Mark was the CIA's go-to man in the fight against al-Qaeda and the Taliban throughout the Middle East. He had just spent the last several years along the Afghanistan-Pakistan border hunting the Taliban and al-Qaeda leaders, including Osama bin Laden. In terrorist circles, Mark was known as Murad Mitchell.

Mark had met al-Awlaki in Afghanistan years before and had become a close confidant to the al-Qaeda leader. He still kept in touch with him through the Internet, even after Anwar had returned to Yemen. It was Mitchell who had helped to arrange the marriage of Aminah to Anwar in hopes that she would lead the CIA directly to him.

The plan had been a simple one. Mitchell would send Anwar's new Western bride to Yemen with a GPS tracing device hidden in her luggage. The CIA would then target her location and take out al-Awlaki from high above using one of their latest drone aircraft. But Mitchell's plan had been thwarted at the last moment when Aminah was instructed by al-Qaeda operatives to bring nothing with her to Yemen.

Though the plan had failed, Mark was not one to concede defeat, and he had requested a CIA operative base be established in Sana'a, the capital of Yemen. He set up a satellite and phone tracking operation in Yemen as a means to find and take out al-Awlaki.

Washington and the CIA worked fast to secure an operational site with the cooperation of the government of Yemen, driven by the prospect of finding and eliminating this major al-Qaeda cell. The White House was equally convinced of al-Awlaki's plots against the West and had issued a *signature strike*, authorizing the tracking and elimination of al-Awlaki and any of his top henchmen. Mark's latest tracking station was linked to the CIA's voice recognition supercomputer at Langley, as well as to a drone aircraft operations center the US was assembling on the outskirts of Sana'a. Along with drone aircraft operating out of Qatar and from a newly fashioned airfield hidden in the desert of eastern Yemen, Mark's work meant that al-Qaeda would soon be hard pressed to advance any plots against the United States or its allies.

But for now, stopping al-Qaeda meant finding the man who was responsible for the latest bomb shipment out of Yemen and killing him. Mark was scheduled to arrive in Sana'a, Yemen, on board a US Air Force C-130. The hunt for Anwar al-Awlaki was on.

DEPARTING

S cott called the Raine office as soon as the raft was loaded, but the phone lines were busy. He was not surprised. He had tried calling several of his friends; even some he knew were on the road, all with no luck. He still did not know who had been on board the doomed Raine Air flight.

With all their gear loaded in the camper and raft, there was no reason to return to their campsite. They could drive straight to Anchorage and arrive home by early evening.

As they drove up and over mountains and in and out of cell phone service, Scott continued to try and reach someone at Raine with no success. He knew each pilot at Raine and worried for the families of whoever had been lost. The thought of their loss put a chill down his spine. He hoped it wasn't any one of his closest friends.

They arrived at Scott's home mid evening, time enough to repack Maggie's things and get cleaned up. He knew their time together was now terribly short; Maggie had been able to book a flight to Washington DC that left in about three hours.

Scott carried her travel bags from the camper upstairs to the master bedroom. He could hear the shower running. The thought of Maggie standing naked under the warm water made his heart quicken, and he felt the palms of his hands warm. Even with the stress the turn of events had just brought, Scott was always in the mood to make love to Maggie, and this would be their last chance for weeks to come. *Men are pigs*, he thought with a smile.

He lit the dozen candles that were strategically placed around the bedroom, and then he drew the blinds over the never-ending daylight that streamed into the bedroom even this late in the evening.

The campfire smoke and fish slime on his hands, he knew, would not make for a romantic scene. He grabbed a clean pair of jockey shorts and made his way to the guest bathroom down the hall for a fast but thorough shower. He was combing his hair in front of the full-length mirror next to his bed, clad only in his tight black shorts, when Maggie walked out of the bathroom wearing only a soft white towel around her wet hair. Scott turned and met her gaze with a smile.

"I could smell the candles burning," she said as she wrapped her arms around his shoulders.

"You look wonderful."

"So do you, honey—and wow, no more fish smell. I love it when you wear those shorts."

Scott put his hands around her small waist. She was still slightly wet. Scott felt his shorts get even tighter as he caressed her soft skin.

The kiss started slow and soft, their hands moving slowly over one another's bare skin. Maggie reached up and pulled the towel from around her head, letting it drop to the floor. Scott ran his fingers through her wet hair, pressing tightly against her head. She wrapped her arms around his waist, pulling him close, and then reached into his tight fitting shorts.

As she stepped back, Scott followed her, gracefully kissing her as she eased back onto the bed.

They made love as if it was their first time, not knowing when they might be together like this again. They remained locked in one another's arms until the clock forced them apart. Maggie had a plane to catch.

A scramble with her luggage, a big hug to Bair, and they were soon out the front door and headed to the airport. The sky was still full daylight, even at eleven p.m.

The drive was consumed with phone calls, Maggie trying her DC contacts, waking her assistant at home. It was three o'clock a.m. in Washington. Scott's attempt to get through to Raine Airways was still unsuccessful. They must have shut off the incoming lines, he decided. He had been able to reach several friends, none of whom knew no more than he did at the moment.

"Call me as soon as you arrive in Chicago, please," Scott said with a smile.

"Oh, you can count on it, baby," she replied, sadness showing in her eyes. "I'm sorry I have to end our vacation with something like this."

"Not your fault, love," Scott said. "You have an important job to do, and you're going to be busy. Looks like I will be too. I should know my schedule by the time you get to Dubai."

They hugged and kissed like it was their last for a vastly long time to come. Scott waved good-bye as she disappeared from view at the TSA security checkpoint, and then he turned and headed back to his truck in short-term parking.

*

Scott arrived at the offices of Raine Airways on the Perimeter Road at the edge of the Anchorage Airport. It was close to midnight, the parking lot was full, and he could tell as he drove up that things were immensely busy inside the offices.

The first person he saw as he walked through the front doors was Jenny Christine. Scott had known her for over fifteen years. She was tall and thin with long dark hair, very attractive, and Scott had always had a soft spot for her. He had watched her handle some of the most stressful situations that had come into this office over the years, and he had always admired her for that. But as she turned and met Scott's eyes, she wore no smile.

Without words, they met and held each other tight, like siblings who had lost a close family member. They had. Everyone at Raine Airways was a part of the family.

"Oh God, Scott, what a travesty," Jenny said, trying to hold back her tears.

"Who was on board?" Scott asked, not wanting to hear the answer.

"It was Don Lambert and Mike Barrett," she said. She looked into his eyes as if she wanted him to tell her it wasn't real.

"Jesus," he said. "Were there any jump seaters?"

"No, just the crew."

"Do we know any details yet?" He looked around the lobby for familiar faces. He saw many, but no one he needed to speak with.

"Almost nothing so far," Jenny said. "We know the crew had a fire on board and declared an emergency shortly after takeoff from Dubai. No one has given out any further information than that."

Several people had entered the office, and Jenny had to leave to greet them. Scott continued toward the staircase leading to the chief pilot's office. He smiled and shook hands with several acquaintances on his way, but he kept his quick pace and did not start a conversation with the people he encountered. He needed to talk with John.

John Fenton was the chief pilot of Raine Airways and the biggest reason Scott still flew for this company. John was a great leader, and in the tumultuous world of the airline industry, Scott figured John's ship was the best to be a crewmember on.

The top of the stairs was free of people, and Scott gazed out at the Chugach Mountains that filled the windows along the wall leading to John's office. He had made this walk a hundred times, but this walk seemed the longest.

"Hello, John," Scott said as he opened the door and reached out to shake his boss's hand.

"It's a sad day, Scott, but I'm glad you're here," John replied, motioning Scott to sit down in one of the modest but comfortable office chairs that faced his desk.

"I've heard it was Don and Mike. Is that right?" Scott asked as John walked around the side of his desk.

"Yes," John confirmed. "Both were on their assigned line, headed to Cologne."

"What do we know so far?"

"Not much that I can share with you. We do know that there was an onboard fire, and we know that the crew was attempting to return to Dubai. There seems to have been smoke in the cockpit, enough that the crew couldn't see anything. They went down just to the southwest of the Dubai airport. The only good news is that no one on the ground has been reported hurt or killed."

"Has the Go Team left yet?" Scott asked, referring to the prearranged team of experts that would go to the accident site. The group included someone from each area of expertise who would assist with each facet of the investigation, as well as with the recovery of the aircraft and the crewmembers' bodies.

"They left late this afternoon," John said. "We arranged a charter to get everyone in position as soon as possible. Patty and Mark from Human Resources are on their way to meet with Don and Mike's families, and we're setting up counselors for anyone who needs to talk about their loss or deal with this in any way. We're coordinating all the efforts from the first floor conference room." He reached for a note from Jenny, who had just walked in the door, and read it as he slowly sat down.

"What do you need from me?" Scott asked after a moment.

"Did you know Don or Mike closely?" John asked.

"I knew them both, but only as acquaintances. I've never had the opportunity to fly with either of them," Scott said.

"Don and I flew together in Nam," John said. "We have been distant friends for thirty-five years. Damn shame. Mike was new here. I had only met him a couple times."

There was a long pause as both men tried to find the right words to say. This was the first major accident for Raine Airways and the only loss of life. It felt like Scott had lost family members, and he knew that it would take a long time for life to return to normal. They both knew it.

"I need you in the cockpit, Scott," John finally said. "We still have the Flight 6 Dubai-Cologne weekly flight that will need to be covered. We'll have to postpone next week's flight, but our shipper will be ready for a reschedule in less than two weeks. We have numerous crews involved with the Go Team and the family support, and I don't know if we can cover all the flight segments. Can you fly some legs for us?"

A dozen issues raced through Scott's mind at once. *You want me to fly out of Dubai? Didn't they just find explosives on FedEx out of there? Maybe that's what brought down Flight 6. Isn't the FBI doing anything about this?* And then: *Maggie is going to Dubai.*

"Sure thing," Scott said finally. "Maggie got tagged with the investigation and left this morning, so I can help with whatever you need."

"Great," said John. "I already gave crew scheduling a list of contacts that I thought would help out, and you're on it. Call them as soon as possible, and they will give you a new schedule. It's going to be a rough time for all of us, Scott. Keep sharp out there."

He stood up from behind his desk and extended his hand to Scott. They shook hands, and John's body language was enough to tell Scott he needed to be on his way.

"I'll be in touch," Scott said, and he turned and headed to the empty office across the hall. He needed to call crew scheduling and find out how his life was about to change.

ASSIGNMENT

The next morning, with Bair's food and schedule coordinated for the next several weeks and the newspapers and housekeeper cancelled, Scott was on his way to the airport in Anchorage. His new schedule showed almost three weeks of flying, with layovers in Hong Kong, Cologne, Shanghai, and Dubai. Maggie was in Dubai, he thought; he might get the opportunity to spend some time with her.

He parked his truck in the crew lot and made his way through security, heading across the large pallet staging area toward the cargo building. He could see the flight line and the numerous jets parked in a row waiting for their next crews to take them airborne. Even after all these years, the prospect of flying a 747 all over the world was exhilarating. He loved his career and his responsibilities. A light rain began to fall, and he quickened his pace.

There were major advantages to being a cargo pilot over a passenger pilot: Rarely did Scott have to deal with passenger terminals, TSA searches, tired flight attendants, and masses of people while getting to and from his aircraft. Most passenger pilots had also taken huge concessions in their pay over the past five years, while cargo pilots had generally fared much better. *Even if we sometimes have to walk through warehouses to get to the jet*, Scott thought as he entered the cargo building. The concrete was wet from the tugs and trucks driving in and out of the rain, and he was careful where he stepped.

Talk of Flight 6 filled the crew ready-room as Scott walked in, greeting and shaking hands with his fellow pilots. The large office space was lined with long tables, and fluorescent bulbs lit the room. The tables were filled with pilots reviewing the flight plans, as well as crews waiting to catch a jump seat home or into their next flight schedule. Scott made his way toward the large window at the back of the room that separated the ready-room from the noisy and intensely busy dispatch office. At the window, the dispatcher handed Scott his paperwork with a kind smile and a thanks. He sat down in a chair near the end of one of the long tables to review it while he listened to bits of the conversations going on around him.

There was little, if any official information available as to the cause of the crash. The lack of media coverage when a cargo aircraft was lost to an accident had always rubbed Scott the wrong way. The media wanted sensationalism, and although the loss of Flight 6 had been in the paper on the day of the accident, it had been several pages inside the fold, and Scott was sure that nothing new would be written about the crew or the accident outside of aviation circles. Speculation within the airline community was that a bomb, like the ones found on board the FedEx plane at London's Heathrow airport, had been the cause of crash. That thought had many pilots around the world on edge.

Soon Scott's crew, first officer Greg Cochran and IRO Andy Owen, arrived. Polite and somewhat somber hellos ensued. They all had known each other for years, having flown together many times, and the loss of their fellow crewmembers had taken much of the joy from the normally lighthearted meeting. Within minutes, they had joined in on the discussion of the only subject on everyone's mind.

"Your girlfriend works for the NTSB," Greg asked. "Does she have any insight into Flight 6?"

"She's involved with the investigation," Scott confirmed, "but she can't share any info with me until it's made public."

"You should at least ask," Greg said. "We could use some insight into this thing. What if it's a damn terrorist? Remember, you and I fly the next Flight 6."

"If I get the chance, I'll ask her if she has info that she can share," Scott replied, trying to dodge the issue. "Don't get your hopes up."

The possibility of terrorists being responsible was real. It made Greg concerned and it was obvious why: In several days, he and Scott would be flying the first Raine Airways flight from Dubai to Cologne after the crash of Flight 6, and like all the other crew members, he was a little anxious about the loss. Greg was forty-two years old and had been flying with Raine Airways for over five years now. His background was the US Air Force, flying the F-16. This was his second year flying the 747–400, having started with Raine Airways as a 737 copilot. Scott knew Greg was glad to be flying with him. Greg was a good pilot; he just made no secret of the fact that he liked having someone with years of experience flying four engine heavies around the world alongside him. And Scott was glad to being flying with such a competent pilot like Greg—especially on a flight like the one they would soon be taking.

After a moment, they each began their review of the paperwork. Their first flight segment would take them to Shanghai, China, and was scheduled for nine hours and forty-five minutes. Any flight scheduled for more than eight hours meant that Scott would have an additional co-pilot, an International Relief Officer, along for that leg of the trip. The IRO made it possible for each crewmember to rest during the flight. Each pilot could expect about two and a half hours out of the cockpit to eat, sleep, or catch up on his reading. These breaks made a long flight enjoyable and even seemed to shorten the flight time.

In addition to his crew, three other Raine crewmembers were jump seating to Shanghai to begin their flight schedules from the Asian city. Raine Airways 747s held ten first class seats, and on international flights, many of these seats were occupied with traveling crews. Scott always had passengers. He was thankful that no jump seaters had been on board when Flight 6 went down, keeping the loss of life to a minimum.

Scott, Greg, and Andy were driven to the flight line in a white GMC van, where they dropped their luggage at the rear of the aircraft. Scott began his exterior preflight, walking around the plane. As he walked, his mind wandered, imagining what the crew of Flight 6 had gone through. The fire had to have been intense, the heat and the smoke uncontrollable. He pictured his plane engulfed in flames, spewing a trail of smoke as it plummeted towards the ground, himself in the cockpit fighting to gain control.

"Get a hold of yourself, dude," he said to himself out loud. He could handle this, he told himself. *No way can this happen again, so just relax.* He shook his head and continued with the preflight.

The crew completed their pre-flight, and the Boeing 747–400 was soon airborne. Speed Flight 81 was Scott's flight number today. Takeoff and climb to altitude was uneventful, smooth and by the book. Their airplane was not fully loaded with cargo, as were most westbound flights, allowing for a high cruise altitude of forty thousand feet.

Their flight was routed over Nome, Alaska, across the

Bering Sea, and then, turning south along the Russian coast and into China. They would stay north and west of North Korea before finally flying southeast into Shanghai.

Shanghai—what an incredible city, Scott thought. He had been there many times and always enjoyed his visit. This trip had a one-day layover in Shanghai, offering plenty of time to venture away from the hotel for shopping and sightseeing. But his Dubai layover—where Maggie would be—was the one he looked forward to.

As the crew settled into the cruise potion of their flight, they divided up the break time, with Scott picking the middle two hours. Andy was first in the bunk and headed to his break. Scott reviewed the flight plan, double-checked that they were on course, and then reclined his seat and looked out the window. Flight 6 still filled his head, as it did all the pilots at Raine Airways. *What could have caused such a fire in such a short time? Why couldn't the crew fight the fire as called for in the checklist, and why did it end in a crash? Had it been a bomb? Was it hazardous cargo of some kind? Were terrorists involved? It was coming out of Dubai, the center of the Middle East, for Christ's sake.*

It was all speculation at this time, he reminded himself. Let Maggie do her investigation. She would find the answers. Scott was confident she would discover the reason for the crash of Flight 6.

The flight seemed longer than normal—conversation between Scott and his crew was more intense than usual, with Flight 6 on their minds—but they arrived early with a flight time of nine hours and forty-three minutes. Scott made a smooth landing on runway three-five left and taxied to the Raine Airways gate on the west side of Pudong International Airport.

They had flown their time machine almost halfway around the world, and it was still early afternoon: the time here was just three hours later than when they'd left Anchorage, and a day ahead. *What a job*, Scott thought as he climbed into the hotel shuttle car. The process through customs and the ride to the crew hotel would take over an hour. They would all be ready for a cold beer and a fine meal by the time they arrived at the hotel. If they weren't too tired, maybe Scott would share a bottle of sake after dinner. Tomorrow morning, he would have a few hours to spend shopping, during which he could make a stop at his favorite pearl market—and then, tomorrow night, he would be in Dubai, and with any luck he'd be having dinner with Maggie. That would be the highlight of his trip.

He was still thinking about Dubai when he and his crew entered the hotel lobby. They were greeted with a news report flashing across the lobby's large screen TV.

ALJAZEERA NEWS

AL-QAEDA CLAIMS RESPONSIBILITY FOR THE
DOWNING OF
RAINE AIRWAYS 747 IN DUBAI

ARRIVAL

Margaret gathered her belongings around her first class seat. The stewardess brought her the light jacket she had worn on board. *I won't be needing that for a while,* she thought, folding it into her carry-on bag. It had taken her almost twenty-four hours to get to Dubai. *There's got to be a faster way to go half way around the world,* she thought as the aircraft door was opened and the few passengers in front of her began the mass exodus. The jet way was so hot it took her breath away. It was a thick, moist, stifling heat, like a steam sauna turned up past the point where someone could enjoy it. *This,* she thought, *is going to be a rough assignment.*

Her senses started to recover as she entered the terminal building and made her way to baggage claim. She was impressed with the small, yet tastefully designed terminal and greatly thankful for the air conditioning. Arab and Middle Eastern families of all types and dress were making their way through the airport gauntlet. This was Margaret's first time in an Arab country, and though she had seen the traditional dress before, the burqas were new to her. She had received the State Department's briefing on operations in UAE. There was not a strict dress code for the women in this country, but she had bought several veils, including the white silk one that she was currently wearing.

She continued to people watch as she reached the baggage claim turnstile, hoping to spot her point of contact, surprised at how quickly the luggage from her flight started to appear on the belt. The workers on the loading crew at this airport must be uncommonly efficient, she thought. Soon, her two black Samsonite rollaways were by her side. She criticized herself for packing too much, looking at the large bags that she would have to drag to the taxi. *It's a desert, for God's sake. How many clothes do I really need? Well, a woman can never have too many clothes and besides I've never been here before,* she reassured herself. But the briefing she had gotten from the State Department in Washington left much to be desired on the proper dress for Dubai. First, it explained that visiting women should wear the traditional Saudi attire, but then it went on to explain how modern and forward thinking Dubai was and that a women's attire could be as Western a fashion as she wanted. This uncertainty was one reason she had flown home to Washington from Anchorage to make a clothing stop-and-buy.

She had found an Arab clothing store in College Park, Maryland. The Garb Gallery on Niagara Road was only a twenty-minute drive from her home in Alexandria, Virginia. Mohamed, the elderly storeowner had instructed his wife to help outfit Margaret with the latest in fashionable Arab clothing for women. Margaret looked stunning in the gold tinted headscarf with black lace fringe. Even so, she hoped to not have to wear veils while trying to accomplish her work in Dubai.

Margaret's thoughts drifted to her home on Glendale Avenue in Alexandria, Virginia. She had lived there for six years now in a two story Victorian house she purchased shortly after her husband Ethan was killed. He had been an NTSB scientist when they met. It was love at first sight for her and theirs was a short courtship. They had so many things in common; life had been wonderful with Ethan. They were talking of starting a family and buying a newer, larger home when he was struck by a car and killed. Ethan had been riding his bike, his exercise passion when a teenage girl, texting while driving missed the light change and so, ended Ethan's life changing Margaret's life forever. Her five-year marriage had ended.

She had dated several times since the loss of Ethan, but it was Scott that had brought her soul back to life. She smiled at the thought of him and lifted her chin slightly, trying not to feel sorry for herself.

She pushed those thoughts from here mind and focused on her task at hand. The officers at each passport control station wore the traditional white thawb and ghutrah with a double-banded black ogal. She waited in line only a moment before she stepped in front of the customs agent and handed him her passport.

"How long will you be staying in Dubai?" he asked without looking toward her face.

"Several weeks, I believe," she responded.

He looked over the computer screen in front of him, appearing to take note of something, and then handed the passport back.

"Enjoy your time in our country," he said, again without making eye contact.

"Thank you," she said with a smile.

Near the exit doors, she saw a man in traditional western attire, polished Mezlan shoes, and a bright red silk tie holding a paper sign with *Margaret Hurley* written in large black letters. She walked over and held out her hand with a smile.

"Hello, I'm Margaret Hurley," she said to the gentleman with the sign.

"Good morning to you, Ms. Hurley," he said in perfect English. "I am Da'ud Hassan, the investigator in charge for the UAE General Civil Aviation Authority. We've spoken through e-mail, if you recall." He had a Wisconsin accent, she thought as he lightly shook her hand.

"Yes, I recall," she said with a smile. "It is nice to meet you, Da'ud. I didn't expect a personal welcome."

"Please, call me David." His eye contact with Margaret was quite short, and only while he spoke. He was extremely attractive, she thought, and then: *Stop it*. "This is our driver," David continued. "Please, allow him to take your bags."

She smiled at the driver as he quickly turned, stacked the bags on a hand cart, and headed to the waiting auto.

"I appreciate your advance emails," she said to him as they walked. "My briefing said I would be working with you, but I didn't expect you to meet me at the airport. Thank you again."

"It is my pleasure, Ms. Hurley. We are at a slight standstill in the investigation until we have the NTSB's expertise. We are all extremely glad you have arrived in such a short time."

"Please, call me Margaret. We're happy to help. Can you brief me on what you have so far?" she asked as they stepped through the outer doors of the terminal building.

The heat was all consuming, wrapping around her like a blanket, the bright sun screaming for her to don sunglasses. Her first breath felt as if she had inhaled air inside an oven, almost stumbling as the change of temperature caught her by the throat. Maintaining her composure, she walked as if she hadn't noticed the heat and casually put on her sunglasses.

"I have a briefing packet for you in the limo, and I will give you what we've found so far this morning on our way to the hotel," he said. "I see you are booked at the Fairmont. We have set it up for you to have a suite with an office area. I hope that this will be okay?"

His hospitality seemed genuine, but not what she had expected. "That will be fine, thank you," she said. "You speak excellent English, David. Did you study in America?"

"I was born in Saudi Arabia, but my mother was American. We moved to Milwaukee, Wisconsin when I was two. I grew up a Green Bay Packer fan. My father taught me Arabic and the ways of the desert." He smiled and looked to see her reaction to his small joke. "I went to University of Wisconsin and worked with the FAA for several years out of school, and then I moved here three years ago to work with the UAE's Aviation Authority. Is this your first visit to Dubai, Ms. Hurley—excuse me, Margaret?"

"Yes it is. I wish it was under different circumstances though."

Their transport to the hotel was in the longest limousine she had ever seen, a white Hummer with huge aftermarket rims and wheels. It could fit forty people, she thought as the driver opened a side door and motioned her in. She stepped up into a cool, almost cold leather interior. It was bright daylight, but the tinted windows shaded the rays of the sun, and she had to remove her sunglasses to find her way to a seat. She sat facing forward, and David followed in after her, facing the rear. The driver closed the door, and then he entered the limo himself, passing two cold, water soaked towels from a small cooler back to his passengers. David wiped his forehead and neck as he watched Margaret out of the corner of his eye. She was glad to be wearing the veil now that it was hiding the sweat trickling down the sides of her face.

I have just walked through that heat for no more than two minutes, she thought, *and I'm dying here.* But the towel was immensely refreshing, and she followed David's lead, holding it in her hands to absorb the cold moisture and then carefully wiping her brow and neck, trying not to interfere with her veil. *A few cold towels each day and I may make it through,* she thought as she passed the towel back to the driver.

"Would you care for a water?" the driver asked as he reached into a side cooler and pulled out two bottles of water, dripping wet from the ice water they had been stored in. He wiped them with a white towel and handed one to David then one to Margaret.

David handed her a small blue folder. "This is our progress as of yesterday evening," he said.

He allowed her time to read through the paperwork as he looked out the windows of the limo. He enjoyed seeing an American woman again and occasionally gazed in her direction, anticipating her questions that he felt sure she would have. He loved his Arabian heritage and was proud to be working and living with his people, but his life in America had taught him to love the outward beauty of women and David preferred Western girls. He was ever the professional and would never allow his loins to interfere with his work, but he always had a hard time not glancing at a beautiful woman and Margaret was just that.

"Have the boxes been found?" Margaret asked, breaking the silence. She was referring to the so-called *black boxes*, which by now she guessed everyone in the world knew were not black, but a bright orange color to help investigators find them after a crash.

"We located the cockpit voice recorder this morning, but we are still searching for the flight data recorder," David said with some hesitation. "As you can see, the crew reported an onboard fire shortly after takeoff. The crash scene strongly supports that. Even with the fuel fire at impact, a large section of the forward fuselage is broken away and appears to have suffered extensive fire damage prior to the impact."

"Have the bodies been recovered?" she asked.

"As of last night, no," David said as he looked away. "I have not been briefed on the situation yet this morning."

"OK," she said. "Have the Raine Airways people arrived?"

"Yes, several of their representatives have arrived. They are staying at the Fairmont as well. We have tried to keep all interested parties on the same floor for ease in communications."

"Wonderful. Do you have any contact names for their people?"

"All the names and numbers are listed on the red bordered sheet at the back of the briefing."

She looked over it briefly; Scott wasn't here yet. He was the one person she looked forward to seeing arrive. "How far is it from the hotel to the accident site?"

"About a thirty minute car ride. As you can see on the map, the site is less than one mile from the airport in an open area. We were damned lucky that no one on the ground was killed."

"Or maybe the crew was that good," she replied. "I'm sure we'll know when we have the recorders."

The Dubai government had no means of analyzing the tapes on the data recorders and would be counting on the NTSB to do it. Margaret was confident that it would at least ensure an accurate account of the events leading up to the accident. She yawned. It was nine a.m. here in Dubai, but her body reminded her that she was still on Eastern Standard Time: i.e., two a.m.

"Have you taken delivery of the NTSB equipment?" she asked.

"Your supplies have arrived, and I am assured that they will be on-site early this afternoon," David replied. The NTSB had sent four large secured aircraft shipping containers that were equipped with a portable laboratory, along with everything Margaret and her team would need to conduct a thorough investigation.

"Wonderful. My team arrives tomorrow morning on this same flight," she said.

"We have their itinerary," David confirmed, "and my assistant will be meeting them at the airport. I was hoping that the two of us could be on-site by tomorrow," he said.

"Tomorrow? I would like to be there this afternoon, if possible," she said. "Just give me time to freshen up, and I'll be ready to head out there."

"That would be outstanding, Margaret," David said, sounding relieved. "I will make sure your equipment is available when you arrive. We have a car and driver at your disposal that will be waiting at the hotel."

"Thank you," she said as she peered out the limousine windows for the first time. *I hope to get to see some of this country before I leave*, she thought as her eyes slowly closed. She hoped David wouldn't mind her sleeping in front of him like this; somehow she doubted he would.

ON-SITE

The car that waited to transport Margaret to the accident scene was not a limo, but a black, new-looking sedan of some type. Margaret didn't know her cars that well, but she recognized the logo as a Mercedes.

Her driver was a young Arab man in a tailored Western suit who introduced himself as Omar Tyagi, speaking English with a strong Arabic accent. She had been at the hotel for only a short time; although she was tired, she needed to see the crash scene and meet her colleagues from the UAE General Aviation Authority. She ate a salad at the small cafe along the side of the large hotel lobby and took several of the power bars she had brought in case it turned out to be an even longer day that she hoped.

She wore a long cream colored dress made of light cotton with a matching head scarf and flat-soled brown loafer-style sandals. She hoped that she had dressed appropriately for work in the desert environment, but supposed that if the area was different than expected, she could modify her attire for tomorrow's work on-site. She carried a large handbag that contained her laptop and Nikon camera equipment, hoping to at least get some preliminary documentation done today. That would give her briefing points to offer her team when they arrived the next day.

The drive through the city was exciting for her. She was fascinated by the difference in the architecture, the attire, and the beautiful Arabic language that was written on all of the signs and billboards. The cars on the streets all seemed to be new and expensive, so many styles that she had never seen before. It appeared to have no trash or litter, and she didn't see graffiti anywhere that she looked. *Big difference from DC,* she thought. She was impressed that a city so large could be so clean.

After taking the airport exit, Omar slowed the car as it approached a security checkpoint at the entrance to a sand-covered road. This was the access point to the accident scene. Yellow caution tape lined the sides of the road, and several wooden barricades blocked the entrance to the area. Two armed security guards in blue uniforms stood against the barricades as Omar turned the car onto the access road. One guard approached the car holding a clipboard. Omar rolled the driver's window down to greet him, and Margaret instantly felt the desert heat roll into the car through to the back seat.

After a brief conversation in Arabic, Omar pulled the car forward past the barricade and into a makeshift parking lot. David was approaching the car from what she assumed was the accident site. Margaret opened the car door, put on her sunglasses, and stepped out into the heat. A thick smell of jet fuel filled the air. She scanned the area around her trying to get a feel for the landscape and the local environment. This would start the twenty-seventh and largest plane crash investigation of her career. *This desert heat could soon make it the most difficult,* she said to herself.

She turned and greeted David with a smile and a handshake.

"Good afternoon, Ms. Hurley," David said.

"Hello again, David," she replied.

He was dressed in Western attire: Levi's blue jeans, short sleeve shirt, loafers, and a green baseball cap with a yellow *G* on the front.

"So you *are* a Packer fan, I see," Margaret said with a smile.

"I even have green blood," he replied.

"I enjoy watching your quarterback play," she said. "He's quite the athlete." *Always worthy politics approving of another person's team*, she thought. "David, I just want you to know that the NTSB is here to help you and your investigation in any way we can. Please let us know whatever it is you need."

"Thanks, Margaret," he replied. "I'm afraid we will be counting on you and your people for most of the expertise. We have little in the way of accident investigation personnel or equipment. We're getting there, but right now we are not set up to handle an accident of this size."

"I'm sure that between your team and all the interested parties, we'll find the cause. Can you give me an overview of the scene?"

"We have two major debris fields," he explained. "This path leads toward the main section of the fuselage and the larger of the two areas. Almost nothing remains of the aircraft wing section due to the fire. The largest part of the cockpit area is further ahead."

Small whiffs of smoke were still rising from burned spots in the sand as they passed. "Have you been able to recover the bodies?" she asked.

"The flight manifest shows two crewmembers on board with no jump seaters listed. We have found one crewmember's body so far in this vicinity of the fuselage,"

David said, pointing to the small area map he held. "We have yet to find any remains of the second crew member."

"What about the recorders?"

"Our people recovered the second recorder this morning. We're hoping the NTSB will do the analysis on them," David said.

"Certainly, we'll get them off to Washington immediately. Do we have an indoor facility available to do field analysis?"

"We have arranged for a UAE hangar to position recovered articles and to do any of the field analysis that we might need. It's located about ten minutes from here. Do you think that will work?"

"That will do very well," Margaret said with some amazement. She was not accustomed to foreign countries treating her so accommodatingly while she was on an investigation. She had extensive foreign experience, having worked twice in Central America, once in Europe, and once on an investigation in Australia, but she'd found the power struggling aviation departments in each country going out of their way not to be overshadowed by the elite scientists of the NTSB—even when they knew they needed all the help they could get to make accurate findings.

"Also, your equipment containers have arrived. You can see them stationed about one hundred meters from here," he said, pointing toward the lineup of four large white shipping containers. "Would you like to go there first?"

"I would like to see the accident site first, if you don't mind. Could we get shipping container number one moved to that hangar? It has most of our lab equipment."

"Absolutely, I'll get it moved immediately," David replied as he raised his two-way radio. He spoke Arabic to the man on the receiving end of the radio, and in a moment he'd turned back to Margaret. "It's on its way as we speak."

"That's outstanding David," Margaret said, feeling that the

investigation was starting off on the right foot. "I didn't expect to get an overview today." She was impressed with his demeanor and attitude—as well as slightly smitten, she was aware, over his good looks.

They began walking over hard-crusted sand toward the crash scene. Many people in the area were wearing ventilators and full HAZMAT suits. There was no sign of vegetation anywhere in the area, and the smell of jet fuel was terribly strong. Margaret found herself swallowing hard, her eyes beginning to water. She could identify several pieces that appeared to be parts of an airplane's landing gear. The smell of jet fuel was almost overwhelming now.

"This may be far enough until we get suited up, David."

"I agree," he said. "You can see the largest remaining piece of the fuselage from here, lying about two hundred meters ahead. We allowed most of the fuel to burn away to aid in the HAZMAT cleanup, but a large portion was absorbed into the sand. Our people are currently searching for human remains. If you'll follow me, I'll show you the access path to the other major debris area." They both turned and retreated from the odors.

"David, can we get a helicopter to see the site from above? I would like to get some aerial photos."

Again he spoke Arabic into his radio. "They're arranging it right now," he said to Margaret when he'd finished. "But I don't know yet if we can get one yet today. It may have to be scheduled for tomorrow morning."

"Tomorrow will be fine. Thank you."

He led her further to the southwest on a small footpath in the sand that had been matted down by the workers already at the scene. Even though they were further away from the initial sight, the smell of jet fuel hung thick in the hot desert air. The fumes from the fuel decreased, however, as they approached the next large piece of aircraft structure rising from the sand. It was obvious to Margaret that this was the nose section of the plane that contained the cockpit area. It was broken off from the main section of the fuselage and lay on its side, crushed to half its normal size, but it appeared to have escaped the inferno that had engulfed the previous section.

"One of the human remains was located in this forward fuselage area," David said. "A crane will be here this afternoon to lift this section as soon as your team gives the okay—maybe we'll find the second body underneath."

Margaret did not respond, but instead removed the digital thirty-five millimeter camera from her bag and began to photograph the scene. She walked around the entire perimeter, careful not to step on anything that could be evidence. Once she'd made it around the entire area, she stepped closer and photographed the inside of the wreckage, paying close attention to fine detail, such as the burned marks around the broken section. She took several photos through the broken windows of the cockpit and then the nose landing gear area.

After about thirty minutes, Margaret walked over to David, who had spent much of this time on his radio. "Are you ready to get out of here for now?" he asked.

She was still feeling the time zone change, and she was looking forward to getting some sleep in a cool hotel room. "I am," she said. "I'm glad I was able to see the accident scene, but yes, I think this is all I can accomplish at the moment. I'll look forward to the aerial perspective tomorrow."

"About that," David said. "I have just been told that a helicopter is standing by to take us up. Would you like to do it yet today?"

The thought of getting another important step in the investigation completed gave her a second wind. "Absolutely," she said. "When can they pick us up?"

Again David spoke into the radio. "They are on their way. They'll set down near the parked cars. If we start that way, we should be back when they arrive."

They followed the same path back toward the parking lot through the strong odor of jet fuel again. Margaret could hear a helicopter now approaching from the direction of the airport. As they neared the cars she could see it: a Bell 206, small and old, but fine for this short survey.

The Bell circled around and made a short approach to the asphalt road near the barricades where Margaret and her driver had entered. The chopper kicked up a large sandstorm as it descended onto the road. Margaret held her scarf close to her face and closed her eyes, waiting for the sand to settle, while David acted as if this was nothing in the way of blowing sand and watched as the helicopter came to a stop. Its pilot reduced the collective to neutral, and the sand quickly settled.

David looked at Margaret and motioned for her to follow. They approached the helicopter and David opened the side door, took Margaret's hand and helped her into the back seat before following her in and closing the door. She and David put on their seatbelts and donned the green David Clark headsets that hung from small hooks mounted on the wall behind them.

"Test, test, can you hear me?" David said into the microphone.

"Loud and clear," the pilot responded. Margaret looked at David and gave him a thumbs-up signal.

"Where do you want to go?" asked the pilot.

"We want to circle the crash site first," David responded, looking at Margaret for her agreement. Margaret gave David a thumbs-up again, and the helicopter spooled to life.

The sand storm returned as they rose from the ground. It lasted several moments, but slowly they rose above the small desert storm and the view became clear. As the helicopter turned to the south, Margaret was able to see the entire crash site.

She made mental notes as she snapped the camera shutter. At first sight, it appeared to her that the plane had been heading in a southeasterly direction, having begun an attempted landing before going around and crashing shortly beyond the airport. A large cut in the sand was apparent, highlighting where the right wing tip must have made ground contact first, causing the plane to start a cartwheel. This probably caused the nose section to break off and come to a stop away from where the main fuselage section had come to rest and burn.

The debris field was quite large. It appeared to be over a half mile, stretched along this lone section of isolated sand. Everyone in the surrounding area was enormously lucky. Housing units and large luxury condominiums lay on both sides of the accident site. *It's a miracle no one on the ground was injured,* Margaret thought. She could see the crane David had mentioned being brought in to start moving the wreckage. Small columns of smoke were rising in and around a large, dark black crater that the main impact had smashed into the sand. Margaret's thoughts turned to the crew who had lost their lives in the surreal scene below, and then to Scott, who was flying a jet just like the one that lay below her.

Margaret cleared her thoughts and focused her mind on the task at hand. It seemed to her that the debris field appeared textbook. No surprises and no ground structures to contend with. *Now I just have to find out why this happened in the first place*, she thought.

The pilot continued to circle the site, making five complete circuits of the crash while Margaret took more photos. Finally, with several hundred shots taken, she turned to David and said, "I've got all I need here."

"Okay, Captain, we've seen enough. You can take us back now," David announced into his headset. The pilot gave David the thumbs-up sign and pointed his bird back toward the road.

But as the helicopter turned with a slight bank, there was a loud bang, and Margaret felt her seat drop several feet. She grabbed for the handle attached to the inside of the cabin with one hand and David with her other. There was another loud bang, and she felt the chopper lose power.

"What's wrong?" she asked over her headset, but she got no response. Her seat dropped again, and this time it didn't seem to stop. She looked out the window to see the ground coming up at a quick pace, but they were still moving forward some. They were going down frightfully fast.

The pilot's voice came over the headset: *MAYDAY MAYDAY MAYDAY, chopper Alpha six three-delta niner, emergency landing three miles west of the field. Please send emergency equipment.* She couldn't quite hear the reply. This was no hiccup: She could see the rotor blades still turning and could hear the engine running, but it seemed much quieter. They must have lost most of the engine power.

Trying to remain calm, she thought quickly. Helicopters could glide without an engine—*auto-gyration* was the name of the fast descent procedure, she recalled. *Holy shit, this is a fast descent,* she thought. They weren't that high to begin with. Several hundred feet, she figured, not more than a thousand. *What does that matter?* she thought. *A fall from a hundred feet is no better that a fall from a thousand feet.* She had to stay calm. *Jesus, I can't believe this is happening. I come to investigate an air accident, and now I'm about to be in one.*

They still seemed to be headed to an open area below. Margaret could make out the cars in the lot where she had arrived. The pilot seemed to be attempting to land close to the large open sandlot. She looked at David again as he looked at her.

"Hang on," he said. "This is going to be a rough landing." He grabbed the handhold on the left side of the cabin and held onto Margaret's hand with his right. The ground was close now, and their descent was not slowing. In fact, she thought they were going down even faster.

She gripped David's hand ever tighter as they neared the ground. "We aren't going to make it—we are going down way too fast!" She thought this, or said it, or yelled it; she wasn't sure. *Power lines*—she could see power lines all around her now.

And then she felt her body gain in weight. *Added G force,* she knew. The helicopter must have slowed its descent, so fast that it drove her down into her seat. The sand storm reappeared all around them, and she couldn't see anything as the helicopter hit the ground hard. Her shoulder straps pulled tight against her body, and she was certain this was the end.

She waited for the fire, the explosion, or whatever was supposed to come next. But slowly, she realized that they had stopped. The engine was still running and the blades were still turning, but the sand storm seemed to be dissipating.

"Everyone all right back there?" came the pilot's voice over the headset.

David looked at Margaret. "You okay?"

She began to relax her body and felt the death grip she had on David's hand. It seemed to startle her, and she withdrew.

"Yes, yes, I'm okay," she replied, surprised at her answer. She looked out the window: The sandstorm had all but disappeared now, and several men were running toward them. The large overhead blades were slowing their rotation: Either the engine had quit or the pilot had shut it down, she wasn't sure. She took off her headset, wanting nothing but to get out. In a flash, the pilot was opening her door.

"Let me help you," he said as he assisted her with the safety harness that now seemed to trap her inside. As soon as the strap was off, she grabbed her camera bag and began her escape from what she found herself thinking of as *the box of death*. David came running around the helicopter, his full attention on Margaret.

"Are you sure you're okay?" He held her shoulder and took the heavy camera bag from her. "Is your back all right?"

"Yes, I think so," she replied. "I feel okay, a little tense but okay."

The blades had stopped now, and the sand had all settled as they walked away from the helicopter. The men she had seen running toward them were gathering and asking whether anyone was injured, she assumed. They all spoke in Arabic, and she felt a little left out as she watched the pilot describe what had happened. Once they saw that everyone was alive and unharmed, their attention turned to the wounded beast that sat broken in the sand. She could hear sirens in the distance.

"Let's head to the cars," she suggested.

"I'm sure the medical technicians will want to look us over before we go," David said to her on the way back to the parking lot. "Are you sure you are okay?"

"Yes, I'm good," she said. "It was a scary ride, huh?"

"I don't ever need to do that again," he replied.

They walked slowly through the sand toward the parked cars. Emergency trucks adorned with bright flashing lights and loud screeching sirens roared into the parking area, all trailing a cloud of sand behind them. The lead fire truck approached the crash survivors, and the sirens all came to a stop.

After David had assured the fire-fighting crew in Arabic that no one was injured and given them a quick description of the scene, several smaller fire trucks headed on to the awaiting helicopter. Two medical personnel approached David and Margaret, offering them a quick examination and escorting them to the air-conditioned ambulance. After a small battery of tests and numerous questions, they were confident that the passengers were unharmed and released them without a ride to the hospital. They both walked toward the parked cars and Margaret's waiting driver.

"Thank you for all your help, David," Margaret said, extending her hand as they reached the black Mercedes.

"My pleasure, Ms. Hurley," he said as he shook her hand. "What an exciting first day, wouldn't you say?"

"Maybe a little too exciting. Let's keep it to an on-the-ground type of excitement, can we?" She smiled, feeling a little closer to this man that stood there in the sand.

"I am truly sorry," David assured her. "There will be a thorough investigation into this accident and into the operator of the helicopter, I can guarantee you. How are you feeling? Are you ready for a return to your hotel?"

"Yes, I do believe I've had enough for today," she said. "I should get some sleep and be ready for tomorrow, in case you have more excitement planned."

"I'll do my best to keep your excitement level to a low roar from now on," he said. "Tomorrow will be a full day, I'm sure. I hope you get some rest. If there is anything you need, please don't hesitate to call my cell phone. It's listed on the top of the briefing packet I gave you this morning." He opened the rear door for her.

"Thanks again, David," she said as she got into the car. Before closing the door, she turned back to shake his hand one more time. Or was it to see his handsome face, she wondered. "See you tomorrow."

At last she settled into the car and sank into the soft cool leather of the back seat. *Home, James*, she thought as the jet lag and the adrenalin rush of the day's events began to overtake her.

Her thoughts filled with Scott. Had he made it safely to Dubai yet? She had always worried a little when he was flying, always waiting for that call telling her he was safe on the ground. Seeing that plane spread across the desert—one that Scott had surely flown in the past—all balled-up in a crash scene drove her fears home. *Wait until Scott hears about my exciting day,* she thought. *Maybe he will have to worry about me in the future.* She felt her eyes beginning to close.

LAYOVER

Culture change was a way of life for Scott, having flown to so many foreign countries over the years. Two days ago he was in the American scene—or at least his Alaska scene—comfortable and relaxed, knowing what he could expect and what was acceptable in every situation.

From there, he had flown to Shanghai. Into a culture that mixed Western and European styles, yet with a distinct Chinese flair and a language that Scott would never be able to read or speak. He only knew a few choice words that could offer a polite hello or order a beer. But the people were wonderful, many of them from outlying provinces who had transplanted themselves to this giant city to discover prosperity and enter the middle class.

Now Scott was in Dubai, a city where long cotton garments and turbans were the norm. Where the people struggled to be so much other from the West. Where more riches and oil wealth flowed than Scott could ever get his head around. Almost everything here seemed new and first class: their limousine ride to the hotel, the artwork, the architecture, and all the amenities. Again, a difficult language in which Scott only knew a few choice words, but at least here most people spoke some English, if not always fluently.

The heat took away from the luxury, Scott thought as he left his jet. *A visit is one thing, but I don't know how these people can live in this heat.* He smiled at the ground crew waiting at the bottom of the stairs. It didn't seem to bother them in the slightest.

"Right this way, Captain," the chief of the ground crew said with a smile, turning to lead the way. He was dressed as many of the workers here, wearing a light blue polo shirt, faded jeans that appeared to be of a European make, and sandals that looked as if they'd been made from brown paper. Scott didn't ask.

He and his crew were escorted to the main airport terminal, where they cleared customs and were then escorted to a waiting limousine. The driver attended to their bags as the crew made a dash for the car's air conditioning. Once in the back seat, the driver quickly offered ice-cold towels to his hot and now sweaty riders. It was late morning in Dubai as they drove toward the crew hotel. Scott turned on his cell phone and called Maggie.

"Hello, this is Margaret Hurley," she answered.

"Hello, Maggie. Scott James here calling from Dubai. How are you?"

"I am doing great hearing your voice, but I'm cooking in this heat. Did you just get in?"

"Yeah, we're on our way to the hotel as we speak. Dinner tonight?"

"That sounds wonderful. I don't know what time though; this promises to be a long day. My team arrived yesterday, and we're hard at it. Can I call you on my way to the hotel?"

"That sounds like a plan. I'll wait for your call. What hotel are you staying at?"

"The Fairmont. Isn't that your crew hotel?"

"Yes, and they have a wonderful restaurant on the top floor. Let's meet there."

"When do you leave for Cologne?" she asked suddenly.

"Not for almost a week. We head back to Hong Kong tomorrow, and then we go to Shanghai before we make our way back here. Our Cologne flight is after all that." He hesitated, knowing her answer to his next question before he asked. "Have you found anything yet?"

"You know I can't talk about an investigation," she said. "I have to go. Love you, see you tonight."

"I love you. Have a great day."

Some poolside time in the sun, maybe a nap, then dinner and cocktails with my girl. Shaping up to be a good day, Scott told himself as the limo pulled into to the hotel's grand entrance. He counted nine bellmen; all assembled in a long line and dressed in bright white thawbs, summer ghutrah scarves, and black ogal headbands. They stood almost at attention as they waited to assist the arriving patrons.

Scott and his crew were shuffled into the hotel with white gloves. Their rooms were of course ready, and they headed to the elevators.

"What do you think, pool in about thirty minutes?" Scott asked his crew.

"Not me—I'm out of here in nine hours," replied Andy, Scott's IRO. Scott's next flight was from Dubai to Hong Kong, which was scheduled at under eight hours, so Andy would meet up with a different crew headed to some other distant port that lay over eight flight hours away. The elevator door opened on the twenty-first floor, and he stepped out. "I'm grabbing some room service and sleep, gentlemen. Good night—nice flying with you. Have a safe flight tomorrow."

The elevator door closed.

"Thirty minutes?" Scott repeated, and Greg nodded.

The entire skyline of Dubai was on display in Scott's thirty-second floor room as it met the deep blue water of the Persian Gulf. Boats of every size and shape dotted the coastline, sending Scott into thoughts of a long, warm vacation wrapped up with Maggie aboard a sailboat.

Scott loved the view, but he enjoyed it several steps back away from the window. He was afraid of heights—or ledges, he liked to remind himself—and these windows covered the entire wall from floor to ceiling, offering a definite ledge sensation if you stood too close to the glass. He was always amazed at the number of pilots he had met and trained over the years who were afraid of heights but who had no fear or even sensation of height while flying. The restaurant on the top floor had the same grand view as his room, and he was looking forward to meeting Maggie there for dinner.

His first line of business was getting his laptop up and running. Any issues from his world back in the States usually found him through email while he was on layover. Nothing immediate jumped off the screen at him after a quick scan through Gmail, so he changed into swim trunks, found his suntan lotion, and donned the white bathrobe and slippers that hung in his closet. He grabbed his room key and sunglasses, heading for the pool and sunshine.

He walked around the pool area on the eleventh floor, taking in the sights and sounds while his body attempted to adjust to the overwhelming desert heat. Even on the eleventh floor, he could hear the busy bustle of the city from below. He had made it down before Greg, so he found a sunny spot and pulled a lounge chair around to face the sun. *Not many people here today,* he thought. A pool attendant approached Scott and offered fresh towels and cold water. Scott ordered a Heineken and sat down. *Thank God they allow alcohol in this place,* he thought. Dubai was one of the desperately few places in this Muslim part of the world that allowed alcohol of any kind. *Dubai was the Las Vegas for Muslims*, Scott thought with a smile. *What they can't have back home, they can get here.*

"Way too hot for me, man!" Greg said, announcing his arrival. He wasted no time in heading for the pool and jumping into the water, where he made a quick lap to the shallow end and back before returning to the chair next to Scott's.

The waiter approached with Scott's beer. "You want a beer, Greg?"

"Sure, I hope they have Bud Light. Bud Light!" Greg said extra loud, just in case the waiter didn't speak English.

"Bud Light," the waiter replied, nodding his head. Greg smiled.

"So did your girlfriend give you any insight into the crash?" he asked Scott again.

"No, and she can't until the findings are final," Scott said. "I shouldn't have asked her. I think it put her in awkward position."

"It was worth trying," Greg insisted. "Maybe there would have been something she could have shared. After all, we are flying the next Flight 6 in less than a week."

"True, but I think the Taliban or al-Qaeda or whoever the fuck it is that says they took down Flight 6 is blowing smoke," Scott said. "My money is on a cargo fire. And if it was a cargo fire, I'm afraid that the odds of ever finding what caused it to start will be a million to one. Besides, they changed our flight number. We'll be Flight 25 to Cologne now."

He hoped all of this would ease Greg's concerns. Privately, Scott wasn't convinced that it was a fire, but he would keep his thoughts of a bomb to himself until Maggie had found evidence of an explosion.

"Changing the flight number doesn't make me feel any

better," Greg replied. "I sure hope they find something."

Soon Scott found their conversation going back and forth over the same speculations and possibilities about what could have caused the crash, the same conversation that had taken place on their flights from Anchorage to Shanghai—and on every Raine flight since the accident, Scott was sure.

After twenty minutes in the sun, Scott was getting overheated. It was his turn to cool off in the pool, so he finished the last of his beer and jumped into the water. After a short cool-down, he said his farewell to Greg and headed to his room for a nap. He wanted to be fresh and rested for his date with Maggie that night—and although it may have been one in the afternoon here in the desert, Scott's body was reminding him that for him, it was one a.m.

*

Captain Lamar Wallace rolled down the driver's side window feeling the warmth of dry desert air roll into his vehicle. He was in the middle of the Nevada. The sun was beginning to light the sky from below the horizon presenting another clear, beautiful sunny day. He held his ID badge up as he slowed his red Dodge Durango approaching the guard shack and the well-armed security force at the main entrance to Creech Air Force Base home for the 4320 Air Wing and headquarters for the US UAV operations.. This was the first of three security checkpoints he passed through each day as he entered to do his job. The airman looked at his ID badge closely, even though the two saw each other almost every day. The guard smiled, saluted Lamar and opened the yellow gate allowing him to continue into the base.

He was an ex-F16 pilot and part of the Air force's new wave of pilots tasked with flying an aircraft that they would never sit in. Captain Wallace was a drone pilot. His office was in an air-conditioned singlewide trailer complete with all the pilot controls and monitors to operate the Grim Reapers he flew on the far side of the world in search of high value targets. He would operate his latest aircraft using computers through a satellite data link and television monitors as cockpit windows. The operation was as close to a sophisticated video game as one could get, but with real life consequences.

Wallace's Sentinel, *the Air Forces' latest term for a drone co-pilot*, tonight and through his entire four-month scheduled duty was Captain Olivia Rose. Her responsibilities include the cameras, munitions, and systems operations. She would be the eyes and ears of the latest high tech anti-terrorist weapon. Both crews, dressed in all-in-one khaki flight suits, sat side by side in aircraft style leather chairs positioned in front of TV monitors, computer screens and the cockpit controls. Their office floor was covered with carpet and other than the hum of computer cooling fans, was quiet as a library.

A CIA agent, referred to as the Operative, accompanied the pilots and would direct the operation. A drone pilot and his operations crew are just part of the almost one hundred and eighty people it takes to bring each of the US anti-terrorist drones to the heart of al-Qaeda and the Taliban.

The outgoing crew had briefed the latest UAV crew in a small office area inside the trailer. Their plane was an MQ-9, known as the Grim Reaper. This drone, codenamed Fisher, had been airborne for almost three hours now, having swapped out the previous drones that had been launched from several airbases within flying distance of central Yemen. Mounted with a 1,000 pound external fuel tank, this Reaper had been armed with two AGM-114 Hellfire air-to-ground missiles in anticipation of a possible strike mission and would stay airborne for the average mission time of eighteen hours.

It was 0600 in Indian Springs, Nevada, but it was the next day in Yemen; 1600, ten hours' difference. Today's mission was to track and monitor Anwar al-Awlaki, the American born Islamic preacher and leader of al-Qaeda in Yemen. He, along with his top four henchmen, had been monitored for more than four days from high overhead; they were showing a pattern in daily activities and providing an opportunity for their demise. Together, this team of drone pilots, ground crews, and CIA operatives would strike a heavy blow to the al-Qaeda leadership.

Because the operating pilot sat seven thousand miles away from his aircraft, a two second time delay existed between the joystick moving and the aircraft responding. This wasn't a concern as the drone flew high in the sky, but it was a serious enough lag that a crew at the airfield completed the launch and recovery of each aircraft through direct contact with the drone's antennae. Thirty minutes after takeoff, control of the Reaper was handed over to the crew in Nevada, and thirty minutes prior to landing, control would be returned to the ground crew on-site.

On the ground in Yemen sat CIA agent Mark Mitchell. He would be monitoring the scene and would call the shot when it was time to take out al-Awlaki and his henchmen.

CONFIRMATION

B y two in the afternoon, the desert heat made it almost impossible to think, let alone carry out a proper investigation of a major airline accident. That was the general consensus of Margaret's team, but tough duties came with the job, and the NTSB was home to the toughest and hardest-working scientists found anywhere in the world.

It had been six days since the accident, and the full investigation team was into their third day on-site. They plugged along, drinking water by the gallon, occasionally retreating under the tents equipped with portable air conditioning units that they had set up at several key areas around the accident scene.

The large tent Margaret was currently in had been erected near the main entrance to the crash scene. A stiff outdoor carpet had been laid out on the ground to offer some semblance of a floor, but even that could not keep the sand out. Margaret could see a small film of dust covering everything in the tent, and she hoped all of their electronic equipment survived this assignment.

From outside, the tent looked and felt like a giant white circus tent, but instead of big rings for entertainment, it was furnished with desks and chairs for serious work, including a small desk and work area for each investigator's laptop. The tent had been outfitted with portable air conditioning units, phone and fax systems, and high-speed Internet service. *Just missing the elephant poop,* Margaret thought.

The UAE government officials had worked around the clock to provide the needed assistance, with David as the driving force. Margaret now knew that part of David's goal was to learn as much as he could from the NTSB's investigation procedures in order to better prepare his own team for any future events in the UAE. One procedure that would be hard for David and his department to duplicate, Margaret knew, would be deciphering the airplane's data recorders. The NTSB's Washington office was home to the world's most advanced laboratory for analyzing both the voice and flight recorders, and while many countries handle their own crash investigations, most relied on the NTSB for analysis of the data recorders. Flight 6's recorders were found soon after the start of the accident investigation and sent to Washington DC for analysis. Separate teams were investigating the results of the recordings, and they shared their daily findings with Margaret.

Margaret was spending the hottest part of the day as time in the focus meeting with her team. An NTSB investigation team was organized by field of specialization, and normally, the teams that investigated aircraft incidents included Operations, Structures, Flight Crew Factors, Air Traffic Control, Weather, and Human Performance. Each specialty area included one or sometimes two team members. Margaret's entire on-site team had eight people, all potentially working in different areas with little chance to communicate. So this meeting was the opportunity for each specialized group within the team to share their findings and ask questions of the other members and the different agencies working on the investigation. The meetings could last anywhere from one to three hours, and as overheated as Margaret was at this moment, she was hoping for this meeting to run longer rather than shorter. She sent a group text message to all team members to meet in the main tent in fifteen minutes. She was sure that no one would be late.

As the team members filed in, she logged into the NTSB secure website to check her email, hoping for additional findings from the data recorder team in Washington. Because there were no surviving crewmembers to interview, the Flight Crew Factors member, Captain Rusty Latenser, was stationed in Washington to assist with the data recorders, and Raine Airways had also sent one of their 747 captains on the Go Team to Washington to assist with that facet of the investigation. But despite the number of people working on the problem, there was no news in her email as yet, beyond the material she was about to present to her teams on-site.

Her mind drifted to the previous evening's events. Dinner with Scott had been wonderful. They'd dined at the Cavalli Club on the top at the Fairmont. The meal was first class, the view of Dubai was spectacular, and Scott, as always, was delightful company. They had shared her room for the night. Thinking of it now still gave her goose bumps, a small consolation for their vacation together in Alaska having been cut so short.

She thought of Scott's next scheduled flight. Less than a week had passed since the crash of Flight 6, and Scott would be operating the first Raine Airways flight from Dubai to Cologne since the loss. She had been worried about him flying ever since the bombs had been found on board the FedEx plane in England. Those bombs had been traced to Yemen and had transferred aircraft through Dubai. *What if that was what brought down Flight 6?* she thought. *And what if whoever had planted them tried again when Scott was flying?* She shuddered at the thought. *He will be fine,* she told herself. *They're looking for explosives even more closely now at every airport.*

She refocused her mind on the task at hand. Several of the team members were already working at their desks, and others were entering the tent and making their way immediately to the water cooler. As she joined them, filling her water cup for the second time, she noticed a box full of pills sitting on a small table and above it a hand written sign taped to the inside tent wall that read, *Salt Tablets Help Yourself.* She swallowed two as she downed her water.

The last of her team members were entering the tent, along with the Raine Airways representatives. Several of the manufacturing representatives were also present. She could see Ken Egge, who represented the engine manufacturer General Electric, talking with Ed Hash from Boeing. Everyone was here in support of the NTSB and the UAE government during the investigation, but the Raine Airways folks were also tasked with the recovery and the return of their lost crewmembers.

As the last of the team members sat down, Margaret looked around the table at the over-heated crew. Everyone continued to drink water as they sat in the refreshing, cool air of the tent, and most were still wearing their white cloth HAZMAT suits. Margaret gave her usual welcoming smile.

"Good afternoon, everyone, and thank you for putting a hold on your work for our briefing. I would like to continue to have this meeting here each day at 1:30 to get us out of the sun for a while, unless there are any objections." Soft applause began, and she smiled wider.

She gave a short pep talk, thanking everyone for their hard work in such trying conditions. Her team was modest and highly professional and shrugged off the praise. "First up, I just want everyone to know that the second crew member's body was discovered early this morning. Pending the autopsy and toxicology findings, which are being conducted by UAE at this moment, both bodies should be released for return to the States by the end of the day." She looked at David, who gave her a nod yes. "Raine Airways," she said, looking at the two Raine pilots at the far end of the table. "You gentlemen are coordinating the return with the families and US authorities, correct?"

"Yes, ma'am. Our team and family members have arrived. We have the repatriation scheduled to begin tomorrow," Raine Airways Captain Dan Schmidt answered.

"Very good, thank you Dan. Let's go around the room—everyone give me what you have so far. Tony, we'll start with you."

"Good afternoon," said Tony Bartinelo, her Structures engineer, who, along with his two team-members, were responsible for analysis of the aircraft structure and its components. "So far we have marked and photographed all major pieces and moved the largest parts of interest to the UAE hangar. We should have all the items marked by each team moved into the hangar by the end of today. If any of you discover any pieces you are concerned with, please let me know and I will have them tagged and sent to the hangar. We are going to direct our efforts toward the forward section of the fuselage, which appears to have suffered the highest heat. It may prove to be the starting location of the fire. We are most interested in the tears found in the metal that showed evidence of an explosion. They are not too extensive, and we've only found them around what's left of the forward, main cargo deck floor. The fire consumed almost everything else. We'll be doing chemical analysis for positive verification. Sandy and her group are set for that testing yet this afternoon; I will let her brief you on that. At this time, we still have found no evidence of structural failure in any of the major flight controls. That's what I have so far." After looking around the tent, Tony slowly took his seat.

"Thank you Tony. Anyone have any questions for Tony?" Margaret asked. The tent was quiet. "Sandy, please bring us up to date."

"Good afternoon, everyone," Sandy said as she stood to address the group. "We've been working with Tony and have found several large sections of fuselage that show the highest temperatures received during the event. It appears that forward container positions three, four, five, and six sustained the most fire damage beyond that which was caused by the fuel fire on impact. It also appears that the floor and the ceiling in that general area literally melted away. The adjacent areas that remained intact show evidence of outward tearing. I hate to use the word explosion until I have the chemical results back, and as Tony mentioned, we have gotten those pieces to the hangar within the last hour. Most of you know Jewel, our chemical engineer on the team. She is running the chemical analysis on those pieces as we speak. She should have results to you, Margaret, any time now. I'm headed there after we break from this meeting, and I'll keep you posted."

"Thank you, Sandy," Margaret said, giving her "nice job" smile.

So far, there had been no questions. Each afternoon's briefing had kept each team up to speed on the different aspects of the investigation. More questions and discussions would occur in the evening at the hotel conference room. The hotel also provided appetizers and cocktails, offering each investigator a short but relaxing social event after what was normally a long, hot, and at times stressful day.

The afternoon meeting continued with an update from each group and input from the manufacturer's representatives from Boeing, Honeywell, and General Electric. After all were finished, Margaret gave the team an update of the data recorder findings from Washington.

"The recorders have been played, and they show some startling evidence," she began. "I will give you an overview of what we have so far. I am told we should have printed transcripts for each of you to read by the end of the day.

"The recorders show a normal takeoff from Dubai International Airport on runway three-zero right at approximately six thirty-three p.m. on the night of July eleventh. The aircraft takeoff weight was 792,000 pounds, the total fuel on board was 181,000 pounds, and it was carrying 247,000 pounds of payload. Twenty-three minutes into the flight, as the plane climbed through 31,000 feet en route to 36,000 feet, the main deck fire warning system indicated smoke on the main cargo deck. The flight crew stopped their climb at 32,000 feet. The Captain broadcast a MAYDAY with Bahrain Center through his oxygen mask microphone, then requested an immediate return to Dubai Airport due to an on board fire."

She looked around the table at the team's reaction to the recorder's evidence. Although they had speculated that this was the case, this was their first hard evidence of an onboard fire. Margaret went through the rest of the report on the flight recording, including the final transmissions between Don and Mike: *Roger that. Get back fast. I can't see shit.*

"As far as we can tell," she concluded, "the captain never made it back to the cockpit, which may explain the location of his body on-scene. As they descended into the Dubai airspace, the UPS aircraft relayed: *Speed Flight 6, Dubai approach requests that you descend on the approach. You are cleared to land any runway.* The first officer said: *Roger.* That was the last transmission. Flight 6 impacted the ground seven minutes later."

Margaret paused for a moment, both out of respect for the lost crewmembers and to allow her team to grasp the horror that must have been going through the Captain and First Officer's minds as they realized that their fate was sealed in a jet that they could not breathe in or even see to control. No one spoke. Most had their heads down waiting for Margaret to continue. This was always a hard moment in the aircraft accident investigation business. The loss of life made it that much more important to find the cause of the accident in order to help prevent the same occurrence from ever happening again.

"We received the data communication log from Raine Airways this morning," Margaret finally said. "It also has some important information in it for all of us. I have copies for each of you." She passed a stack of paper to Sandy who was sitting to her immediate right.

The Boeing 747–400 had been equipped with a state-of-the-art feature that provided additional real time data about the events as they unfolded. Through a constant satellite data link, any abnormal indications that the airplane sensed were immediately relayed to the Raine Airways Operations Center in Anchorage. The company had several pages of faults and equipment failures that had been sent from the aircraft as the fire began and that continued until the data link was lost about one minute prior to the crash in the desert. Margaret had received copies of the data log with its list of failures overnight from Raine.

Once everyone appeared to have a copy, she gave a short synopsis. "As sad as it seems, it may be that our crewmembers were not alive or that they were at least unconscious at the time of impact. As you can see, on the second page, the oxygen tank pressure had dropped to zero eleven minutes prior to impact."

Everyone in the tent knew what this meant. With heavy smoke in the cockpit, the crew would have to be breathing oxygen through their masks to stay alive. With the bottles reading zero pressure, the fire had probably burned through the main supply hoses that allowed the remaining oxygen to escape from the tanks. Once the fire had started, the crew had never stood a chance.

No one had to say the obvious, Margaret knew. It was now apparent to this team of scientist and engineers that Flight 6 had likely experienced more than just a fire on board. The investigation would now turn toward finding out what that cause was—specifically, whether it was an explosion and whether it was deliberate.

Margaret adjourned the meeting, reminding everyone to drink plenty of water. As the groups mingled, some took the time out of the sun to do their needed computer work, while others left the tent to continue their fieldwork. Margaret caught David's eye and walked in his direction. Her cell phone rang.

"Hello; this is Margaret Hurley," she said, turning her direction away from David.

"Margaret, this is Jewel Simmons at the hangar," said her investigator. "I've got a positive confirmation for explosives on board."

A hundred things were suddenly racing through Margaret's mind. "Okay, do we know what we have?" she asked.

"So far I've only tested for plastic explosives, because it was PETN that they had found on the FedEx jet in London. I tested for that first."

"Good work, Jewel," Margaret said. "I'm going to need your written report ASAP. I'll have to let Washington know as soon as they wake up. The White House is going to have to be involved with this now—not to mention everybody else," she added, almost to herself. "This is classified information until you are told otherwise. No one on the team other than Sandy is to know about it until we get clearance to release this finding. Am I clear?"

"Yes ma'am," Jewel replied. "I will have a written analysis to you within the hour."

Margaret hung up her phone and turned back toward David. She couldn't see him in the tent anywhere. *Probably better*, she thought. She would have to share this latest finding with him and the UAE—but not until she'd informed Washington.

*

Mark Mitchell sat on a plastic chair in a small room inside a mud-brick, one story building sitting on the edge of Sana'a, Yemen. The room buzzed with electronic gear, and the portable air conditioner struggled to keep the cicuits at working temperature, including Mark. The summer heat of central Yemen was doing its best to shut down Mark's operation, which had been set up by the CIA and had become fully operational just weeks before.

Mark was the director in country of the drone operations, now at functioning capacity with the Yemen government's blessing. His target here, just as in Afghanistan and Iraq, was al-Qaeda, and Mark was the best in the business.

Al-Qaeda was getting a strong foothold on the African continent with Yemen established as its headquarters. All signs pointed to Anwar al-Awlaki, a US citizen, as the leader and the principal author behind the plastic explosives found on a cargo plane at London Heathrow. The bomb shipments had been traced to Sana'a, Yemen, putting al-Awlaki on the US most wanted list with authorization for an immediate signature strike. Mark had been tracking al-Awlaki for almost three years now, attempting to pinpoint his exact location for a decisive drone strike. Tonight was as close as he had ever gotten.

Just two days after the operation had been set up, the CIA had picked up a cell phone call from someone they suspected of being al-Awlaki. The computers sitting behind Mark sent monitored cell phone conversations to Fort Meade and the NSA's voice recognition software computers. Al-Awlaki's voice was an easy match for the NSA due to all of the public speeches he had made over the years, and the call was quickly confirmed. He had been discovered along with his accomplices in a four-story building just outside the small village of Radda. CIA investigation found that the building had been purchased by Samir Khan, a man considered al-Awlaki's second in command, with monies wired to him through the Bank of Yemen from a known al-Qaeda financer in Pakistan. Drone surveillance had shown that Khan and al-Awlaki now called the building home for them and their families.

The drone team had followed al-Awlaki's exact movements day and night for four days now, and he had shown a small yet faithful routine. Each evening, after prayers, al-Awlaki and his men traveled to this building where his phone signal had first been intercepted. The group of al-Qaeda operatives had driven along a dirt side road from the central mosque in Radda to their homes south of the city. All persons in this group were considered combatants and were targeted for termination, but as this was considered a signature strike operation, all noncombatants had to be avoided. Khan was included in this operation's kill list, and the CIA was hoping to take out both him and al-Awlaki with the same strike.

If they followed the same route tonight, placing themselves on the isolated road away from innocent bystanders, they would be taken out by the powerful, remotely operated Grim Reaper that circled silently overhead. It would be up to Mark to decide when—and if.

RETURN

The air was hot and still, and the voices spoke with quiet reverence. The small contingent of mourners had gathered under a tent erected to shade them from the desert sun. The UAE had released the airmen's bodies from Flight 6 for their return home. Raine Airways had flown their families and loved ones, along with company ambassadors, to Dubai in a company 747-400 to assist with the repatriation.

A large, unmarked panel truck drove slowly through the airport gate towards the 747 and the white tent positioned behind the left wing. Twenty-three people sat in folding chairs in the tent's shade waiting for their arrival. Family members of the lost crew sat in the front row, followed by representatives from the UAE, Emirates Airline, the FAA, and the NTSB. Numerous Raine crewmembers were present, all in full uniform. Margaret and David had taken time out from their busy investigation to attend today's small ceremony.

The panel truck came to a stop at the red carpet laid down for the ceremony, which was lined on either side with dozens of flower bouquets. Uniformed pilots opened the rear doors and slowly removed the caskets that contained the lost crewmembers, and then, stationed on either side of the caskets, carried their fallen crew to waiting biers. They draped each casket with an American flag and then positioned their fallen comrades at the front of the tent.

John Fenton, Raine Airways' chief pilot, stepped forward, standing between his two lost pilots. "Ladies and gentlemen, family and friends, fellow crewmembers. We have all gathered in this distant land to bring our lost family back home after this terrible tragedy." A small breeze caused the open tent to flap loudly, helping to block the sounds of tears that were being shed throughout the tent as John cleared this throat. "Just days ago, we were all shocked and devastated by the loss of Captain Donald Lambert and First Officer Michael Barrett. Both outstanding airmen and exemplary persons to all that knew and loved them. I wish to offer my sincere sympathy to Doug and Mike's loved ones from all of us at Raine Airways." John paused, then read a short passage from the small Bible he had carried with him. "It is now time to take our loved ones home."

John paused again, giving his best understanding smile, and then went up to each of the family members who had come the long distance, offering a heartfelt handshake and condolences. The pallbearers rose from their seats and lined up again on both sides of the biers. A larger memorial ceremony was planned upon their return to Anchorage and at each of the crewmembers' hometowns.

Slowly, the pallbearers wheeled them to the waiting K-loader. The two fallen crews would be the sole occupants of the cargo hold.

As the mourners watched the caskets loaded into the jet, many were running the accident over in their minds. *How could it have happened? What could have caused them to crash so close to the airport?* Both men had been experienced, highly skilled pilots who should have been able to handle almost any emergency. Neither the press nor the NTSB had released any valuable information, beyond the public statement which said that the crew had declared an emergency and reported an onboard fire. Even now, no one outside Margaret's circle knew the suspected cause of the accident. Even David had not yet been informed. Washington—more specifically, the FBI—was still working their investigation. But a bomb had been foremost on everyone's mind even before al-Qaeda's claim on Al Jazeera taking responsibility for the downing of Flight 6 and before the discovery of the bombs aboard the FedEx plane.

The airplane had been fueled and readied for departure prior to the ceremony. Once the caskets were loaded, the returning crew members, friends, and family took their seats on board the jet. The remaining attendees said their good-byes, the tent was quickly removed, and the Raine Airways 747 with its precious cargo was soon on its way home.

Margaret and David walked toward his car after the ceremony without speaking. It was a sad and solemn moment for them both—not just because of the loss of the two men, but because of knowing that finding the cause of this tragedy lay on their shoulders. And it bothered Margaret not to be able to share her team's findings with David. She enjoyed working with David, true, but she wouldn't release the information until Washington gave the clearance. Neither of them could imagine the chain of events yet to unfold before that would be allowed to happen.

*

Mark Mitchell walked inside the Ops room after enjoying a cigarette in the cool early evening air. Yemen did have its days of enjoyable climate, he thought, scanning the screens that lit the otherwise dark room. Each monitor displayed the camera angle from the Grim Reaper circling high over the streets in Radda. Earlier in the evening al-Awlaki and his men had been closely monitored driving from their homes to the city's central mosque, just as they had done each evening. The pictures were sharp and clear: two parked cars and two men holding AK-47's standing guard over them on an otherwise empty street. The scene had not changed for over an hour.

He was now waiting for them to leave the mosque and begin their travels. If the group of al-Qaeda leaders followed the same route along the isolated road, they would be taken out. Mark Mitchell would call the shot.

*

As a fresh drone crew took their seats at the controls in the Nevada operations trailer, the surveillance cameras were focused on a small group of men getting into two white Toyota sedans. The incoming crew had been briefed on tonight's planned targeting of the senior al-Qaeda leaders. Tension built inside the small office that was lined with large monitors displaying clear, real time images of the targets and areas surrounding the city of Radda. Infrared cameras provided an accurate account of people who could be hiding behind walls or inside buildings. At night, the picture showed as black and white images on the monitors, their features highlighted by infrared cameras that could clearly show the entire landscape and its activities. Detailed maps of Yemen and its roads, cities, and towns covered the walls of the operations office.

At the controls of the Grim Reaper was Captain Wallace, with Captain Rose as the Sentinel, controlling the eyes and ears of the of the drone aircraft. Captain Wallace began a slow descent to fifteen thousand feet, keeping well above the target but providing an easier target for the Sentinel to paint with the laser. The MQ-9 Reaper aircraft had a ceiling of over 50,000 feet, but were normally operated at 25,000 and below, ensuring they stayed away from commercial aircraft.

"Targets one through five approaching the two vehicles. Designate vehicles as new targets six and seven," came across Mark's headset from the CIA operative on-site in Nevada.

All crews were highly trained for these missions, but as the targets were close to being taken out, Mitchell could hear the adrenaline in his operative's voice running high, as if he and the crew were actually on board the aircraft seven thousand miles away. The UAV program had revolutionized the art of war, but the act of taking a life remained the same, and none of the drone flyers took it lightly. Even now, the off-duty crew remained to watch the culmination of their days of surveillance.

Pilot," said the operative, "Let's spin up weapons on tail one-zero-seven."

"Roger, pre-launch check list," announced the pilot.

"Entered," replied the Sentinel.

"AEA power."

"On."

"Weapon bit."

"Passed."

"Code weapon."

"Coded."

"Weapons status?"

"Weapons ready."

"Checklist complete."

Mark was watching the same live feed at his location in Sana'a.

"Five human targets entered into two white vehicles, targets six and seven, confirm targets," Mark said.

"Copy," came the response from the CIA operative in Nevada over the headset.

"Sentinel confirms."

"Roger," Mark said. "Keep eyes on targets six and seven."

"Pilot copies. Sentinel, lock onto lead auto, target six."

"Sentinel copies. Target locked."

"Mark, we were expecting six human targets," said the operative. "Any intel?"

"Negative," Mark said. "Continue with operation."

The stretch of road Mark had chosen for the strike was less than a kilometer from the terrorist's home. The section was barren but would have to be clear of all noncombatants, and Mark watched as the cars came within three kilometers of the target area, approaching a sharp bend in the road where they were forced to slow down.

"Area is clear," he said. "Take them out."

"Agreed, all non-combatants clear," announced the operative. "Pilot, Sentinel, you are cleared to engage target at your discretion."

"Pilot, Roger. Launch auto track."

"Established."

"Laser."

"Laser selected."

"Arm laser."

"Laser armed."

"Fire laser."

"Lasing. Target in range. Three, two, one, rifle."

There was a pause as all eyes followed the white autos that had slowed approaching the curve in the road.

"Three, two, one, impact," reported the Sentinel.

The area where the front car had been visible on the screen erupted in a massive fireball.

*

Faria and her daughter were sitting on the small concrete porch of their home in the cool evening air, waiting for Anwar to return home, when the bright flash lit the entire sky in front of them. A loud explosion quickly followed, and Faria's daughter jumped, running to her mother's side.

"What was that, mama?" she asked, still staring in the direction of the explosion.

"I don't know, dear," Faria replied after a moment as a chill ran down her spine. She was afraid that she knew exactly what it was.

*

The hit had showed as a bright white explosion on the monitors. The smoke and fire cleared slightly, and the second car stopped a short distance behind the carnage that now lay in front of it.

"Laser target seven, the remaining car," said the pilot.

"Lasing. Target in range. Three, two, one, rifle."

Again there was a short pause as all personnel watched the big screen monitor. The white auto began to back up, swinging around in an attempt to retreat from the fireball that moments ago had been their colleagues. It was too late.

"Three, two, one, impact."

Mark watched as the remaining target, with all its occupants, erupted into a second fireball.

"Two confirmed hits," came his operative's voice over the headset. "Excellent job, folks."

*

"There it is again," shouted her daughter. "What is that?"

"I'm not sure," she replied. But she was sure. She feared

her plan had not worked as she had hoped, and she knew her life and that of her family had now just changed forever.

*

Mark imagined the room in Nevada growing quiet as the drone operators collected their thoughts on what had just taken place. Even when it involved an enemy, the taking of human life was a sepulchral business, one that the drone crews dealt with as any soldier on the battlefield. Modest reflection and handshakes went all around as the crew congratulated each other on a successful mission.

With that, the pilot turned the Grim Reaper westbound. Mark continued to watch the monitor as the drone began its climb back to twenty-five thousand feet, where it would continue to orbit and monitor the scene on the ground.

The CIA would keep a constant eye on the al-Qaeda situation as it continued to unfold in Radda and the remote villages of Yemen. They had inflicted a heavy blow to the al-Qaeda terrorists in Yemen tonight by eliminating its al-Awlaki and his henchman. But Mark knew—watching the drone circle from his monitor in Yemen—that this was not the end. For all the he knew, the plot to deliver explosives into Western countries may still have been underway—and who could say whether or not their success tonight might provoke another attempt? And, who and where was the sixth terrorist they had expected?

ADVANCEMENT

Ibrahim sat cross-legged on the dirt floor of a cinder block hut, an AK-47 laid across his legs. He clenched his rifle—shaking with rage, wishing he had the CIA agent who had killed his friends in his sights—while he stared blankly at the bare wall in front of him. The sun's rays leaked in and around the sides of the dirty cloth hung to block the one window. He was hiding from the prying eyes in the sky.

Am I being followed? Did they see me walk into this building? He felt watched, spied upon and unsafe everywhere he went. Anwar was gone. Anwar al-Awlaki, his leader, along with his closest allies, had been murdered, executed from the sky. He was certain that the Americans and their CIA were responsible. *How could Allah have allowed this to happen? How can I bring jihad and death to the Western infidels now? How can I ever get my brother the explosives he waits for?*

So Ibrahim sat here in hiding, fearing for his life. He wasn't afraid to die—he told himself this—but he was afraid that if he was killed, his grand plans would never come to fruition.

All the men whom he had assisted with the first failed

bomb delivery had been killed along with al-Awlaki. He shuddered at the thought. The gathering last night had been intended to devise the group's next step after the bombs had been discovered on board the aircraft. Had Ibrahim not left after evening prayers to purchase khat, he, too, would have been in the cars with Anwar and his men.

He and a friend had been several kilometers behind al-Awlaki's group, and they were the first to arrive at the scene. The site of the bombings was utter destruction. Little was even recognizable as an auto, and in the darkness, they could find no human remains.

The *Yemen Observer* and Internet news broadcasts claimed that the assault had been carried out by the Yemen military, but Ibrahim knew this was a lie. Yemen officials and police from Sana'a had arrived this morning to seize Anwar's house. They had taken his wives for questioning, or prison, or execution; he did not know. They had removed everything of value from the house and left. *They would make the women talk, tell all that they know about Anwar's life and our plots of jihad,* Ibrahim was sure. *But how much did they know?* Very little, he tried to convince himself. *They know nothing of the targets. Only that some packages had been shipped. What about Faria? She probably knows little or nothing. She wouldn't even know what she had helped us ship. Anwar never shared any planning with her. I bet she doesn't even care that Anwar is gone.* Then he thought about Aminah. *Anwar shared his vision with that woman. She knows more than she should. But she doesn't know I'm alive. She would think that I was in one of the autos and killed with the others.*

Even the Americans may not know Ibrahim was still alive. This could be his greatest advantage until the authorities verified who had been killed in the attack, if they ever could. The thought brought a slight smile to his face.

Yet he knew the US drones were still up there watching,

waiting. Waiting for him to make a mistake by showing himself. *Did they even know of me?* he wondered. *How could they*, he thought. *No one ever thought to give me a chance before.*

Anwar never gave me a chance. Never trusted me. Never thought I was smart enough to do anything but build bombs. Well, I can. I can make this plan work. I can get the packages to my brother using my own plan. I can be the next al-Qaeda leader—and I have an advantage.

The Americans would not know him or target him, he assured himself. He was merely a foot soldier compared to al-Awlaki, just a meager bomb maker. He had never made public speeches or brought any attention to himself. *No one would know who I am.*

But how had the CIA found Anwar? He had been in hiding for so long. *We allowed only trusted men into his inner circle,* Ibrahim thought. *We shared his location with no one. Everyone in our evening salat group was one of his protectors. Did someone betray our leader? Is there a spy among us? First the plane crashes in Dubai and we lose our bomb, and then the bombs are discovered on board the plane in London, and now the murder of Anwar and our leaders of the jihad—*

Ibrahim had always considered himself a smart man, but these questions lay heavy on his mind, and he had no answers. He only knew that if the jihad in Cologne was to be carried out, the responsibility now lay solely with him. *Maybe the demise of Anwar is Allah's plan, his plan to make me the leader of his holy jihad.*

Ibrahim knew he could lead this effort. He had no choice. Now more than a foot soldier, he had become the de-facto leader of this operation. If not the leader of AQAP—yet—he was at least the leader of the bomb plot for Cologne. His brother still waited in Germany for a bomb, the bomb he had promised before these setbacks and the bomb that Ibrahim would now have to rebuild and somehow smuggle in. The jihad that al-Awlaki had begun was now Ibrahim's driving force more than ever, his only reason to carry on.

So, alone, he contemplated his next step. With Samir Khan killed in the attack, there was no longer anyone in Yemen with the Pakistan connections necessary to get the bomb material. He would have to devise a way to get explosives from another source and then construct new bombs.

Further, with the last bomb delivery foiled, he would have to find another way to get the explosives to Cologne. Shipping them from Yemen was no longer an option; all packages were being opened and searched. Al-Awlaki's contingency plan had been to hide the bombs on board westbound aircraft themselves. But how was Ibrahim supposed to do that?

He remembered the man his friend in Dubai had told him about—the one he had followed home from the airport. A worker he had spotted who might easily be persuaded to assist with their demands.

A smile grew across his face as he saw his plan begin to come together in his mind. The best chance he would have for bomb material, he know, was to contact friends in Iran. He could make that call right away he thought, get that side of the plan working. It was all too simple.

He stood up, walked to the window, and looked up at the sky. Then he turned on his cell phone and dialed the number to a friend in Iran.

At that same moment, Mark Mitchell's computer flashed a message across the screen.

WAYLAID

T hanks to Margaret's team's work, leaders in Washington were now convinced that the bombs found on the FedEx plane had exposed a conclusive chain of events that led back to AQAP. Now, with Anwar al-Awlaki dead, the White House felt confident the bomb plots had been stopped. Thus it was finally time to inform Dubai about the explosives found at the crash scene of Flight 6. The duty fell to Margaret. *Finally*, she thought as she requested a briefing with David, in the conference room that had been set up at the Fairmount hotel.

She had wanted to tell David of their findings the day they had discovered them, but she knew that decision was high above her pay grade. Now, with the directive from Washington to inform the UAE authorities that explosives had been found on and at the crash site of Flight 6, she knew that it was important to present the information carefully. Thus she had arranged the meeting to be offsite. Partly, this was because diplomacy was key: She wanted David to have a moment to digest the information, giving him time to decide how to handle it. She hoped he would not be forced to cover up the findings, that the UAE would cooperate with the investigation into who put the bomb on board. But partly, the hotel venue was just to give them a chance to relax. Both of them were coming from the crash scene, having just finished the latest afternoon briefing from Margaret's team in the large tent that had been set up for the NTSB investigators.

It had been another extremely hot, cloudless day for all of the investigators, and the strong odor of jet fuel continued to make their work an even greater challenge. The accident investigation at the scene would soon be coming to a close, with most of the needed information collected and the pieces of wreckage that required further investigation moved to the Emirates Airline hangar for analysis. The NTSB investigators would be wrapping-up on-site and returning to Washington to complete their findings in the comfort of their offices, and the crash scene would be released to a hazardous material response unit for cleanup.

Beyond all that, though, Margaret thought a quiet discussion with David away from the accident scene might be nice regardless of the reason. It would have to be short, though; she was meeting Scott for dinner at eight p.m.

Her driver, Omar, was still assigned to her, escorting her today in a black Audi A7 with all the trimmings, even a mini bar set up with the finest beverages money could buy. She looked at the arrangement of bottles: Lordanov Vodka, Woodford Reserve Bourbon, Cruzan Gold Rum, Aberfeldy Single Malt Scotch, several others she had never seen. She didn't recognize the wines, but she still wished she had time to open a bottle and try the red. *Not until after the briefing*, she thought.

Omar's car pulled to the front of the Fairmont, and the usual nine porters stood eagerly waiting, only to be disappointed as Margaret stepped from the SUV with no luggage to offer for their support. She was beginning to tolerate the heat, but she still looked forward to each time she entered an air-conditioned building.

Her room was on the twenty-ninth floor, and she went there to freshen up. A quick shower and clean attire was in order. She had brought along numerous new slack outfits and blouses, several she had yet to wear. The job site had been so hot and dirty, and she had found herself sporting a HAZMAT jumpsuit every day, making her clothes filthy and wet with sweat by the end of each day.

This briefing would be different: clean, cool, and well dressed. Besides, she wanted to look her best in front of David, as well as for dinner with Scott. She wore her favorite pantsuit, a light summer tan with long sleeves and small folded neckline that showed just a small thought of cleavage, accented with a black pearl pendant and earrings. Her long dark hair lay just over her shoulders, and she thought she looked stunning.

Two handsome men in one evening, she thought, smiling as the elevator door opened to take her to the conference room.

*

The soccer ball rolled fast down the dirt road into the doorway that led into the ghetto-like workers' camp that Agib called home. The air was a mixture of stifling heat and sandy dust that rose up in the shade of the whitewashed walls on this desolate street.

Soccer was Agib's only escape from his studies and the boredom of his temporary life, as his father called it, here in Dubai. Agib was tall and rather muscular for age eleven, a handsome boy who always wore a smile that could melt hearts and dark hair that he wore too long for his father's taste. Today, Agib wore the traditional white, one-piece dress that he found the coolest for playing in the afternoon, as well as the new Nike tennis shoes his father had bought him. The shoes were his pride and joy, and he only wore them for playing soccer.

Agib was almost twelve; his birthday was one week away. He had hoped that he and his father would return to celebrate his turning twelve in their hometown. *That would be a grand birthday present,* he thought. He did not enjoy much of his life here. There were few boys his age to play with, and he was homeschooled by his father. Thus Agib spent most of his time with his studies in their one-room flat with its vinyl floor and steel bunk beds, or else kicking his soccer ball up and down the dusty streets.

He had been yelled at sometimes when he practiced on other streets, the ones that led in and out of the workers' city. Those were the ones filled with lost souls—human slaves, it seemed, even to an eleven-year-old boy. Not Agib's father, of course. He was a skilled worker and master craftsman who could apply his trade of fine woodworking back home, back where Agib's friends were, back where life was happy and he attended a real school, back where his mother had died.

Agib had finally found an open space to kick his ball, one not filled with men coming and going or women cooking onions and tomatoes on small propane stoves along the sides of the streets. Several months ago, he guessed that this street would have had many construction workers mingling, but few now remained in this area of the city. Many had retreated to their homeland as the world's economy had slowed, bringing many of the new construction projects to a near halt. But on other streets, many workers remained, some employed on the few large construction jobs being completed, but many more stranded with no job and most with no money to return home.

It was a place that Agib could have all to himself to practice his football. He was going to be a star player someday, he knew, the pride of Pakistan—that is, if he and his father ever returned to their homeland.

The only thing Agib did enjoy about Dubai—unlike his father—was the heat. He never felt too hot, and he didn't look forward to the cold winter nights that he remembered of northern Pakistan—when, one day, they returned, as his father swore they would.

His ball had come to a stop in a doorway. Standing there was a large and scornful-looking man, who gave Agib a dirty grin as the boy approached. Agib smiled back, and then he reached down for his ball.

The man in the doorway reached out for Agib's hand. He gripped the boy hard, pulling him in. Agib began to yell, but his cry for help was quickly muffled by the man's massive hand gripped tightly over his mouth. The man wrapped his arm tight around the boy and wrenched him off the ground.

"Quiet, you little shit!" said the man in Arabic as he clamped a bear hug down hard on the boy.

Agib's heart raced. *What is happening,* his mind cried out while he continued his struggle to get free. But the man gripped harder, squeezing the air from Agib's lungs. He couldn't breathe! *Need air*, Agib's mind screamed. He calmed himself, and the man eased his death hold slightly. Agib breathed in hard, filling his lungs with the hot desert air mixed with the taste of sand and the smell of his abductor's sweat. He stayed still as his thoughts screamed for release.

The man covered Agib with his loose fitting djellaba and walked quickly down the sand-covered side street with Agib in his arms.

Why was this man after him? he wondered. Had he done something wrong? His ball had not hurt anyone, and surely the man didn't care that he was kicking the ball down this empty street. Why had this man grabbed him from his quiet soccer field?

He thought of his mother and it made him struggle again, only to be squeezed tighter. He stopped struggling, hoping for an escape but he could see little other than the top of the man's hand that held back his screams. Flashes of the sandy-brown street and white walls of the ghetto passed by as his captor walked at a fast pace.

"Father!" Agib tried to scream.

Where was his father when he needed him so? Why was this man hauling him down this lonely alley? What had he done? Where was he being taken? The questions raced through his mind, and he began to cry.

*

The back alley was still empty as Hadid al-Otaibi carried the airport worker's son toward his goal. It was a lucky break, he thought, that the kid played on this street: there was no one in sight, and there were few windows as well. It was an easy take.

Hadid al-Otaibi had been born in Quseim, a nomadic city in the Najd region of Saudi Arabia. His father was the infamous Juhayman al-Otaibi, leader of the 1979 rebel uprising that attempted to overtake the Grand Mosque in Mecca in defiance of the Saudi Government. Juhayman and his men had held the mosque for almost two weeks until the Saudi National Guard had overtaken them with the help of the Jordanian Special Forces. Soon after the rebels were captured, Juhayman, along with sixty-seven of his henchmen, was publicly beheaded, ending the largest dissident movement against the Saudi king and ending any chance of a respectable and fruitful life for his son Hadid.

Because of his father's dealings, Hadid had been shunned

as a young man by neighbors and leaders of the Saudi tribes. Along with his older brother Omar, he found himself shuffled from family to family around Saudi Arabia. Hadid had watched his older brother die during a scuffle with common street thugs after arguing against the Saudi government. Shortly after, Hadid had been sent to an orphanage—the Imam College of Islamic Law in Saudi Arabia—to keep him from further trouble.

Hadid spent over a year of his life in this home for troubled boys. It was here that he had met Ibrahim al-Asiri and his brother Karim, and the three had become lifelong friends. All three grew up together and were the attentive students of the radical cleric Abdullah el-Faisal, their inspiration. Hadid was somewhat of a folk hero at the radical mosque due to his father's failed takeover. Hadid, however, was bored with the radical jihadist teaching, and as soon as he was of age, he fled to Iran. Here, he met with radical young capitalists who were attempting to change the Iranian regime. Although their beliefs were more in line with his thinking, after several years of near poverty and sheer boredom, he fled to Dubai where he could find work and avoid the deadly fanatical politics that seemed to follow his family.

Hadid never minded the fight, just the cause. Islamic jihad seemed too distant, too uncontrollable, not worth the struggle. Why should he become involved in matters that he couldn't change? Hadid needed involvement with smaller issues, issues that affected him immediately, directly—issues that put money in his pocket.

Hadid's lack of interest in radical Islam brought him to the United Arab Emirates. It was his need for income that brought him to his daily job. Hadid was a large man, taller and broader than most, and at the age of thirty, this gave him an edge in working for the Minister of Interior, His Highness Lieutenant General Sheikh Saif bin Zayed Al Nahyan. Specifically, Hadid was stationed in the workers' housing areas as a watchman. Officially, he was a peacekeeper for the workers, but everyone here knew that his real task was to keep the media and nosy tourists out of the workers' ghetto in an effort to help hide the living conditions of the workers from the rest of the world. There always seemed to be reporters trying to make a name for themselves by attempting to show an appalling side of exquisite Dubai.

Despite his steady work, however, Hadid was always willing to help a friend if it paid well. So he had been happy to hear from Ibrahim offering a lucrative side job. *Today, retrieve the boy, unharmed, no questions asked.* Perfect for his line of work. An easy nab that would pay 1,500 dirhams, about 400 US dollars. It would take him almost a week to make that as a watchman. *Not a bad take*, he thought.

The Toyota Highlander was waiting with the engine running. The back door was open, and a man wearing a white thawb, a black ogal headband, and dark sunglasses waited beside it. Hadid approached the SUV quickly, looking around for peering eyes or danger of any kind. As he reached the opened door of the truck, the Arab grabbed the boy's head by his hair and lifted him in. As Hadid removed his hand from the boy's mouth, he gasped again for a lungful of air and started a loud scream, only to be quickly muffled by a band of duct tape and a dark cloth bag over his head. The two men threw the boy into the back of the SUV, and the Arab followed him in, placing his knee on the boy's back, pulling his hands together, and then binding them with a long zip-tie. He jumped from the truck, slammed the back door closed, and tossed Hadid a small pouch.

"We will be in touch, my friend," said the Arab. "There is one more task for you." He quickly walked to the driver's door of the SUV, slammed the door shut, and sped away.

Hadid turned and walked down a small adjacent alley.

That was easy, he thought to himself with a smile as he counted out his dirhams from the pouch. He wondered what the other task was. He didn't like getting involved with his friend's politics, but he did hope to get more easy work from them. *I do like their money*, he thought with a grin as he rounded the corner and disappeared onto a busy street.

INFORMED

It was dark each evening by the time Jafar arrived home from the airport to his one-room flat in the slum. He always looked forward to this moment: There was no air conditioning in his flat, but the cool poured concrete walls provided a small relief from the day's scorching heat, and he always enjoyed the chance to ask his son Agib about his day. Dubai held the swelter of the day for much longer than the barren desert did. Even with the higher temperature, Jafar preferred the idea of being in this city to the endless desert sands he that knew lay just beyond the nighttime glow of this iron and glass oasis.

He unlocked the steel door and pushed it open. To his surprise, the single light in his home was not on. Agib was always here waiting for him, reading, trying to fulfill his father's demands to study. After a pause, Jafar turned and stepped back into the street.

"Agib!" he called down the dark sand covered neighborhood. There was no reply.

He stepped back inside and turned on the light that hung from the ceiling in the middle of the room. There was a man standing in the corner.

"What is this? What do you want?" Jafar demanded,

startled.

"Close the door," the man said.

Jafar hesitated, but then he turned slightly and closed the door.

"I have a message for you, Jafar. A message from some dangerously important people," said the man.

Jafar studied the man. He wore a filthy ghutrah and smelled of smoked fish and hashish. His ogal was dirty and crooked on his head, and streaks of sand and food stains covered the front of a once white thawb. The man wore a janbiya, a curved dagger, on his belt.

"Why are you in my home?" Jafar demanded as he stepped closer.

The man placed his hand on the hilt of the dagger. "These people have your son, Jafar," he said.

Jafar's heart stopped. He stared at the man telling him this news with disbelief. "Why? Why would they take my son?" he asked. "I have no money! What do you want?"

"It is not money that they seek. They ask only a small task of you," the man said as he reached inside his ghutrah for a cigarette.

"What kind of a task? Tell me where my son is!" Jafar said, angry and pleading at the same time.

"Your son is fine, and he will remain so if you follow their instructions," the man said as he lit his cigarette. "They would like you to place a small package on board an airplane. That is all. It will be very simple, and then your son will be returned to you."

"What kind of a package?" Jafar demanded, his voice sounding nervous.

"You will be told what you need to know," said the man. "You will receive it tomorrow on your way to the airport. A man will hand it to you on the Metro. Take the package and do not speak to him. Do you understand?"

"Yes, yes! Then what?" Jafar asked, becoming desperately angry.

"The package is to be placed aboard the aircraft that is flown by Raine Airways. Do you know this airplane?"

"Yes, I assist in loading their planes each day," Jafar said. "But I do not have security clearance to enter the airplane!"

"Keep your voice down. Remember, it is your son's life you are working for now," the man said, and Jafar's face grew cold. "It is a very small package and it is a very big airplane," the man continued. "All you need to do is hide the package inside."

The man stepped toward the single wooden table in the middle of the room that separated him and Jafar. As the man came closer to the light bulb, his face came into view. Jafar had seen this man before. This was the man who had been on the Metro. This was the man who had been following him, and now he stood here in Jafar's home.

The man pulled a small rolled parchment from inside his left sleeve and unrolled it onto the table. Jafar glanced down at the paper. It was a drawing that looked like an airplane, a 747, from the top. It showed all of the cargo container locations on the main cargo deck.

"Tomorrow, a Raine Airways 747 is flying to Cologne," the man said. "You are to walk up the main stairs only. Place the package here between these two container positions." The man pointed to a small area between containers three and four. "Place the package far enough down that it cannot be seen and leave the airplane."

"I do not know where the airplanes are going," Jafar lied. "I just drive the cans to the airplane." Maybe if the man thought he couldn't accomplish this task, he could get Agib back, end this here and now.

But the man didn't move. "There is only one Raine Airways flight tomorrow," he said, "and it is the one going to

Cologne."

"But how do I get the package through security before I ever get to the airplane?" Jafar protested. "And what do I do if I get caught with this package?"

"The package will not alert security going into the airport," the man assured him, smirking. "As far as getting caught goes—it is your son's future. So I suggest you do not get caught."

"What is this package? What is it for?"

"That information is not for you. Even I do not know what is in this package. I am only a messenger."

Jafar felt sure the man was lying. "How will I know this man on the Metro tomorrow?" he asked.

"He will know you. Enter the Metro at the Al Jafiliya station as you have each day. If you go to the authorities, or if things do not look safe to him, he will leave the Metro, and you will never see your son. Do you understand?"

"When will I get Agib back?" Jafar asked after a moment.

"You will have your son back after you do this small task," the man said as he walked around the table. He kept his eye on Jafar and his hand on the janbiya. "Don't even think about going to the police. If we see anyone following you, your son will be killed. We will be watching you closely. Don't screw this up."

With that, the man turned, opened the door, and stepped out into the darkness.

Jafar stood there under the one bare light bulb, his fists clenched and his body shaking. *What was this all about? Why me? Why Agib?* He began to pace, walking in circles around the small table. Finally, he stepped to the door and looked outside onto the dark street. There was no one outside moving.

Who are these people? What should I do now? Where can I get help? The questions burned in his mind. He had no one that he could count on to help. He didn't trust the police, and the man had said they would be watching him. And there was no one else in this city that he knew.

Jafar finally sat down on the wooden chair at the table, slouching over and resting his head on his hands. His body was still shaking, and he began to cry. It would be a surpassingly long and sleepless night.

CABAL

The night was exceptionally warm. A light sea breeze blew against Ibrahim's face as he motored the boat quietly out of the harbor and turned the bow toward the open water. The smell of dead fish mixed with the salt air was strong, and he looked up at the bright stars shining between the scattered high clouds. Small banks of fog lay close to the shoreline, but the path ahead looked clear.

As the small craft broke through the waves of the Iranian coast, he advanced the throttle and the boat picked up speed. When he was far from shore, he turned off all the lights on the boat. He did not want to be seen by any patrol boats as he entered UAE waters.

He rarely looked at the small GPS map display on the console; he didn't even need navigation equipment on a trip such as this. Soon a massive glow of yellow, like that of a distant fire, would begin to show on the horizon to mark his destination. The lights of Dubai were the perfect beacons to sail by on a night like this, when high, thin clouds reflected the desert city lights.

It was a nice boat and just the right size, large enough to make it safely across the Gulf yet small enough to elude the radar along the UAE coast, a twenty-five-foot fiberglass pleasure boat that was fast and safe on the open sea as long as the waves stayed small. The boat had been "borrowed" by a friend and smuggled into the Iranian harbor for use on trips such as these. Ibrahim had made this journey twice before, sailing his friend Hadid to Dubai several years ago in a craft similar to this one and his cousin Atash several months ago in this exact boat. His hastily laid plan was coming together.

The waves were generally light and the tide swells small. The distance across the Persian Gulf from Bandar-e Lengeh on the southern coast of Iran to the rendezvous point east of Dubai was almost exactly two hundred and thirty kilometers. He would make the trip in five and a half hours provided he maintained close to twenty-five knots, which would allow him enough time to arrive before sunrise.

It had been a fast and furious several days, and he was feeling tired yet driven. Smuggling himself from Yemen across the Saudi desert and into Dubai had been easy enough to arrange. His boat had remained moored in the small Dubai harbor where he had left it, the slip rent paid for the entire summer. After a six-hour cruise to Iran, he was able to quickly fashion two new bombs out of the extra printer cartridges he had carried from Radda. He obtained homemade plastic explosives from his Iranian connections, a simple yet deadly explosive material made from the mortars and rocket propelled grenades now in large supply since the end of the Iraq War, many of which had found their way to his friends in Bastak, Iran. The material was not as powerful as the PETN they had obtained earlier, but it was explosive enough. Ibrahim had added extra material to the bombs just to be sure.

The patrol boats were the next obstacles he had to

overcome, he reminded himself as he settled into the trip and the rhythm of the waves. The Persian Gulf had many boat patrols compared to years before. But with a sharp eye, he would avoid detection.

Ibrahim felt proud as he stood with his back straight, making a determined face even with no one around. He was a young man. He had turned twenty-nine just last month. Not a tall man—but not short either, he reminded himself—and a man of purpose and determination, for he was the author of this masterful plot. He was the one who had chosen the target, and it was he who had organized this small band of allies. He knew they could achieve greatness for this act of martyrdom, and it was he who would ensure its success.

The one-kilogram bombs, like the ones he had crafted before with a simple detonator, could destroy a bus or a train car. The two-kilogram bombs that he carried tonight could destroy a church. *A giant infidel church*, he grinned as the thought raced through his mind. They had been so close to achieving their goal. For two years, Anwar and his group had been planning each detail of this operation. The crash of the plane and loss of bombs, the murder of Anwar and his colleges; they all seemed like minor setbacks now. Soon, Ibrahim and his remaining small band of jihadists would have their satisfaction upon the Christian infidels.

Getting the explosive material was easy in a country like Iran. Making the concentrated plastic explosive was manageable with the help of the Muslim clerics who taught at the school where Ibrahim's friends had attended, and it all came together with the financial backing from supporters in Saudi Arabia—including his old mentor at the orphanage, Abduallah el-Faisal, who had provided the travel and living expenses for his men.

But as Ibrahim had expected, getting the explosives from Iran to Cologne had proven a daunting task. The cargo screening any receiving Western nation required was not in place in Iran, and thus all packages arriving to or from Iran were tightly watched and examined. It would be almost impossible to get a package of explosives to Cologne directly from this terrorist labeled country.

The bombs were to be transported to Cologne on board a cargo airplane, just like the last shipment that hadn't made it to Cologne. Ibrahim still wondered about the crash of Flight 6. Had the bombs exploded and caused the plane to crash? Or was the plane crash just an unforeseen delay in his quest? The explosives were relatively stable, and had they been handled properly, they should have made the flight safely. Ibrahim did not know the reason for the crash, and the authorities would not announce anything while the investigation was still underway.

But he knew the accident investigators would soon find evidence of the bombs and tighten airport security, making it impossible for another package to be delivered. He was now forced to smuggle the explosives into Dubai and place them on board an aircraft themselves.

Ibrahim had packaged the explosive more carefully than the ones that had been seized from the FedEx plane, using a stronger plastic container inside two ink jet cartridges that he had sealed as if they were new. Even if the cartridges were to be discovered, he hoped their explosive nature would go undetected. Surely they would get through to Germany this time. The cargo loader from Pakistan would get them through—or else he would receive his son's head in a basket.

Ibrahim's brother Karim remained in Cologne to carry out the demolition of the cathedral. Karim was employed as an armed airport security guard with access to the cargo aircraft landing in Cologne. It had taken Anwar almost two years to place an operative at a major German airport, but Karim's job as a security officer could not have been better. He would get the package from the plane, and he would set the explosive in the cathedral.

Ibrahim and his brother would bring this giant monstrosity to the ground, just as Bin Laden and his men had brought down the towers in New York. Had it not been for the loss of the cargo plane carrying the precious explosives, the job would have already been done. But Ibrahim would be stronger than Anwar had been. He would not allow any more setbacks; everything must go as planned. Soon the explosives would be on their way to his brother in Cologne, and their jihad would be close to reality. Ibrahim smiled at the thought. Perhaps after the bombing in Cologne, he would be the next inspiration to emerge from the Muslim world.

Several fishing boats appeared on the horizon, and Ibrahim turned his small craft to avoid them. They should be no problem, he thought. Of more concern were the high-speed cigarette boats that the rich Saudis ran along the Dubai coast, even at night. Staying far away from them was in his best interest. It would be difficult to get out of their way if he couldn't spot them in time.

The city lights of Dubai now rose from the horizon as Ibrahim motored closer to the shoreline. Giant buildings, some of the tallest on Earth, cascaded before him. He steered further east, keeping the city off his starboard side. The bright glow was inspiring and made him proud that such a place existed in the Muslim world.

The GPS screen showed the small entrance to the inlet waterway that led to the marina. He continued motoring further along the coast, watching for the green and red-lighted buoys that marked the small opening along the sea wall. This led into a long estuary lined with moored boats of every size, where he could dock and leave his boat in his rented slip until he needed it again. A white flashing light was the signal for Ibrahim that the area was clear and that it was safe for him to approach the marina, where he would rendezvous with Hadid and his cousin Atash, who had assisted in the kidnapping of the airport worker's son. After more than ten minutes on his eastern course, Ibrahim felt he had gone too far, and he brought the boat back around to the west while he continued to scan the shore.

He was about two hundred meters off shore, just outside the breakers that ran parallel to the coast, when he pulled a cell phone from his pocket, turned it on and hit SEND.

"Yes?" a voice answered.

"Are you there? I am two hundred meters out."

"Yes, cousin, our light is on," Atash answered. "All is clear. You are mooring in slip three-fourteen."

There was the light, thirty degrees to starboard one hundred meters ahead. "I see you," he said, and he pushed the END button on his phone and placed it back into his pocket, leaving it turned on.

He motored the boat toward the buoys and turned his navigation lights back on, all the while watching for cigarette boats. This area of the coastline was pitch dark, and he could feel the waves against the bow as the small boat heaved up and down cutting through the water. But he knew how to navigate the breakers, and he continued towards the shore and Atash's flashing light.

The seawall finally came into view, and Ibrahim steered his boat into the breakwater. He raised a hand toward his colleagues, who motioned him towards the next pier. The lighted sign was marked *PIER 3,* and he turned, slowly motoring the boat through the no-wake zone, where Atash pointed to slip fourteen, the open slot along the line of boats. Ibrahim threw a bowline ashore to his waiting crew and then hooked rubber fenders to the starboard side of the boat. He turned off the engine, raised the outdrive from the water, and pocketed the keys. His small ship was quickly and safely tied off.

For a desert people, we sure know our boating, Ibrahim thought, feeling his sea legs waver as he stepped onto pier three. Tall lights mounted along the pier made shadows, and Ibrahim looked around for anything or anyone that looked out of place. He glanced up at the sky, remembering the drone that had taken his friends' lives.

"May Allah be with you, cousin," Atash greeted.

"May Allah be with you," Ibrahim replied, embracing his friends one at a time before handing his cousin a brown cardboard box. "Here is our package. Handle it with care."

"And we have our other package as well, Ibrahim," Hamid said. "He is in safe keeping."

"And our delivery man?" Ibrahim asked. "Is he willing to deliver our package?"

"He will be willing, or he will have his son's head delivered to him," Atash asserted.

"Very well—then it will be delivered tomorrow, as planned," Ibrahim said. "Allah will help us with our holy mission."

And it is I, Ibrahim that has made this jihad successful. Where Anwar failed, I have succeeded. My plan has come together and the Americans have no clue. Wait until they see what I have planned for them. It was the proudest day of Ibrahim's life.

The three men turned and walked from the marina onto the streets of Dubai.

INTERNMENT

The room was hot. The young boy lay on a straw filled mattress, duct tape over his eyes and mouth. His hands and feet were bound with a hard plastic strap that cut into his wrists and ankles. He was thirsty, and his stomach growled from hunger. No one had been into the room for a achingly long time. Agib had no way of knowing how long. No way to tell how long he'd been here, no way to tell where here was, no way to tell where his father was. All he knew was that he needed water. He could hear a noisy ceiling fan running overhead and felt the small relief it offered as the mild breeze hit his face.

He had given up trying to escape his bindings. His wrists screamed with pain, and he could feel the dried blood that had trickled down his fingers. Each time he tried to stand up, he just fell over. His entire world had collapsed into a closet of fear and pain. The constant hum from the fan and the occasional noise from somewhere outside, beyond his world, were all he knew.

Where am I? Why am I here? What have I done to be taken by these thugs? Where is my father? Is he looking for me? All of these questions continued to race through his mind as he tried again to get comfortable.

A door closed somewhere in the distance. He heard footsteps approaching. Then another door opened, and he could hear a person walk toward him.

"Sit up," said a voice. He felt a hand grab his arm and pull him up to a sitting position.

"If you want food and drink, I must remove the tape. If you yell out, I will cut your throat. Do you understand?" the voice announced.

Agib nodded his head yes. A hand touched his face and then pulled hard against the tape across his mouth. It hurt, but he was glad to have it off. He stretched his mouth and licked his parched lips.

"Here, drink," the voice said.

Agib felt a straw at his mouth. He was so thirsty that he didn't even worry about what he had been offered, but instinctively he took the straw in his mouth and drew in a mouthful of the liquid. To his delight, it was cool water, and he drank as fast as he could, fearing that the straw would be taken from him.

"That's enough for a moment, or you will get sick on the floor," the voice said as the stranger pulled the straw from his mouth.

Agib panted and licked his lips, trying to savor every last drop of the refreshing drink.

"Here, eat this," said the voice, and Agib felt a spoon being thrust into his mouth. He chewed fast. Some kind of a rice mixture with a chicken flavor, he thought. The spoon was back to his mouth before he was done chewing. He quickly swallowed and took the next bite.

This went on for several minutes, and then the voice offered more liquid. Agib drank like a man dying of thirst until the straw was pulled from his mouth. He breathed heavily, hoping for more water, and then he heard the draw from a roll of duct tape. His face was bound again, and the man pushed him back down onto the bed. He heard footsteps walk away, followed by the door closing on the far side of the room.

The ceiling fan was again his only companion. Food and water had relieved his immediate pain, but now he could feel his wrists hurting. He felt overwhelmingly alone and began to cry, but he tried hard to stop himself, remembering how hard it had been to breathe with his nose all stuffed and the tape over his mouth. His tears began to back up behind the tape that covered his eyes.

He listened for clues that might discern his location or who the persons were that had interned him in this hell. But everything was silent, other than the faint footsteps treading in a distant room.

Finally, he began to drift off. Nightmares filled his sleep.

Part III

TAKEDOWN

BRIEF

Margaret was waiting for David in the conference room before her meeting, reviewing her papers and trying to discover some way to put a positive spin on her findings for the Dubai authorities. Washington had seemed somewhat unconcerned about Dubai's reaction toward the discovery of explosives and the possibility that terrorists had brought down the jet. Margaret, along with the leaders in Washington involved with the crash investigation, knew that the UAE would most likely put their own conclusions on any results of the accident investigation that they did not agree with. As much as she might wish, this was not an open democracy, and she knew that the government would not publicize any Arab involvement in the crash. Still, she hoped the information she was about to drop on David could be made part of the final report.

The conference room, like her hotel room, was huge, with ten-foot ceilings, beautiful carpet, tasteful artwork, and windows that took up the entire exterior wall. A mixture of different styles and sizes of chairs, all vastly comfortable, sat along the walls and tables, and a grand couch adorned the long interior wall that faced the windows. The view was spectacular, looking out over the city and the deep blue Persian Gulf. She had pulled the drapery all the way open to let the evening sun fill the room.

She had ordered an appetizer to be delivered; neither she nor David had eaten since the small lunch during the midday briefing. It was now nearly six p.m., and she glanced at the wine selection on the side table under the window.

"Calm yourself," she said aloud. Why was trying to predict David's official reaction to the news giving her so much concern? *Is that what has me concerned?* She needed to stay focused, disciplined. She thought of David's eyes. She was a professional woman, she reminded herself; no colleague or fellow associate had never smote her in all her years on dozens of investigations. Further, she was happily involved with Scott, and she was hoping and expecting more from him in the way of commitment. *So what the hell?* she asked herself. *Am I starting menopause?*

Plus, David was too far out there—an Arab, a foreigner. *Although he was really a Cheese Head,* she reminded herself. She almost laughed aloud as the door to the conference room opened and David walked in.

"Good evening, David," she said, calming herself down. "Thank you for coming."

"My pleasure, Ms. Hurley," he replied with a smile, closing the door and approaching the table that Margaret stood over. She walked around the table, her hand extended, greeting David with her finest smile.

"Please call me Margaret, David."

"That I will, Ms. Margaret," he replied with a smile. "You look beautiful this evening. We've had little opportunity to talk personally in the days since our exciting helicopter ride."

Margaret blushed slightly. "That was an exciting first day here," she said, adopting her best professional voice. "Any news on the helicopter or the operator?"

"The operator is clean and has a great safety record. So far, it looks like some fuel contamination to the engine. That's what caused the power loss and our extremely hard landing, anyway. The investigation team is looking for the cause of the contamination, but it will probably turn out to be a sand plug. Not uncommon in the desert environment as I'm sure you know."

"That's some good news, I guess," she replied, walking to the table. She hadn't thought for days of the fear she had felt during the crash. It had been a very dangerous but frightfully exciting experience they had shared together, and she hoped it would make the news she had to tell him easier. "David, please have a seat. I have some information regarding the accident findings that I need to share with you."

David turned and sat at the large conference style table just to his left. Margaret sat down across the table and opened a blue folder brimming with papers.

"I'll cut right to the chase. Our worst scenario may have become a reality," she began. "I'm afraid we have found evidence of an explosive device on board Flight 6." She handed him a copy of the test results that confirming the presence of PETN. She gave him time to review the papers.

There was a light knock on the door, and it opened to admit a waiter who pushed a catering table in and across the room. He turned and left, leaving the trays and their warm aroma behind. David was still reading the packet of papers intently. Margaret stood and walked to the catering table, lifting the dome off the tray. She was hungry and helped herself to one of the servings of smoked chicken with vegetables wrapped in pita bread.

Finally, he turned to meet her eyes. "Are you confident of these findings?" he asked.

"Perfectly confident, David," she replied, setting down the pita. "We've run our analysis several times to be sure. We are positive there were explosives on board."

David shuffled in his seat. "Are you saying that an explosion brought down Flight 6?" he asked.

"We have yet to confirm that, and we may never be able to. There is evidence of an explosion, but it appears minor compared to the damage that would normally result from PETN. We have sent several of the pieces of evidence to our explosives lab in Washington. They're doing further analysis."

"What do you propose I do with this information?" he asked, his face neutral.

"I have been instructed to inform you and your agency that explosives were found on board Flight 6. At this time, we can neither confirm nor disprove that the explosives were the cause of the crash. How you act on this information lies in your court. It's your investigation."

David didn't speak, his shoulders stiff. Margaret stared at him, waiting for a reaction. He knew as well as she, that this information was likely to start a storm within his government.

"Have you eaten?" she asked, attempting to lighten the mood slightly.

His concerned posture relaxed. "No," he said. "And I'm starving now that I smell all that food."

"Please help yourself. It's been a terribly long day, and we don't have to discuss this on empty stomachs."

"That sounds great." He looked at her strangely. "I'd sure like a beer or glass of wine with it. Are you open to a bottle of wine?"

She reached across the table and handed him the wine list that she had looked at earlier. David walked to the phone and dialed room service. Speaking in Arabic, he ordered a bottle of wine, hung up the receiver, and turned back to Margaret.

"I'm afraid there's little I can personally do with this information, other than pass it on up," he said. "It will go all the way to King Rashid, I'm sure."

"Yes, I figured it would," she said. "But given the latest findings of explosives on FedEx, Washington felt it was important that you and your team should be made aware of what we have found."

"Are you placing blame?" David asked sharply.

"Blame isn't my job, David," she replied. "Finding the true cause of this aircraft accident and the loss of two innocent lives is."

"What are you thinking?" he asked. "Was it a bomb planted in Dubai? By who?"

"Some of those questions will have to be answered by the FBI and your law enforcement agencies," she said. "We are here only to assist you with the investigation. What happens with that information lies with the politicians, I'm afraid."

"The politicians," he laughed. "Things operate differently here than what you and I are used to in the States, Margaret. If the FBI finds that Arabs were at fault, then the cause of the Flight 6 crash will be blamed on a fire—or worse yet, on the American pilots who were flying the plane. If a bomb was the cause of the crash, it's you and the NTSB who'll have to release the findings, if that information is ever to go public."

"We don't know what the cause was yet," Margaret cautioned. "And you know that we won't be able to publicize anything your government doesn't sign off on. Besides, I think Washington will put the blame on al-Awlaki, the al-Qaeda leader that was just droned in Yemen. Seems they fingered him for the bombs on the FedEx jet, so he was probably responsible for what was on Flight 6 as well. It's your investigation, and the final report will have to come from you and the GCAA."

David will never convince the authorities to release this information. It will be held and the accident will be blamed on a cargo fire and nothing to do with Muslim terrorism, she thought as she watched him look over the findings. *But I can't let this affect my investigation or my attitude. The information is now passed on, and it's out of my hands.*

There was a light tap at the door and a waiter entered

pushing another wheeled table draped in a white cloth, this one bearing a wine decanter.

David stood and greeted the waiter, thanking him in Arabic. He handed him a tip while escorting him out and locked the door as he closed it behind him. Then he walked back to the small table and poured two glasses of the French red wine, handing one to Margaret. "To new friends," he offered as a toast, and he clinked her glass.

"To new friends," she replied, standing up from the table with a smile and taking a sip of the wine. She had not had any wine since her dinner with Scott several days before and the thought took her from the moment.

She liked David, she thought. He was an educated, successful, and good-looking professional. So was she. And she was fascinated that he was an American, one whom she had met in the Middle East.

She had not dated anyone but Scott since the day they had met. *Nor do I have any interest in anyone else*, she reminded herself firmly. She took another sip of wine. They were standing exceedingly close to each other now. She turned and took a step toward the windows.

"Do you like the wine?" David asked her.

"Yes, wonderful choice, David. What is it?"

"A 2005 French Bordeaux, Chateau Haut-Bergey from the Pessac-Léognan appellation," he replied with his best French accent.

"You know your wines, I see," she said. "And your French."

"I know some French wines," he agreed. "My mother was born in France, so I studied some French and visited there several times."

"You speak French too?" she asked, somewhat impressed.

"Oui, mademoiselle. Mais pas selon les francaises."

"Tres bien pour un americain," she replied.

"Brilliant," David said. "You speak the language well, Margaret."

"Just enough to get myself trouble."

"To the French," David toasted, and they both enjoyed another taste of the Bordeaux. "How did you learn French?"

"I took four years in college and visited France twice," she said. "That's not enough to speak it well, and I have little opportunity to speak it with anyone these past few years." For some reason she felt tense and excited at the same time. "How about you?" she asked. "Where did your mother grow up?"

"A small village in the center of France called Lucenay. That was my mother's maiden name. They spell it De Lucenay. Je voudrais vous montrer la ville."

She translated in her mind: *I would like to show you the city.*

The sun had set, and the lighting in the room was mesmerizing. Dim sconce lights glowed along the walls, and the evening lights of the city rose into the windows.

"I see," she managed to utter as he turned his head slightly and kissed her. He did it slowly and her heart skipped a beat. She could tell, under her closed eyes, that he was waiting for her reaction. Her mind raced with dozens of thoughts.

Finally, he paused, and Margaret stepped back. She looked into his handsome eyes.

"I'm sorry, I can't," she said. "I have someone else especially important in my life right now."

He looked into her eyes. She looked back at him, watching a deep disappointment rush over him.

"I am sorry too, Margaret," he said. "I find you incredibly attractive and extremely intriguing. Are you sure this someone fills your life?"

"Yes, at this time he does," she said. "In fact, I am meeting him for dinner very shortly."

"Oh, he is here in Dubai? Someone I may know?"

"He's a Raine Airways captain," she explained.

"He is also a lucky man," David said, taking another sip of his wine and then setting his glass on the table. "I will review your team's findings and report to my boss," he said after a moment. "Is this copy for me to take?"

"Yes," she said. "It should have all the information that your team needs."

"Thank you. Please enjoy your evening," he said. He extended his hand, shaking hers goodbye. He offered a warm smile, turned, and left the conference room, closing the door behind him. Margaret watched as the door closed behind him and then sat in the nearest chair, feeling light headed.

A moment later, her cell phone rang and startled her back to the moment. "Hello, this is Margaret Hurley," she answered.

It was Scott.

ENSCONCE

Jafar slept little that night. His mind raced, and he found himself pacing and sweating on and off all night, finally getting some broken sleep just before sunrise. Still wearing the thawb he had worn the day before, he shuffled the few dishes he owned on the table. He lit the small gas burner to warm some water, still smelling the man's cigarette from the previous evening: a sharp reminder of his predicament. Not hungry, he settled for a cup a tea.

The morning light was beginning to creep into the small, solitary window in Jafar's single room home. He boiled his black tea with crushed cardamom and cinnamon and poured the strong liquid into his cup through a screen. The aroma normally helped to wake his senses, but not this morning. He sat down on the large rug that covered the center of the room and pondered the deadly situation he found himself in.

Going to the authorities was out of the question. Jafar didn't trust the police, and the man in his room last night had scared him. He knew the man who'd visited him had told the truth: These men would not hesitate to kill his son. Following their demands seemed, at the moment, to be the best chance to get Agib back.

For the love of Allah, why do they need me to put this package on board? Why can't they just ship it? It's a cargo plane!. That plane that crashed the other day was a cargo plane too. Do these same guys have anything to do with that? I bet this package is a bomb. Why else would they need me to do it? Do they want to blow-up this plane? Why would they want to blow up a cargo plane? Why would they want to blow up anything?

Jafar could never understand the violence done by would-be Islamic terrorists. *Do I want to be a part of this?* he asked himself. *They are going to kill somebody with this bomb, and it will be with my help if I do what they are demanding, demanding using Agib as their bargaining chip. What can I do against these thugs that won't get my son killed? I have no choice but to help with this insanity. Oh, Agib, I hope you are all right—*

He finished his tea and put several dried dates in his pocket. Hunger would come later, and it was sure to be a desperately long day. It was earlier than he would normally set off for his job at the airport, but he could sit still in this room no longer. The tears began as he stood, his body still trembling. Taking a deep breath, he pulled himself together, slid his cell phone into his pocket, and stepped through the door.

The usual morning heat was there as he stepped outside. The street was empty for now, and he felt slightly relieved as he turned toward 20 B Street, walking past the Karama Fish market on the shortest route to the train station. He walked slowly; his regular metro connection would not arrive for almost an hour, and his normal walk time was less than forty minutes. As he neared the elevated walkway that crossed over the busy Sheikh Rashid Road, the number of people rapidly increased, and he soon found himself in small sea of humanity, all of them headed out on their morning commute.

Are they watching me now? he wondered, looking behind him for a moment. *How did they find me? Why us? There are so many workers at the airport, why me?* Then the answer hit him. *It's not me; it's us—Agib and me together. I'm a worker with a son who they can exploit to do their dirty work. It must be highly illegal for them to go through all of this. It must be a bomb. What if it blows up on this plane? What if I blow up? What if I'm caught? How will I ever get Agib back?* The questions would not leave Jafar's mind.

His walk took him around Zabeel Park and onto the bicycle trail that led close to the Metro station. This was close to the same path he had taken when that man had followed him from the Metro. He had forgotten all about that man until he'd showed up in his apartment last night. *Was that the first day he had followed me?*

He held back from the increasing crowd of commuters, staying in the shadow of the small building that belonged to the Emarat gas station at the end of the street. It would be several minutes before his train would arrive. He scanned the area, trying to spot anyone who might be watching him, but he saw no one who looked out of place. They all seemed to have their own destinations, and no one was giving Jafar a second look.

His train was approaching, and he walked the steps to the elevated station. The building, along with the Metro system itself, was all new construction. Jafar had trouble imagining the situation he was in while he was surrounded by such a wonderful place. He scanned his NOL card, walked through the turnstile, and headed straight for the open doors of the rail car. He shuffled through with the mass of riders and found a seat, all the while searching from the corner of his vision for whoever was watching him. There were so many people.

The train speaker announced that the doors were about to close. The last few riders scurried in as the doors slid shut with a smooth gliding sound. A moment later, the train began to accelerate toward its next stop. Jafar's stop was Rashidiya, ten stations away and the last station on the Red Line. Within two minutes, the train slowed to the next stop, Al Karama. Riders rose from their seats and waited next to the doors. Jafar watched them closely, scanning the people who were still sitting. No one even looked at him. *Where is this man,* he thought?

New riders entered the train. There were five separate cars on the train, and Jafar had no way to see them all. The next four stops were all the same. People got off the train and new ones entered at each stop, the crowd seeming to grow smaller. There were several people toward the back of the car and three or four businessmen wearing Western style suits who were reading their morning paper and drinking their coffee, all of them headed to the airport along with Jafar.

Deira City Centre, an underground station, was the next stop. The bright sunshine faded as the train descended into the tunnel, but the interior was still bright with fluorescent lighting. The train came to a halt. Jafar's shoulders stiffened: entering the train was a young Arab man in clean but worn clothing who carried a paper sack with handles. The man made eye contact with Jafar as he walked past to sit down in the seat just behind him. The doors closed, and the train started its forward movement. This must be the man.

Jafar could hardly sit still. He wanted to turn and choke the life out of this Arab bastard who had his son. But instead, he made a fist with both hands, trying hard to control his rage.

After a moment, the man leaned over the seat and spoke into Jafar's ear. "Do not cause a scene," he said.

"Where is my son?" Jafar demanded.

"Quiet!" the man replied. "Your son is alive, and if you want him to stay that way, you will do as you are told."

Jafar said nothing, but he kept his fist clenched. He saw several of the businessmen look at him and then go back to reading their newspapers.

The man placed the paper sack on the seat next to Jafar. He looked at the sack with distaste, wanting to throw the thing across the train and demand to have his son back.

"Be especially careful with this package," the man said in a voice just above a whisper. "It is fragile, and it must get to its destination without any problems, or you will not see your son alive. If you are questioned by anyone, tell them that your package is merely printer cartridges for your office photocopier."

Jafar continued to look at the paper sack that sat next to him but said nothing.

"You will place it in front of the number four container position," the man said in his most threatening voice. "Four. Do you understand?"

Jafar turned, staring coldly at the man. He was wearing dark sunglasses, and Jafar could not see his eyes. "Yes, I understand," he replied in as loud a voice as he dared. "Do not hurt my son!"

The sunshine quickly returned through the windows as the train raced up the ramp to the elevated portion of the rail system and began to slow. "We are approaching Al Garhound station," a pleasant voice announced in several languages.

The man was already up and headed for the door. Jafar watched him, trying to memorize his face through those sunglasses. The train came to a smooth stop, and the doors slid open. The man stepped out and never looked back. As doors closed and the train began to move forward, Jafar could still see him, his back still to the train, walking down the stairs and disappearing from sight through the exit.

Jafar looked down at the sack that sat next to him. He felt frightened, scared and all alone. What could be in such a small package that could cause all this trouble in his life? Did he dare look inside? It felt like everyone around must be watching him. He looked around the train. No one seemed to be paying any attention to him, and he felt slightly more at ease. He picked the sack up by the rope handles and set it on his lap. It felt heavy for its size

"We are approaching Rashidiya Station," the speaker announced.

Jafar jumped as if he had been woken from a dream. He had not even noticed the last stop, and suddenly he was faced with his destination. He rose from his seat, holding the sack tightly, and moved to the doors. As the train came to a stop, he glanced around the car. There was an Arab man who was sitting on the back wall of the train, someone whom Jafar had not noticed until now. He was staring directly into Jafar's eyes. Trying to remain calm, Jafar turned and walked from the train. The doors closed behind him.

He could feel the fear and anxiety begin to overtake him as he walked toward the stairs that led to the terminal entrance and the security checkpoint for airport employees. Certainly they would catch him with this package at the checkpoint, he thought. Abruptly, he turned to the left and entered the men's washroom. Several men were inside washing their hands, and two stood at the urinals. Jafar walked further, entered a stall, and closed the door behind him. He stood with his feet toward the door, so it would appear that he was seated to anyone watching from the outside.

He had to think. What was he going to do? How would he pass safely through security? He felt as if he would soon be in jail. He looked down at the sack in his hands and slowly opened it. Inside was a package wrapped in brown paper and tied with a white string. He removed it from the sack, untied the string, and carefully lifted the paper's edge. Inside the wrapping were two long, narrow boxes decorated with pictures of a large photocopier. They each read *Hewlett Packard Printer Cartridge*.

He placed one of the boxes back in the sack and hung it from its rope handle on the stall door coat hook. Gently, he turned the remaining box over in his hand. He cut the tape on the box with his fingernail, slowly opened it, and removed something that looked and felt just like a new black plastic printer cartridge.

He turned the cartridge over in his hand. *Why is this so important that these men would steal Agib just to get them on an airplane?* he thought. The cartridges wouldn't be a problem to get through security, he was sure; the officers rarely looked through the employees' bags, just sent them through the x-ray machine. *They won't even question me about printer cartridges,* he told himself, *and if they do, I'll just say they are for the cargo office. They will buy that.*

He slid the plastic cartridge back into its box and reassembled the package, and then he flushed the toilet and left the washroom, heading straight for the security entrance in the terminal. He had to do this right; it was for his son's life. He tried his best to wear a smile.

A small line of workers had formed in front of the x-ray machine, each of them waiting their turn through airport screening. Jafar reached into his pocket and placed the dates he had brought for his lunch in the sack with the printer cartridges. Two Arab men motioned each worker through the metal detector. Jafar was now next in line and placed his sack on the conveyer belt. It was quickly swallowed into the machine. *I hope it doesn't blow up,* Jafar thought.

He was motioned through the metal detector by one of the security guards. He stepped through the white arch, but there was no sound, and the Arab guard gave him a smile and waved him on. Jafar turned to find the other security agent holding his sack and looking straight at him.

"What is in this bag?" the man asked.

Jafar hesitated. *Say it,* he told himself. *Just say it.* "My lunch and printer cartridges for the office," Jafar replied.

The guard handed the sack back to Jafar. He took the sack and slowly walked on through the security area and out the door to the tug office. He still felt a huge lump in his chest and his heart was racing. On the far side of the ramp from the tug drivers' office, he could see the Boeing 747 that he was about to load.

The cool air of the office hit his face as he walked inside. Workers were gathering around the counter, waiting for their load sheets. He didn't want to talk with anyone. What if someone asked about the sack he carried? *It is my lunch,* he would tell them. He stood behind the line of tug drivers, remembering to say good morning to his dispatcher as he reached for his load sheet.

He had been assigned tug number forty-one. A schedule of the day's aircraft was posted on the wall of the office, and each driver was given a copy to review throughout the day. Raine Airways' plane was below three other 747s on the list. Several hours would pass before he would load it. Jafar left the office with his schedule and bag in hand, headed for his tug, walking into what was already a damned long day.

*

The afternoon sun scorched the cement of the tarmac, and Jafar's only relief came while he was driving the tug, where the oncoming air offered a slight reprieve from the appalling inferno. He looked down at the package on the floorboard of his tug. It was almost time. He drove to the dolly line-up area where he would be given his loading sequence. His next pull, five dollies that had already been hitched together, was to be delivered to the Raine Airways craft.

An experienced ground crew could load a 747 in about an hour, which was how much time Jafar had to make his move.

The main deck of a 747 is loaded from an aft cargo door on the left side of the fuselage using a K-loader, capable of lifting two containers or pallets at a time to the aircraft's main deck. As each pallet enters the plane, electric wheels mounted in the floor roll it forward and then lock it into position. Although much of the loading is automated, several workers are on board the aircraft to operate the rollers and lock down each pallet. A supervisor who stands on the ground next to the K-loader coordinates the loading and is responsible for the container positions on board the aircraft. The loaders position the cargo pallets two across, with the main deck holding up to thirty positions. Container position is subject to change and each tug driver is directed, primarily with hand signals to pull the appropriate dolly into the unload position.

Despite the complexity of the process, Jafar's only concern today was with when and how he would get on board the plane without being caught. He had security clearance to be on the ramp and around the aircraft, but he had not been trained on loading yet and was not authorized to be on board. The man on the train had instructed him to place the package in front of the number-four container position. That position was in the forward section of the plane, and it would be one of the first containers loaded.

The tug only had a top speed of ten miles per hour, and it took Jafar almost ten minutes to reach the plane from the cargo staging area. As he approached the K-loader, he scanned the area, looking for a reasonable place to park his tug, somewhere that would let him quickly enter the plane and get back without drawing any attention to himself. The area in front of the aircraft was wide open, but soon there would be several service vehicles parked around the front of the stairs that led to the main crew entrance door three stories above. He would wait for the area to become crowded, which would offer him the best cover.

Driving slowly, he pulled his small train of dollies into position following the load supervisor instructions. As his last dolly was unloaded, the next tug driver moved into position behind him. The service vehicles from the companies that cleaned the cockpit, loaded the catering for the flight crew, and serviced the lavatory had not yet arrived. Sweating, he returned to the staging area to collect his next set of dollies.

His heart was pounding. He felt that the sweat dripping from his brow was from the tension and fear running through his body rather than the heat from the desert air. It was taking all his concentration to steer the tug where he needed to go. It felt like police cars were sure to surround him, and he would be arrested at any moment. *If I'm arrested they are sure to kill my son*, he thought. *I have to do this right on the first try.*

When he returned to the loader with the next round of cargo, the service vans and trucks had arrived and sat parked around the front of the 747, blocking sight of the stairs. This would be his best chance. He sat, waiting in line behind the train of dollies being off loaded onto the plane, shaking as if he were cold even in the one hundred fifteen degree heat that now baked the air around him. He rehearsed the plan in his mind: There may be someone walking up or down the stairs leading to the crew door. What would he say if he was questioned? *I needed to use the lavatory,* he would reply. His supervisor had told him specifically on his first day that the loaders were not allowed to use the aircraft facilities. If questioned, he would just have to lie and insist that it had been necessary.

If he were caught, he knew it would mean the death of his son. If he were locked in jail, what reason would the Arabs have for keeping Agib alive? The police would never be able to find Agib in time. This had to go right.

He watched as the last container on the dolly in front of him was pushed onto the K-loader. As the tug and dollies in front of him pulled away, Jafar drove his into position. He would make his attempt after this load. Assigned only three dollies on this trip, he was just moments away from his task.

Loading of the main deck was almost complete. As the last container was unloaded from his dollies, he drove slowly forward, making a large arc as if he were driving back to the staging area. But instead, as he drove around the front of the giant 747, he pulled his tug between two large service vans, one with panels that read *Delicacy Gourmet Fine Airline Catering*. The deliveryman was just leaving the airplane and headed back to his van. Jafar swallowed hard, picked up the sack, and headed toward the stairs.

The stairs consisted of two tiers with a small landing at each level. *Three stories high*, Jafar thought as he walked up toward the plane. He tried to make it appear as if he knew what he was doing, but he trembled inside. He had never been on such a large airplane before—in fact, he had been on an airplane only once in his life, on the flight that had brought him and his son to Dubai. Nearing the top landing, he missed his footing, and he reached with both hands onto the guardrail to steady himself. The sack slipped from his hand. He tried to catch it as it fell, but he missed, and the sack containing the box of ink cartridges tumbled down several steps. Jafar froze in horror for a moment, but then turned and followed the sack down the steps to catch it. There was a man in a pilot's uniform climbing the stairs. Without pausing, he grabbed the sack and continued up the stairs without missing a step. He held the sack out to Jafar with a smile.

"Thank you," was all Jafar could think to say, not able to meet the man's eyes.

The man smiled, continued past Jafar, and entered the plane. Jafar followed and watched the pilot climb the yellow ladder that led to the cockpit. There was no one else in the cargo area, and position four was just to his right. Taking several steps toward the back of the airplane, he pulled out the paper-wrapped package from the sack, still wrapped in its white string, and placed it between positions three and four as instructed. It fit snugly between the two containers. It was not fully concealed, but he assumed that since the aircraft was almost fully loaded, no one would be left to see it. His heart was pounding with fear. Trying to remain outwardly calm, he wrapped the sack in a ball, placed it under his arm, turned and left the plane.

He walked quickly to his waiting tug and drove off. He never looked back, only headed for the staging area and his next series of dollies. There was always another plane to be loaded. He looked at his watch. The whole thing had taken less than three minutes. Sweat dripped of his forehead onto his watch, and he realized at that moment that he was shaking almost uncontrollably. He concentrated, trying to calm himself. The task was done. He had done as he was told.

They have to give Agib back now, he thought, *but when?* The men had not said when they would be in contact with him again. Suddenly he became angry with himself: He should have demanded a time and place where he could find his son. *What am I going to do now?*

PLOT

It was twelve days since the crash of Flight 6, but the story was still big news in Dubai, and although Raine Airways had retired the flight number—Scott and Greg would be crewing Flight 25 that evening along the same route—there was still a great deal of tension in the air. Scott and Greg shared their concerns with each other as they made their way to the airport, following the same routine as the crew of Flight 6 had.

Foremost on their minds was the article printed in this morning's Dubai newspaper, the *Khaleej Times*. Again, apparently, al-Qaeda had claimed responsibility for the downing of Flight 6. The authorities had neither confirmed nor denied the claim. Scott had called Maggie after reading the newspaper.

"All I can give you is the official UAE and NTSB response," she had said. "An onboard fire brought down the jet, not a bomb." But Maggie's tone of voice had said it all. He could also tell that she knew more than she was willing, or allowed, to share with him, and she was concerned with his safety. The issue was at the forefront of their conversation all through dinner and wine the night before, taking a reprieve only for lovemaking.

"Be careful," she'd told him as she said goodbye on the morning of the flight.

And he would be. An onboard fire is always the greatest danger while flying commercial jets, and all flight crews are trained to handle the emergency. Landing the plane as soon as possible is the primary concern, although finding a close, suitable runway while traveling over some foreign countries can be a serious challenge. So Scott and Greg had reviewed all the in-flight procedures and checklists associated with fires and had listed all the available airports with suitable runways for a 747 along their route of flight. They had a clear diversion plan if a fire started on his flight along any point en route to Cologne.

But Scott reminded himself: The crew of Flight 6 had been through all of the latest training for an onboard fire, and they had been relatively close to a usable runway. Neither of these things had saved them. *Hell, they almost made it,* Scott thought. *That fire must have been intense.*

The crew van drove around the Raine Air 747 tail and made its way to the front, where the crew stairs were stationed. Scott climbed out of the van and looked up at the jet he was about to take airborne. *Funny how this bird seems to get smaller over the years,* he thought, pulling his bags from the back of the van. Crews were still loading the aircraft, and trains of cargo containers pulled by tugs were being driven in every direction. Even after having watched this for over twenty years, Scott still always thought of this scene as controlled chaos.

The pilot's luggage was normally loaded into the aft belly compartment to save the long bag-drag up the stairs. Scott rolled both his and Greg's suitcases to the aft of the aircraft, walking under the massive jet's fuselage. He set the luggage next to the small conveyor belt loader that led to the cargo hold, and he began his walk-around and exterior pre-flight of the aircraft.

The aircraft had been thoroughly inspected by aircraft maintenance prior to the crew's arrival. It was the obvious things that Scott was looking for on his pre-flight, the big things that could get you into trouble: oil leaks, broken hydraulic lines, missing panels. Over the years Scott had rarely found anything wrong by the time he did his inspection. What he usually found were worn tires or frayed hoses, issues that maintenance had usually already discovered and found to be within tolerance and safe for flight. This was all the better to Scott, who would always rather go flying than go back to the hotel due to an un-airworthy plane.

He smiled and nodded hello to the loaders and tug drivers he passed as he made his way around the jet. It looked as if the main deck was almost finished being loaded, and the conga line of tugs had been reduced to just one, which was currently loading the last of the belly compartments. Soon, the large K-loader would be backed away and driven to another plane.

As Scott made his way back to the front of the plane, he found it odd to see an empty tug sitting at the base of the stairs with its engine running. Tugs normally drove all around the jet, but cargo loading and unloading was done at the rear or on the right side of the plane. The loading crews did not normally park tugs near the front of the jet and use the crew stairs.

The crew stairs had a landing halfway up and another at the top, allowing for a less steep climb than the old-style stairs that rose in one flight from the ground to the entrance door twenty-five feet above. A man—by the look of him, the driver of the abandoned tug, Scott thought—was climbing the stairs above. He carried a paper sack on his shoulder, and just as he was about to reach the door, a package wrapped in white string fell out of it and began to tumble down the stairs.

Without breaking stride, Scott picked it up and offered it to the man, smiling politely. The man raised his gaze as he took the package, but offered no smile and failed to meet his eyes.

"Thank you," said the driver.

Scott continued onto the plane, hearing the driver follow him on. He climbed the next set of stairs that led to the cockpit, where Greg was already working on his portion of the pre-flight. But something about the driver was nagging at him. He sat his flight bag down at the top of the stairs and returned to the cargo area just as the man was leaving. He seemed to be in something of a hurry. Scott walked to the door, standing just out of sight, and watched the man continue down the remaining stairs and climb aboard the already running tug.

Thirty large pallet size containers sat locked into position on the main cargo deck. A full load, each container filled with every size and shape of box and package. *So why was a member of the load crew leaving the main deck using the crew stairs,* Scott wondered.

There was a two-foot wide path between the wall of the plane and the cargo containers, which provided a walkway around the entire main deck to allow for inspection of the cargo. All of the cargo packages were locked inside the containers, so it was unusual and not required for a member of the flight crew to visually inspect any of this. But after the loss of Flight 6, Scott thought—and after the encounter he had just had on the stairs—it felt like the right thing to do.

He turned from the doorway and started to walk aft along the outer edge of the containers on the left side of the cargo deck. Several containers aft, he saw it. A paper-wrapped box, the size of a long, large shoebox, lay wedged on top and slightly in between two containers, just three pallet positions back from the entrance door. It was the same package he had picked up and handed to the tug driver on the stairs not five minutes before.

Scott continued to look at it for a moment, collecting his thoughts. Priorities and procedures compiled themselves in his mind. In no way was this package supposed to be here. He needed to get Greg and everyone else off this jet immediately.

He turned and headed back toward the yellow set of stairs that led to the flight deck. After a quick scramble up and through the flight deck door, he scanned the seats and galley area. All Raine Airways 747s were equipped with ten extra seats in the large upper deck for traveling crews and company personnel. No extra passengers were currently on board. Greg was alone in the cockpit.

"Greg, we need to get off this jet now," Scott said. His tone had told Greg all he needed to know. A heartbeat later, Greg pushed his seat back and followed behind Scott, exiting the plane.

The stairs seemed endless to Scott now that he was eager to see the last step. His mind was in a far away dream scene as he scrambled down. *We need to get far away from this jet as fast as possible. Is this what happened to Flight 6? What the hell did that guy think he's doing? Did he think he could get away with this?* And, in the back of his mind: *What if it isn't a bomb and I'm freaking out for nothing?*

He made it to the tarmac with Greg right behind him. The fast pace of two crewmembers descending the stairs caught the attention of the aircraft mechanic who walked towards them from his truck.

"Captain, is there a problem?" he asked as Scott approached.

"I just did a walk through the main deck and found a box stashed between two containers," Scott replied.

Greg looked at Scott, alarmed.

"I met some guy, a loader, coming down the stairs as I went up," Scott continued, speaking more to Greg now so that his copilot understood his concern. "He acted suspicious, so I went looking. I need to get the gateway manager involved right now. Can you get a hold of him on your radio?" he asked, turning his attention back to the mechanic.

"I shall call inside," said the mechanic. He started speaking Arabic into his hand held radio.

"I think we should call Operations in Anchorage," Scott said to Greg. "I feel a departure delay coming on."

"Yeah, that's probably a good idea," Greg replied, looking up at the jet.

A moment later, the gateway manager was approaching Scott. He had a phone in his ear and seemed nervous as he ended his call and reached out to shake Scott's hand.

"Greetings, I am Carmen Antar, on-site manager. What seems to be the problem, sir?"

"Scott James, nice to meet you. I found a box lying by itself, lodged between two containers on the main deck."

"That is very odd," said the manager. "Can you show it to me?"

Scott frowned. "I don't know if that's a good idea, all things considered. You know what I mean?"

Carmen pondered for a moment. He speed dialed a number on his phone and spoke forcefully in Arabic. After a minute, he ended his call and turned his attention back to Scott. "Our load master is on his way."

"I saw a man leaving the plane as I was going aboard. He seemed dang suspicious, and he dropped what looks like the same package I just saw lodged between two containers on the main deck."

"Could you identify this man?"

"Probably."

The phone in Carmen's hand rang, and he turned away from Scott to answer it. Scott reached in his pocket for his cell phone and dialed Raine Airways in Anchorage. As he informed the assistant chief pilot on duty of their situation, several airport police cars arrived next to the plane. Since the jet was not in the air, Scott was not in charge, but merely a spectator in the unfolding events. The airport police talked with Carmen and then quickly moved everyone far away from the plane. They asked Scott about the box and its location as the Dubai police arrived, along with a large van and bomb squad members dressed in heavy black gear.

So much for flying, he thought. At first he had hoped to get this box removed and continue on with their flight to Cologne, but he now realized that the authorities would not release the plane—nor would Raine Airways—until it was completely unloaded and thoroughly inspected.

Shortly after their arrival, the bomb squad emerged from the plane and slowly walked down the crew stairs. They were carrying what appeared to be a bomb blast container. As they loaded it into their waiting truck and drove from the ramp, a man in plain clothes approached Scott, Greg, and Carmen, who had been moved back to the edge of the cargo ramp along with all the other gateway personnel.

"Excuse me, Captain," said the man. "I am Detective Barad with the Dubai Police. I understand you saw a man leaving your airplane. Did you see him with the package you found on board?"

"Yes, and then I watched him come down the stairs in a hurry," Scott said. "He got on his tug and drove away."

Barad looked at Greg for a moment. "I didn't see him," Greg offered. "How did you find the box, Captain?"

"It was easy to see if you were looking. Is it a bomb?"

"We do not know yet, but we take this issue extremely seriously, as you can see," said Detective Barad. "Would you be able to identify the man you saw leaving your airplane, Captain?"

"Probably," said Scott. "How do you propose we do that?"

"We have someone at the main office who will provide us

with the employee identification photos to review," said Detective Barad. "If you will follow me please, I have a car waiting."

"What about my F/O here?" Scott asked gesturing toward Greg.

"Did you see this man?" the detective asked Greg.

"No, I was already in the cockpit."

"Very well, you are free to leave."

"I'll stay and get our bags, Scott," Greg said. "Meet you at the hotel when you're done."

"Thanks, Greg, see you soon," Scott said, shaking Greg's hand and punching his shoulder.

*

Once inside the office, it took Scott only ten minutes to find the picture of the man he had seen leaving the plane. Jafar Khah Hamdard was the name under the photo. The detectives immediately printed copies for distribution throughout the airport and to all airport staff.

The arrest was almost a textbook procedure for the Dubai police. The airport and all entrances and exits had been locked down immediately upon word of a possible terrorist bomb. Jafar had been easily found and arrested at the cargo tug office, all within an hour of Scott finding the box on board his jet.

My jet that's still sitting on the ramp at the Dubai Airport, Scott thought. It was nearly six p.m. now, hours after he had made the identification. He had had his fill of police work.

He was looking through the glass at a man sitting, his hands bound with a plastic tie wrap. *The infamous one-way mirror that's in every detective movie,* Scott thought. *Glad I'm looking through this side of it. What's in this guy's mind? Why would he want to blow up my jet? Shithead! He's looking really pathetic now.* He stared at the man on the other side of the glass for a moment and then turned to face the detective.

"Yeah, that's the guy I saw leaving the jet. I'm sure of it," he said, sealing the fate of the man in the adjoining room.

APPREHENSION

Detective Josh Barad paced in his small cubicle of an office looking at the growing stack of papers on his latest case. He had little or nothing to go on at the moment. A man was accused of placing a package onboard a cargo plane. Not the most offensive of crimes, unless of course the package was illegal contraband, or worst, a bomb. After the recent loss of Flight 6 from the same airport, he was taking no chances. Jafar would remain in custody until the all the facts were known.

His phone rang. "Barad," was his greeting. "Yes. You are sure?" He took several notes listening intently to the caller's news. "Thank you. Please keep me informed," was his response as he hung-up the phone, staring at the photo of Jafar on his desk. Barad knew he was now in the middle of an international terrorist investigation. The police lab had just confirmed that the package found onboard the Raine Airways 747 was indeed a bomb. Its exact chemical analysis was not complete, but they were certain that the package contained explosive material, inside two printer cartridges with the electric circuitry needed for detonation.

Just like the bombs found on that cargo plane in the UK, the case of a lifetime he thought and one he hoped to play a pivotal roll in. A case that he only dreamt would come his way since his days at the Dubai Policy Academy. He was in the first graduating class at the Academy in 1992 earning a BA degree in Law and Police Sciences. He had worked in London and throughout Northern Ireland for two years with Scotland Yard, chasing the Provisional Irish Republican Army, PIRA until Sinn Fein had called a unilateral ceasefire and the terrorist activities had settled down.

He returned to Dubai and soon made rank of Detective. Life had gotten much quieter than his time in the UK. The largest case he had been involved with since his return had been a major counterfeit operation and it seemed to be his ongoing investigation. Petty theft, auto theft, an occasional murder were some of his past investigations, but on the whole, Dubai's crime scene was quiet compared to cities of the same size and Detective Barad's job was at times boring. His life was about to get much more exciting.

*

The small cell was located on the second floor of the Central Dubai Police Department on Sheikh Zayed Road. It was furnished with a bunk along one wall, a stainless steel toilet, and a tiny sink with cold water in the corner. The walls were concrete, painted an off white color, and one wall was made of bright yellow iron bars with a gate. There was no privacy in this jail cell, but its occupant paid no attention. The only person in the room was Jafar—or, as the police knew him, Jafar Khah Hamdard, the man suspected of planting a bomb on board a Raine Airways 747. He was sitting on the bunk, having slept little during his long, lonely night.

His mind still raced with the questions and fear that had consumed him from the moment that man had left his home. The moment when he realized that he had lost his son. Where is Agib? He had brought his son to this country so he would be safe, so Jafar could look after him and keep men like the ones who had taken him at bay. He had failed. The terrorists would never let Agib go now, and the police where sure to put Jafar in jail for an exceedingly long time for having placed a bomb on board an airplane. He was losing all hope. Should he tell the police everything? Take a chance and let the police find Agib? Could they find him in time? Was he even alive? Would they even believe his story, or just throw him in jail to rot? He had no answers to all of these questions. He only knew that the fate of both he and his son now lay with the men and women in this police station.

*

The ambassador from Pakistan had been notified that one of their citizens had been arrested. Detective Josh Barad was now attempting to control the mad rush of inquiries from numerous countries while the police station filled with authorities from government agencies that represented each of the countries with ties to the bomb plot.

It was still early morning when agents from the US, including the FBI and Homeland Security arrived at the Dubai police station to assist with the investigation into the latest bomb plot. Mark Mitchell from the CIA was among them.

Since this last drone strike on Anwar al-Awlaki six days prior, no other bombs had been discovered on board any cargo or passenger aircraft. Mark had begun to think that the al-Qaeda cell responsible had been completely annihilated, but knew, the moment the CIA had been informed that explosive material had been found at the wreckage of Flight 6, that he had been too optimistic. Mark was on the next C-130 from Sana'a to Dubai. They had either missed someone in the latest strike, he suspected, or money was now flowing to a new cell seeking to achieve the same plot. Mark was here to find out exactly what.

The UK had their interests present as well when Rob Morris from MI5 walked into the room. Each agent had been near or in the country, having been involved in the investigation into the loss of Flight 6 or with the bombs discovered on the FedEx aircraft. Everyone knew each other, and cordial hellos and handshakes ensued as each new agent made their entrance.

Detective Barad gave the agents a briefing of yesterday's events and the information that they had so far. No links to any terrorist organizations could be found associated with Jafar Hamdard. Mitchell was not surprised: *New recruit* was the name of the game for al-Qaeda. But if Jafar did have any connection with a terrorist group, he knew, he and the men and women in this room would find it.

The glass of the one-way mirror lit up when the light in the interrogation room was turned on, illuminating what looked like a small, empty stage. The single door in the room opened, and two officers escorted Jafar in, seating him in one of the chairs. The officers left the room, locking the door behind them. Jafar, wearing bright orange prison overalls, sat alone, looking tired, unshaven, and desperately nervous.

Every agent present had requested to be a part of the interrogation of Jafar that was about to take place, but only Mark Mitchell spoke fluent Pashto, Jafar's native language. He was even fluent in Jafar's regional dialect, having spent the last three years in the Afghanistan-Pakistan border region in the hunt for Osama bin Laden. Mark had learned the Afghani language from his mother, a professor and dean of foreign language studies at Washington University. His mother was born in Kandahar to rich merchants that had fled the country even before the Soviets began their invasion back in the seventies.

Better, more accurate information could always be gathered by using a suspect's native language, everyone knew, so Mitchell and Barad would conduct the interrogation. They entered the interrogation room where Jafar was sitting. Jafar rose to his feet.

"What are you going to do?" he asked in broken Arabic.

"We are going to ask you some questions," Mitchell said calmly in Pashto. "Please have a seat."

Jafar was visibly surprised to hear the agent speak in his own language. He moved back into his chair, squirming as he watched both men rearrange the chairs to face him across the table. His hands—no, his entire body was shaking, Mitchell noticed.

"Jafar Khah Hamdard. Is that your full and legal name?" asked Barad in English.

"Yes, yes that is my name. They have my airport identification."

"Jafar, my name is Detective Josh Barad with the Dubai Police, and this is Agent Mark with MI5." Mitchell nodded; they had thought it best not to give away Mitchell's true identity, given his ties to the al-Awlaki organization.

Jafar gave them both a nervous look, his body still trembling.

"You have been working at the Dubai Airport as a tug driver now for only four days," Mark asked in Pashto. "Is this correct?"

"Yes."

"Jafar, do you know why you are here now?"

Jafar stared ghost-like at his accusers. After a moment, he lowered his head and began to cry. "They have Agib," he let out.

"Agib? Who is Agib, Jafar?"

"My son."

"Who has your son?"

"I do not know," Jafar said, visibly attempting to hold back more tears. "A man came to my room and told me they have Agib, and that if I want to see him again I was to do what they told me."

"What did the man tell you to do, Jafar?" Mark asked with a calm, reassuring voice.

"They said I was to place a box on the airplane I deliver to."

"And what was in the box?"

"They did not say, but I looked inside and saw that it contained printer cartridges."

"Did you think they were really printer cartridges, Jafar?"

"I do not know," Jafar said helplessly. "I looked at it. They looked like two printer cartridges to me. All I know is that they have Agib."

Mark and Josh looked at each other. The detective shared a note he had on his briefing folder, stating that Jafar had entered the UAE with a boy, age eleven, full name: Agib Khan Hamdard. They gave each other a nod.

"Did you see these men?"

"I saw the man who was in my room. I have seen him before. He followed me on the Metro and all the way close to my home."

"Is this the same man that gave you the package to put on the airplane?" Mark asked.

"No, it was a different man on the train."

"Do you think you could identify either of these men?" Mark asked.

Jafar seemed to straighten up. "The man in my room, most assuredly. I do not know if I can see the man on the train. I have tried to remember his face. He sat close to me and I looked at him and watched him as he left the train, but he wore dark sunglasses."

Detective Barad motioned at the mirror for someone to meet him at the door. At the same time Mark opened his Apple laptop computer and turned it on. The door to the room opened and the Detective instructed the officer to cut the zip-tie that bound Jafar's hands. More officers brought in several bottles of water and set them on the table.

"Are you hungry?" Mark asked.

Jafar nodded yes, and Barad opened a water bottle handing it to Jafar, who drained it. After a minute, Mark sat his computer on the table where Jafar could see the screen.

"I have some photos I'd like you to look at. Maybe the man on the train is in one of these pictures," Mark said as he showed Jafar how to advance from one photo to the next. "Take your time. Let me know if anyone looks familiar."

Jafar began to study each photo carefully. As he did, Mark stood up and motioned Josh out of the room. They walked to a quiet area along the adjacent hall.

"I have a good idea who set this up, Detective," he said. "Or at least I'm sure he's involved."

"Who—someone right here in Dubai?" asked Barad.

"You know about the bombs found on the FedEx jet in London?"

"Yes, I do."

"When the Yemenis found out those bombs had been shipped from Sana'a, they took out the heads of AQAP. I think one man may have been missed." Mark said with a frown. "Further, I've gotten word through one of my contacts that an al-Qaeda bomb builder named Ibrahim al-Asiri has been seen in the city. He was on the hit list from the Yemen operation. We have reason to believe that a partial detonation or malfunction of one of his bombs brought down the Raine

Airways 747 thirteen days ago."

Barad nodded, absorbing the information. "If you are correct, then this must be their latest attempt."

Both men returned to the room where Jafar was studying the computer screen intently.

"Have you spotted anyone familiar, Jafar?" Mitchell asked.

"I have not found the man who handed me the package. But as I left the train, I saw this man staring at me." Jafar brought up the photo.

"Ibrahim al-Asiri," Mark said with a grin, turning his eyes to the detective. He closed the computer. "Thank you, Jafar. If you will follow me now, please, I have other photos for you to look at. Maybe we can find the man that came to your home." He motioned Jafar toward the open door.

Jafar rose to his feet. Several empty bottles of water sat around him, and he seemed much more relaxed now. "How will I find my son?" he asked, looking at both men.

Detective Barad glanced at Mark. "We are going to do our best to find him," he said, trying to sound optimistic.

Mark knew as well as the detective that the odds were not in the favor of finding the boy alive. These were ruthless, fanatical killers. But finding Agib alive, Mitchell knew, had just become Detective Barad's primary task.

After escorting Jafar to another room, Mitchell and Barad returned to the viewing room, where the other department agents waited along with the Dubai chief of police. Mark gave them a thorough briefing on the interrogation.

"Gentlemen," he said, "if we're going to have any chance to nab these guys, we have to act fast. The way I see it, the terrorists here in Dubai were either watching that plane—in which case they now know that it didn't leave—or the person who was expecting the package in Cologne informed them that it never arrived as scheduled. They are going to want to know why and if their bombs are still on board. That should leave them returning to our man Jafar for answers. Jafar will inform them that the jet had mechanical problems, but that it will leave as soon as these are fixed—and that their bombs remain on board where Jafar put them. They must believe that the plan is still going forward as they intend."

It was quiet in the room. After a moment, the FBI agent spoke up. "I like it," he said. "Do we have anyone watching Jafar's home now?"

"We searched it for evidence shortly after his arrest," Barad replied, "but we found nothing besides passports for him and his son, as well as a little cash and a bank deposit booklet. Seems Jafar has done well at saving his earnings while in Dubai. We have two officers stationed there now, but so far no one has shown up."

"If that's their only means of communication with him, I suggest we get him back to the house and set up the sting, now," Mitchell said. "If he tells them that Flight 25 will fly as scheduled, only one day later than planned, it will give us time yet today to set up a sting in Germany as well."

There was agreement throughout the room, and Mitchell and Barad left to speak to Jafar. This would give them the best opportunity of apprehending their prey, Mitchell knew, formulating the plan in his head as he walked. He also knew that so many things would have to go just right for this plan to work—but saw no other options if they were to find the boy alive.

STRATAGEM

The Dubai police returned Jafar's cell phone to him, escorted him to his neighborhood in an unmarked squad car, and allowed him to walk back to his apartment while they waited in their car, a block away. The sun was approaching late morning and even parked in full shade the car's air conditioning struggled to keep the men inside cool. They had outfitted Jafar with a hidden microphone to listen to, and record everything said between him and the terrorist. Several police officers dressed as civilians wandered the hot and dusty side streets, radio and weapons at the ready. Barad had just settled in to what he thought would be a long and fruitless stakeout.

As Jafar walked into his home, the memories of the night that the thug had been in this same room all flashed back. He closed the door and looked around the room. Many things were out of place, and all of his and Agib's clothes were in piles on the bunk beds or scattered on the floor. It was obvious someone had searched his home. He started to pick up Agib's things, and the thought of his son started the tears again.

Where is Agib? How could I have let this happen?

He wiped his face with his sleeve and tried to pull himself together. He stepped over to his burner, lit the flame, and put on water for tea. He wasn't hungry, but maybe some of his favorite tea would help him through this—this meeting with a terrorist, a kidnapper, a murderer even. That thought made him sit up straight. *I have no defense against this man, no weapons.* He looked around the room. In the corner next to the bed he saw his son's cricket bat. He placed it on the table at the ready, but it did little to ease his fears. *I've never harmed anyone in my life, but kidnapping my son seems the best reason to start,* he thought, trying to reassure himself.

The water was steaming and Jafar poured it over the tea strainer, the aroma of the strong leaves filling the air as the door to his home burst open, and a man walked inside. It was Hadid, the same man as before. Jafar sat the teapot down and reached for the bat, but the man was there first and threw it across the room as he pulled out his janbiya. He pointed it Jafar and stepped toward him around the table. He was still wearing the same dirty, food-stained thawb that Jafar had seen him in days ago. His hands were black with dirt, and he smelled like Turkish cigarettes.

"Why does the airplane sit at the airport?" he demanded, shaking the curved blade at Jafar's face.

Jafar was startled, even though he had expected the visit. He looked at the man with hatred, this man who had his son, and he stood his ground.

"I was told it had broken and could not fly," he said as rehearsed, trying to remain calm.

"Where is our package?" the man yelled.

"It is where I put it. Where you said it was to be placed. Where is my son?"

"When does the airplane leave for Germany?" the man asked, ignoring Jafar's question.

"Tonight," Jafar said. "Only one day late. Where is my son?"

The man turned and stepped away from Jafar, took a cell phone from his pocket and hit SEND. His Arabic was too quick for Jafar to follow, but it was obvious he was relaying the information to a colleague. Jafar tried to step closer without being noticed; hoping Barad's microphone would pick up the call.

Finally Hadid ended his phone call and put his hand on the doorknob. "We will be in touch," he said to Jafar.

"What about my son?" Jafar demanded.

"You will have your son when the package is delivered as planned," the man said, pulling the fold of his thawb and sheathing his dagger. He kept his hand on the hilt just in case Jafar had any ideas about taking matters into his own hands. He stepped over to Jafar's pot of boiling water and dropped his small flip phone in. He grinned at Jafar, then he turned and walked out the door of the apartment and onto the hot dusty street, where the police were waiting for him.

Jafar was completely exhausted. He pulled his chair over and sat down, not sure what he was to do next. *What does come next?* he asked himself. *What will they do with me know? How will they ever find Agib? This man will never tell them where my son is. I am sure I have lost my job. Do I go back to jail again?* Always so many questions and no answers. The smell of his tea brought him out from the daze he sat in, and he took a sip from his cup.

*

It was almost too easy Barad thought. The sting had lasted for less than an hour before handcuffing Hadid and putting him in the back of the squad car. Barad had spent days on stakeouts while working with Scotland Yard searching for members of the PIRA, many times with no results: bad intelligence, or their position compromised somehow. That always seemed the hardest part of an unsuccessful stakeout: *what had gone wrong?* The answer was usually never discovered.

This had been the shortest stakeout he could remember. The man they had been looking for walked right in as if he owned the place, unarmed other than the Arabian dagger. He had offered no resistance when surrounded by the officers.

"Not bad, and all before noon," Barad had told him happily.

*

Mark Mitchell joined Barad and the police at the station to assist in the interrogation as best he could. He hoped that the man they had in custody had useful information and was willing to talk. The attempt to find the missing boy was a police matter, he knew, but the shipment of explosives on an international flight operated by a US carrier was CIA business. He would have his turn at questioning the handcuffed man on the other side of the one-way mirror, and he would have the answers he needed one way or another.

Jafar was brought in to give a positive ID. He now looked through the one-way mirror from the opposite side, seeing Hadid sitting in the same chair that he himself had been sitting in just hours before.

"Yes, yes that is the man that came to my home," Jafar said, speaking his native language to Mark. "He had the diagram of the 747 and showed me where to place the box."

Mark looked at Detective Barad giving him a congratulatory nod and a smile. Barad smiled back and turned toward Jafar.

"Thank you for your help," he said. "We cannot release

you at this time, but if you will remain patient, I think your freedom will come soon."

"Please just find my son," Jafar replied as a police officer arrived to escort him back to his cell.

"Have you gotten anything from him yet, Josh?" Mark asked.

"He hasn't spoken a word since we nabbed him," Barad said. "I think when we tell him what he's up against, we might get some information from him."

"Let's go in and have a talk with our young terrorist," Mark replied, and they both turned and headed for the other side of the glass.

*

During the night, the Raine Airways 747–400 scheduled as Flight 25 had been unloaded, thoroughly searched for additional explosives, and reloaded. As everyone suspected, no additional bombs or suspicious packages were found. Bomb experts with the Dubai Police had been in contact with US Homeland Security, and the evidence shared between the two agencies revealed the bombs Scott had discovered to be an identical match, except for the composition of the plastic explosive, to those removed from the FedEx aircraft at the East Midlands airport in the UK. Authorities were relatively certain that the two bombs Jafar had placed on the jet were not designed to detonate in flight.

Mark Mitchell and the other agents agreed: The bombs that had come out of Yemen, as well as these now found in Dubai, were ultimately being shipped for use on targets in other cities. This meant someone had to be planted there to receive the packages. This latest attempt at a shipment proved just that, and in this case, the package was going to have to be taken off the airplane by someone involved. As Mark Mitchell tracked down the terrorists in Dubai, then, the FBI would work to find the cell in Cologne. If their plan worked, they would catch the pickup man red-handed.

All they needed, Mark thought, was the cooperation of Raine Airways and a couple of brave pilots.

*

Scott James's phone rang in his hotel room at the Dubai Fairmont. It was the third or fourth ring, and Scott tried to wake up and find the receiver.

"Yeah?" was his groggy hello.

"Scott, this is John Fenton. Sorry to call you at this hour of your day. I'll give you a moment to wake up—thanks again for keeping us up to date yesterday."

"I'm awake now," Scott said. "What's up?"

"I have some information to share with you," John began, "and a request. It appears as though the police and probably every government agency involved wants to try and nab the terrorists responsible for the package you found. They tell me that it was a bomb you found, but it appears it was never designed to take down your jet. The cops seem to think that it was intended for use by someone in Cologne. Now they need some help to arrest whatever terrorist in Germany tries to get the package off the plane."

"I can see where this might be going," Scott said, now wide awake.

"I figured you could," John replied. "They want to fly the regularly scheduled flight tonight and set a trap for the pick-up guys in Cologne. It might include some risk. Do you want the job?"

"Put me in, coach," Scott said immediately. "I'd like to help catch these guys!"

"What about Greg? Do you think he'll go along with it?"

"I'll call him right away. But I bet he will want to put his dog into this fight."

"Great, Scott. Thanks," said John. "You're going to get a visit from the agents involved. I told them they could expect full cooperation from Raine Airways. After your briefing, give me a call with an update. And if anything seems out of line, Scott, give me a call right away."

"Roger that, boss. I'll keep in touch."

Wow, a stakeout, Scott thought, looking at the clock on the night stand and still trying to wake up. *This is great; it will be like an aviation sting operation. And I would love to help nab some Islamic terrorist motherfuckers, especially the ones that tried to put a bomb on my jet.*

After a quick call to crew scheduling in Anchorage, Scott found that Flight 25 from Dubai to Cologne had already been rescheduled for later this afternoon. Departure time was four p.m. local. Now all he had to do was wait for the call from whichever agency would be involved next: the police, CIA, or FBI. He wondered which of them was running the show while he channel surfed the TV and pondered the adventure that lay ahead. Scott's next call was to Greg, who was probably still asleep on the thirty-third floor.

"Greg, Scott. How you doing? Hope I didn't wake you."

"No, I just got back from the gym. What's up?"

"Dude, you're not going to believe the call I just got from Fenton."

As he'd suspected, Greg needed no persuasion and was excited to be in on the plot. It was still mid-morning when the knock came on the door. Scott clicked off the TV and walked to the door, wearing his blue cotton sweat pants and white tee shirt and holding a cup of coffee. Standing in the hallway outside his room were several serious looking people, along with his copilot Greg, who was wearing a grin on his face.

"Come on in," Scott said, and the group shuffled into his

exceedingly large corner hotel room, a room that by most worldwide hotel standards would have been considered a large suite. Its twelve-foot ceilings and full-length windows on two walls provided a grand view of the morning sun over Dubai and the bright blue Persian Gulf.

"I'm Shauna Marshall, Homeland Security," said a woman in a dark suit. "This is Rob Morris, an agent with Great Britain's MI5, and agent Derek Johnson from the FBI."

"Agent Johnson," Scott said, trying to break the tension. "Doesn't every FBI agent have that last name?"

The agent smiled politely. "And this is officer Darzi with the Dubai police department, here on behalf of Detective Josh Barad, who's leading the investigation," Agent Marshall concluded.

Everyone's involved with this fight, thought Scott.

The plan was simple: The agents would place a decoy box containing two printer cartridges—as well as a GPS tracking device—in the exact location of the aircraft as Jafar had been instructed to leave the actual bomb. Rob Morris and Derek Johnson would both be riding in the plane. GSG 9, the elite counterterrorism unit of Germany's federal police force, would be in position on the ground when Flight 25 arrived. They would observe the pickup and track the package once it had left the airport.

"So what do you want Greg and I to do?" Scott asked.

"Nothing out of the ordinary," responded Morris. His British accent made Scott smile. "The perps here in Dubai have been told that your aircraft was broken and that the flight has been re-scheduled for this evening. As far as they know, the explosives remain on the plane where they had been placed."

"But we have another objective with this operation," Agent Johnson chimed in. "We have yet to capture the leader of this latest bomb plot. To help with that, we need the

Cologne cell to contact their supplier here to confirm that the delivery has taken place. That should get us the cell phone tracking we need, which will hopefully pin point the terrorists in Dubai."

"We want you to operate as normally as possible in all cases," Shauna added. "Since we don't know who will pick up the box, we do not know how much he knows about your normal operations. We don't want to scare him away."

"That we can do," Scott said, and Greg nodded in agreement.

"Then if there's no further questions, we will leave you to get ready for this evening's flight," Shauna said, rising from her chair. The other agents followed suit, ending the briefing with handshakes all around.

"We really appreciate your help with this," Shauna added.

"Wouldn't miss it for the world," Scott said with a smile.

"We will meet you at your airport crew area at, say, two p.m. local?" asked Agent Morris.

"Our crew area would be the jet itself, sir," Scott replied. "We don't really have our own crew ready-room here in Dubai."

"Jolly good! The jet it is, then," Morris responded, bringing another smile to Scott's face as he escorted them to the door.

"Wow, Greg," he said, returning to where his co-pilot stood at the center of the room. "We're now part of a covert anti-terrorist operation working with spies."

"And a real James Bond," Greg added.

"You noticed the accent too," Scott said, voice full of excitement. "Now that's something to tell the grandkids about someday."

"Yes, sir—the CIA, here we come," Greg replied.

"This should be a lot of fun, Greg, as long as we don't get shot."

"Yeah—and I wish that FBI guy would have added that as one of his objectives for this operation," Greg added, with slight concern on his face.

RESCUED

Agib had been bound and gagged for days now. He lay on what felt and smelled like a straw mattress on the floor of his lonely prison. He had lost track of time, drifting in and out of sleep, awakened periodically by his captors for food and the toilet—how often, he didn't know. The duct tape across his eyes had slowly loosened from wetness of his tears, and he could see light around the edges, but he couldn't tell if it was from the sun or a lamp.

His wrists hurt from the plastic bindings, and it was almost impossible to get comfortable lying on his side. In the moments he lay awake, his mind raced, tormented, trying to understand how this could have happened. His predicament no longer horrified him; now, only the longing for his father and his lost mother filled his thoughts. His captors had told him nothing of their demands, nor had they spoken to him at all.

My father has no money, not that I know of, Agib thought. *Why would we have stayed in this city if father were wealthy? Father's not in any kind of trouble, is he? Father is always with me or working. Is he looking for me? Why hasn't anyone come for me? Why do these men want me?*

These thoughts molested his mind, repeating over and over with no answers. After hours of mental torment he would drift off into light, restless sleep.

*

The man sitting handcuffed in the interrogation room, Mark had learned, was Hadid al-Otaibi, a Saudi born man with no criminal history in UAE that they could find. His father, however, had been a well-known dissident leader against the Saudi Government, and had lost his head over his beliefs.

The detectives had been unable to recover any data from the phone Hadid had dropped into the boiling water and his interrogation had started out painfully slow. Both Mitchell and Barad knew that men who believe in radical Islamist ideology took much longer to persuade into sharing their information. These men always seemed ready and willing to die senselessly at the whim of their deranged leaders, an ideology that Mark had always struggled to wrap his head around. Sometimes the process of persuading such madmen could take weeks and become deathly ugly—and in today's political environment, it was becoming even more difficult to achieve results. It seemed that the terrorists' civil rights had taken the forefront in the war that was being waged against them.

But as it turned out, Hadid al-Otaibi did not have either his father's calling or his radical beliefs. He believed only in himself and in the money he needed to survive. Mark was relieved to learn this: People who only believed in themselves were easy to threaten, using life in prison as a bargaining chip. Faced with the thought of life behind bars, Hadid began singing like a canary.

Finding Agib alive was foremost on Barad's mind, so the

interrogation concentrated on the boy's location. Hadid did not know the exact street address to which Atash had taken his captive, but he was able to show the agents on a city map of Dubai. The boy was being held in an apartment: a two room, two-story flat attached to the side of an auto repair shop in eastern Dubai—several blocks south, Mitchell noted, of the boat slip registered to one Ibrahim al-Asari. The boy was being kept in the back room of the second story. Detective Barad mounted a small force of Dubai police and headed for the apartment to find and rescue Agib.

Mark Mitchell stayed to continue the interrogation, focusing on what his prisoner knew about Ibrahim al-Asiri and his boat. The interrogation of this man went as quickly and as smoothly as the stakeout had, and Hadid provided answers to almost all of Mark's questions, including the whereabouts of the leader of the plot and the builder of the bombs, Ibrahim al-Asiri.

Hadid requested heavy terms in exchange for his information, and Mitchell had given him everything he had asked for. Mitchell knew it was safe to do this because that fact was that this young man would never stand trial in the UAE. He would be returned to his home country of Saudi Arabia, where kidnapping and terrorist plots were not treated lightly. Hadid would probably find himself behind bars for the rest of his days—or the subject of a swift execution.

*

In the flat, just outside the door where the captive boy was half-asleep, Ibrahim al-Asiri was furious. The plane had never left the airport, and Ibrahim had sent Hadid to the tug driver's flat to discover why the plane still sat at the gate, and where the bomb that had been so costly to produce might be now. Hadid had reported back by phone: according to the tug driver, the plane remained in Dubai due to a mechanical failure. The plane was still loaded with their package in place, and it would depart one day late. Neither Ibrahim nor his cousin Atash had seen nor heard from Hadid since. That had been over four hours ago.

"He is supposed to be here by now," Ibrahim insisted. "It is not like him to be this late."

"Hadid probably found another way to make a quick dirham, Ibrahim," Atash replied, attempting to ease his concerns.

Ibrahim thought this over. *What would Anwar have done,* he found himself thinking.

"I think we shall depart today, right now instead of tomorrow," he decided. "It will be safer."

"I thought we were to stay until the package is delivered to Cologne," Atash replied. "Your brother will have it tonight, and we can leave tomorrow as planned."

"But what if Hadid has been captured?" Ibrahim demanded. "If the police or CIA have him, then it is only a matter of time before he tells them of us and of this place."

"Hadid would never tell them of us, Ibrahim," Atash said. "He is trustworthy. A man of Allah."

"That will not matter," Ibrahim said. "They will make him talk, and there will be nothing he can do to stop it."

"No, Ibrahim, he would die before he tells them anything."

"They will not let him die, not until he tells all he knows." He tried to work it out logically. "If they have him, they will stop the package, and it will do us no good to remain—then we will be captured next. If Hadid is free, then the package will make it to Karim as planned. "We will leave the harbor tonight, as soon as it is dark and if Hadid does not show, then he will remain in Dubai."

Ibrahim was feeling intensely nervous at the thought. If the authorities had Hadid, he knew it was only a matter of time before he told them of this location. What was more, they would also have Hadid's cell phone—and they would now have his as well. He looked up at the ceiling, envisioning a missile dropping through the roof. *Does the CIA have drones over this land?*

"We must leave this building now," he asserted, pacing the floor of the small room. "If Hadid contacts us and all is safe, then we may all leave Dubai together, but right now we have no reason to stay here."

He tried to get a grip on what was happening. *Where was Hadid? Does the CIA know of our plans? Surely the police would not have freed Jafar to meet with Hadid had they discovered the bomb. But was Jafar really free? Maybe the police had captured him and sent him in as bait. And how do we know that Hadid actually met with Jafar? Maybe the police had even captured Hadid and forced him to place the call this morning!*

He had focused so hard on delivering the explosives to his brother, he realized, that he had not planned for this type of contingency. They should never have returned to this place after they had given Jafar the package. His plans were all falling apart, and he had to figure out how to reduce the damage. He had to get control. He walked to the sash hanging from the wooden hook on the wall that held his pistol.

"We must kill the boy now," he stated, looking at Atash with a panic in his eyes.

"That was not our plan, cousin," Atash insisted. "We can merely leave him or release him. He does not know us, nor has he ever seen us."

"We will kill him to show this Jafar that he cannot cross us," Ibrahim yelled. "To show the world we are serious in our jihad against the West!"

"No, cousin! He is just a boy! He can do us no harm and his death will serve no purpose."

Ibrahim stood at the door that led into Agib's lonely hell. He pulled the revolver from the sash and stared at it.

"Ibrahim," Atash pleaded. "The sound of the gunfire is sure to attract attention. Attention we do not want."

Ibrahim continued to stare at the pistol, and then he turned to face Atash. "If ever this boy becomes a problem, it will be you that I kill first." He hung the sash over his shoulder, replaced the pistol in it, and walked out of the upstairs flat. Atash followed him out.

The street was empty, and the heat rose from the scorching pavement in the mid afternoon sun. The two men walked briskly away from their latest hideout, heading in any direction that led them away, any direction that would give Ibrahim time to think.

Now what? Ibrahim asked himself as he looked around the area, feeling that the police were closing in on him.

"Thank you for sparing the boy," Atash said after a moment. Ibrahim said nothing.

They walked north in the direction of the marina. As they neared the large Al Itihad City Park, Ibrahim made a decision.

"We will wait throughout the rest of the afternoon and evening away from the flat," he told Atash. "If we do not receive a message from Hadid, we will take the boat and return to Iran. Back with friends. We can get assistance there, more money to carry on the jihad."

With that, Ibrahim sat looking around the park for anything, or anyone that seemed out of the ordinary. A small market at the end of the street would provide them some food for their dinner tonight and a few supplies for the trip across the Gulf. He reached into his sash and felt the cold steel of the revolver, ready to kill anyone who tried to arrest him, and he looked up past the palm trees that stood motionless in the afternoon desert heat, watching, waiting for the sky to fall on him.

*

Police Detective Josh Barad, along with a fleet of Dubai's finest, surrounded the service station and the small attached apartment building. They blocked the two side streets with their cars as numerous officers approached the building. Several cars were fueling at the petrol pumps. The attendants stared bug eyed as the police took up positions and escorted any bystanders to a safer location.

They found the flat just as Hadid had described it and began their assault up the stairs to the second floor. The door wasn't even locked. They discovered the boy just as the terrorists had left him, alone on the straw mattress bound in duct tape and tie-wraps. He was dirty and smelled of urine.

Detective Barad knelt down and helped the boy sit up. "It's all right now, Agib," Barad said in Arabic as he gently removed the tape from the boy's eyes and mouth. Agib squinted his eyes from the bright light and stretched his mouth. One of the policemen cut the plastic band that had bound his wrists. Dry blood covered his hands and sleeves from the tight binding that had secured him for days. He rubbed his eyes and ran his fingers through his hair.

"We are here to take you to your father now, Agib," Barad said with a smile. Agib was beginning to open his eyes and focus on the men that stood around him. "Can you stand up?"

"Yes, I think so," were Agib's first words.

"Where is my father?"

"He is at the police station waiting for you, Agib. Would you like to go see him?"

"Yes, please Sir." and Barad saw the first smile this boy had worn in a long time. "Let's not keep him waiting," Barad replied.

Detective Barad escorted the young boy to the waiting

police car as the officers searched the empty apartment. The terrorists had left nothing behind. Not even a scrap of paper was found in the rooms. The police would run the apartment for fingerprints and interview the owner of the apartment. Something might show up. With any luck it would be the next lead they needed.

*

Mark, after changing into a clean white thawb and ghutrah with a double-ring red ogal, stepped from the police station, donned his sunglasses, hailed a cab, and headed toward the small marina and the slip where Hadid had told them that Ibrahim kept his boat. He was hoping that, having had no word from his compatriots either here or in Cologne, al-Asiri would make an attempt to escape Dubai, and would make it soon. *A boat large enough to travel across the Persian Gulf,* he thought. A boat Mark planned to take out with his prey in it.

The marina was smaller than he expected as the cab pulled up alongside the single-door entrance. The sign in Arabic read *Mohamed's Slips, Pay in Advance.* Mark paid the cabbie and walked to the access gate at the side of the building. The gate was locked to keep the non-boat owners out. Mark walked to the glass door and into the marina. The back wall of the small building was mostly glass, and Mark could see a lineup of boats all moored to the concrete wall that lead out to sea. Some looked like commercial transports, and several fishing boats floated in the midst. He began to wonder how big Ibrahim's boat really was.

Sitting in front of the glass wall was a long counter covered with sale items. The remaining walls were covered with lines, pulleys, and fishing gear. Props, anchors, netting, and parts of every kind lay in piles on the floor; every available space was full. A man with dark, wrinkled skin wearing a white turban and smoking a Turkish cigarette walked in through a back door. He looked at Mark and gave him a toothless grin.

"What may I do for you today, fine sir?" he asked Mark.

Good afternoon, sir," said Mark. "I am interested in looking at a boat that is moored here."

"And why would you need to see this boat, sir?"

"I am thinking of purchasing it from a gentleman. He tells me that it is kept moored in a slip here. Would it be possible to look at it today?"

"Anything is possible today, sir," the man replied. He took a long drag on his cigarette, dropped it on the floor, and crushed it out next to several dozen others that lay next to it. "What slip might it be in?" he asked breathing out his smoke.

"I am told it is in slip three-fourteen. Do you know the boat?"

"I know this boat," said the man. "The price of my cigarettes keeps going up, you know. How important is it to you to see this boat today, sir?"

Mark understood the true nature of the question.

"I would consider it a favor if I was able to view the boat today, sir," he said as he placed a small stack of dirhams, almost one hundred US dollars, on the counter in front of the toothless man.

"This must be an important boat, sir," the man said, folding the cash and putting it in his pocket. "You will find it on pier three, seventh boat on the left."

Mark nodded at the man and walked out the back door onto the main pier that led along the wharf. He was not nervous, but all his senses were on high alert. Earlier he had considered getting his eyes in the sky—a drone aircraft to cover his ass in case of too many bad guys—but he didn't have time. It would take hours, even a day or more to get approval from King Maktoum for a CIA drone over his country.

He watched closely as he turned onto pier three, walking as if he were a fellow skipper of one of the crafts he strolled past. The boat in slip 314 was simple, about twenty six feet long, Mark figured, blue with an open bow, a pleasure boat that said *LARSON LXi* on the side. It had a white interior and two Honda outboard engines. The registration sticker on the side was from Dubai and was for the current year. It looked out of place among the large multi-million dollar ships that took up most of the harbor. No one was aboard.

Mark did a quick glance around the area and stepped aboard the boat. He sat down in the captain's seat, reached into the pocket of his thawb, and pulled out a small black box, a GPS device. He moved the switch on its side to ON, pulled a small piece of protective paper off the tape, and stuck it up under the dash, completely hidden from view. He stood, looked around the interior, and opened several side compartments, attempting to look like a buyer in case anyone on the pier had been watching.

He stepped back onto the pier and walked from the marina, waving at two sailors who were working on one of the fishing boats.

He would need to stake out the marina for the next several hours, he knew, long enough for Barad to find the boy. If the police didn't arrest Ibrahim at the apartment, Mark expected him to flee on his boat. Mark walked along the street from the marina, stopping at a small café that offered coffee and hookahs outside under the shade of a bright orange canopy lined with a short, decorative black iron fence. He declined a hookah pipe, ordered a coffee, and asked for a newspaper, sitting at a table that faced the marina entrance. *The perfect stakeout position*, he thought as he arranged his photo of Ibrahim al-Asiri in front of him and looked down at his iPhone.

His first call was to Creech Air Force Base in Nevada. It was time to launch a Grim Reaper.

FALL

Scott and Greg met with the agents at the aircraft at two p.m. as arranged. Derek Johnson from the FBI and Rob Morris from MI5 would be riding shotgun onboard Raine Air Flight 25. The flight crew was once again thoroughly briefed on the scope of the plan and the role that they were expected to play. It seemed simple enough to Scott. Just fly the jet to Cologne as scheduled and let the good guys catch the bad guys. It couldn't be easier, at least for him and his co-pilot. The onboard agents would be waiting for the fake bombs to be picked-up from the aircraft and Germany's GSG 9 would be covering the airport grounds, tracking the pick-up man as he left the airport.

The crew of Flight 25 completed their pre-flights and briefed their secret-agent passengers on the safety items onboard the Boeing 747-400. Catering had been provided for the crew and the agents and Scott explained how to use of the galley and its oven. There were no stewardesses on this flight and the meals would all be self-serve.

Engine start, taxi and take off were all routine and on schedule. Flight 25 was soon airborne into the setting sun leaving the Dubai coastline and flying out over the Persian Gulf. Flight time was scheduled at six hours forty-three minute with clear skies forecast along most of the flight route.

With no other passengers or jump-seaters onboard, both agents rode in the cockpit, neither having had the opportunity to see a 747 operated from the front seat vantage point. Initial cruise altitude was flight level three-five zero and as the jet and crew settled into the routine of cruise flight, conversation began on the probable events they expected on arrival.

The agents explained that the big unknown was the bagman. Who would be there to retrieve the now planted, bogus bombs? The Cologne airport police, along with GSG 9 had run a recent and thorough background check on all of the cargo handlers that could be involved with this arriving aircraft. Two men had surfaced with potential drug connections, but no prior convictions and no affiliations with terrorist activity. In fact no association or possible connections to any radical Muslim organizations had been uncovered with the twenty-two people that would be working cargo loading this evening.

One possibility, the agents explained was that of a third party, a victim such as Jafar who had been forced to put the bomb onboard the plane. Someone could have been blackmailed, or even paid to get the package off the plane and deliver it to someone or someplace. That would make the agent's jobs much more difficult and the hunt for the Cologne cell that much longer. The search on the ground continued for other possible suspects as Flight 25 continued their journey to Cologne.

*

Their descent into Cologne was relatively smooth and direct. At this time of the evening most passenger flights are over for the day leaving the skies relatively quite. The night belonged to the cargo operators and Scott enjoyed the quiet radio and empty skies that night flying offered. The weather in Cologne was reported as clear, temperature 11C, with winds out of the north at nine knots. The crew could expect vectors to the ILS for runway three-two right.

They were given their landing clearance and Scott touched down at fifteen hundred feet on the twelve thousand five hundred foot runway. He made the first left high speed taxiway with ease and exited the runway at alpha three. This taxiway led straight into the cargo area and both he and Greg were scanning the ramp area for signs of the GSG 9 troops that would be covering their ass. Nothing looked out of the normal as three flashlight-waving marshalers directed Scott into his parking spot. Scott knew this was a covert operation, so he was not surprised at the lack of police presence as they taxied to a stop. Both agents were seated in the aft jump seat area with the window shades pulled down keeping their presence hidden to anyone who may be watching.

"OK Greg, let the games begin," Scott said looking at Greg with a smile.

"Bait's set. Let's catch us a bad guy." Greg replied.

Ground power was quickly attached to the aircraft and Scott shut down the last running engine that had been supplying the ship with electrical power. Both crewmembers had numerous checklist items to accomplish as the crew stairs were pushed into position. Once they were in place, Scott left the cockpit and descended the yellow ladder-like stairs that led down to the main cargo deck, followed by both agents. The plan was for them to conceal themselves behind cargo containers, watching and waiting until someone took the bait. Derek had even mounted a small hidden video camera pointed right at the phony bomb to document the person taking it.

As soon as both agents were out of sight, Scott opened the main entrance door. He looked out at the immediate ramp area, trying not to look conspicuous. Nothing seemed amiss. He could see several ground personnel locking the stairs into position. He ascended back up the stairs to the cockpit where he and Greg had several remaining items to finish on the secure checklist. They had been instructed to remain in the cockpit, until the all clear was given by one of the agents.

Scott felt his adrenaline rise ever since he opened the door. Here he was, involved in a covert, anti-terrorist operation and he and Greg were about to watch a terrorist take the planted package off the plane. The aircraft tail stand, a tri-pod device placed under the tail section to prevent an inadvertent tipping of the aircraft while unloading, was locked into position as the K-loader drove up to left side of the fuselage. Scott watched his ICAS screen, a color display depicting an overhead view of the plane, show the cargo doors being opened one-by-one. *It won't be long now* he thought.

Looking outside the cockpit window Scott could see two people standing at the base of the crew stairs along the left side of the aircraft. One was surely the mechanic assigned to this jet, the other looked like a security man. Scott could see an arm badge and what appeared to be a handgun on his belt. He wondered if this was a security guard or a GSG 9 man. Armed security personnel around the aircraft were not surprising, due to the high dollar cargo that they hauled on a regular basis. Third party armed security services were present to receive many cargo shipments. Scott assumed he was here for some high dollar pick-up.

The mechanic walked up the stairs and was soon in the cockpit. "Good evening gentlemen," he said with a thick German accent.

"Good evening," was the response from both crews.

"Any write-ups tonight?" he asked, referring to any broken or inoperative items that the crew may have entered into the logbook and would now be his responsibility to repair.

"No sir. Clean jet tonight." Scott replied hoping the mechanic would not get in the way of the operation and at the same time, wondering if he had been briefed on the operation.

"Well then you gents have a nice evening," he said and left the cockpit.

"Wow Greg, do you think anybody is going to show for this set-up?" Scott asked. At that exact moment he heard a loud, fiercely aggressive German voice say something he did not understand. He and Greg looked at each other.

On the main cargo deck, just below the cockpit, the mechanic had stumbled upon the security man walking from the back of the cargo deck area towards the main entrance door. He was carrying a package of some kind under his arm. The mechanic knew immediately that this was not a normal operation for a security man, even if he was there to retrieve a package. That would be done inside the cargo facility, after the packages had been unloaded and cleared for release.

"What are you doing onboard this aircraft?" the mechanic demanded, this attempt in English, his voice rising even further as the man walked towards him ignoring his demand for an answer.

Karim al-Asiri did not hesitate. He drew the handgun from his holster and pointed it at the mechanic's face.

"Get out of my way Mike!" reading the nametag on the mechanic's overalls. His German had a strong Middle East accent.

Mike couldn't believe what he was looking at. The man's accent said it all and he knew he had just walked into something big. He raised his hands slightly and stepped back towards the door, blocking the man's escape route. This was not his real intent at the moment, but he was taken by surprise and was trying to think of a plan. At that instant, agent Morris peered from around the edge of the number one cargo container just behind the defiant mechanic. His weapon, a Beretta 9mm automatic, was pointed at the security man.

"Drop your weapon!" Rob demanded with the best German accent he could muster.

Karim's reaction was quick, one of a desperate man that knew he was trapped. He fired two shots at the weapon-wielding agent hitting Mike in upper left shoulder. Mike spun to his side and fell in front of the doorway. Agent Morris was hit in the right arm causing him to turn and fall over Mike. They both now blocked the exit and Karim's only escape route. Karim chose his only immediate path, the yellow ladder leading up to the cockpit and began a quick ascent. Derek Johnson, out from his hiding spot and approaching the bottom of the stairs, held his shot for fear of hitting Mike or Rob that lay behind his line of fire, but confident he now had the gunman trapped onboard the plane.

The gunshots had been loud and caused both Scott and Greg to jump from their seats in the cockpit. It was only four long strides for Scott's legs to reach the doorway at the top of the crew stairs. He opened the door that separated the upper deck with the main cargo deck below and was greeted by a man racing up the stairs, holding not only a gun, but also the planted package with the fake bombs.

Scott's reaction was immediate. He balled his right fist and punched the advancing man in the face with all his strength as he reached the top of the ladder. The result even surprised Scott. Karim had not had his hands on the either railing as he ascended the ladder and Scott's slug plummeted the terrorist back and over, down the yellow ladder-like crew stairs, over ten feet below to the aluminum floor and the waiting agents.

Scott watched as the man hit the floor, the sight making him cringe. The security guard landed on his back, his head hitting the floor with a dull bursting sound. Blood ran almost immediately from his broken skull. Scott could see both agents, their weapons drawn on the suspect as agent Johnson pulled the gun from Karim's hand, Morris favoring his wounded arm. The security guard did not move.

"Holy shit!" Greg said from behind Scott, looking down the stairs at the crumpled man on the floor.

"Yeah" was all Scott could think to say.

Derek Johnson pulled out his cell phone and called his counterpart at GSG 9 to inform him of the situation. They had two men shot and an on-site ambulance was standard procedure for any operation such as this. It would be the fastest help he could offer Agent Morris and the wounded mechanic. There was no help needed for Karim.

"You guys all right up there?" Derek called up the stairs.

"Yeah we're good, Scott said looking at Greg for his affirmation. Is that guy dead?"

"Yes sir Captain. Looks like you just took-out your first bad guy," Derek said trying to make him feel better. It didn't help. Scott turned and sat down in one of the first class seats behind him.

"Well that sucks Greg. Now how will they find the other terrorists here in Germany?" Scott said, staring at the open doorway.

Derek Johnson was at the top of the ladder stepping through the doorway. "Hey that's our job, we'll figure something out," hearing Scott's concern. "Nice job with the terrorist Captain. No telling how it would have unfolded if he had gotten up here and shot you or held you both hostage. You did the right thing. We'll get the others, don't you worry."

Greg handed Scott a bottle of water from the galley. "You OK man?"

"Yeah, I'm good. That dude had a gun. I'm thinking that's a real bad guy and not some dupe sent here just to pick-up the bomb, what do you think?" Scott asked.

"That would be my guess at this point in time, but we'll see how it turns out," replied Derek. "Give us some time to put this mess together and you gentlemen can head to your hotel. Again, nice job Captain. Thanks for all your help, both of you."

They all heard an ambulance siren approaching the plane. "You sure you're both alright?"

"Yeah I think we're fine, Greg you OK?"

"I'm great."

With that, Derek Johnson headed back down the stairs to check on the wounded men, leaving his latest *secret agents* to sit and ponder the day's events.

DRONED

Nightfall had settled upon the city park where Ibrahim and Atash sat, nervously waiting for word from their co-conspirators. The calls were long overdue, and Ibrahim was becoming convinced that both Karim and Hadid had been caught, or worse. He was sure that it would be only a matter of time before the police, the CIA, or somebody came looking for him, if they weren't already searching. The thought made him look to the sky.

How could this have happened? Ibrahim asked himself. *My plan was foolproof, even better than Anwar's. I so wanted to show him, show the world that I, Ibrahim al-Asiri, am a leader, a planner, and not a poor stupid man. I know I can make this jihad work if only I have competent people to follow me. Hadid was the one who foiled my plan. It is his entire fault. How could it not be? He must have gotten himself captured, the imbecile, and now we are all at risk.*

It was time, almost eleven p.m., and he could wait no longer. Ibrahim stood, motioning Atash to follow as they headed from the park for the nearby pier and the waiting boat. All he had to do was travel back across the Persian Gulf, returning to the small boat harbor in Iran. His friends were there; they would help him with his jihad.

Streetlights lit their path as they walked the distance to the marina. The sidewalks were empty of pedestrians except for the two terrorists, and traffic was light. Ibrahim continued to watch every corner for the police, holding a tight grip on his handgun. Both men quickened their pace as they neared the marina, entering through the large metal gate using a magnetic key.

The pier was dimly lit with yellow lights. Several of the moored boats had light glowing from their bridges, but the docks were quiet and void of people. Their boat was docked where they had left it. It had been re-fueled by the marina and had more than enough fuel aboard to get them to their destination.

Atash got the bowline ready as Ibrahim climbed aboard. He looked up at the sky, at any moment expecting to see or hear a drone circling overhead.

*

Twelve miles from a nation's coast is the internationally agreed upon line marking that counties' *territorial waters*. An imaginary, yet deadly line that foreign aircraft cannot pass over or conduct operations within, without permission from the ruling country. This was the line where Mark Mitchell and his team of drone operators would wait just outside for Ibrahim and his small boat to cross.

Target information and the tracker ID that provided the boat's location had already been uplinked to the satellites overhead hours before. The GPS tracker that Mark had hidden on the boat contained an internal satellite modem, allowing the precise location of the boat to be displayed on a moving map in front of the drone pilot crew sitting in Nevada at Creech Air

Force Base. In addition, the latest generation KH-12 spy satellite was programed to film the boat on its next fly over. Both the GPS and the satellite imagery showed that the boat had not moved throughout the day.

The flight time for a Grim Reaper from the US Al Udeid Air Force Base in Doha on the eastern shore of Qatar to the northern edge of Dubai at twenty five thousand feet was less than two hours. This evening's Grim Reaper, code named Sea Dog was now on station and could hold, circling, watching, and waiting for up to ten hours before it would have to return for fuel. Armament onboard was two laser guided, AGM-114 Hellfire air-to-ground missiles, more than enough fire power to take out almost any ground objective including tonight's target. A replacement drone would be flown into position to replace the Sea Dog before it left station, ensuring that the boat would be intercepted as soon as it left the Dubai coast.

It was exactly 2330 hours when Mitchell, sitting in the dark shadows of the now closed sidewalk café, watched Ibrahim al-Asiri and another man swipe their key at the entrance gate to the marina and walk toward the waiting boat.

"I have a positive ID on Ibrahim," he said in a call to Nevada.

He folded the newspaper, which he had read three times during the course of the evening while consuming numerous cups of Arabian coffee, stuffed it into the waste basket, and walked from the café through the small decorative fence, headed closer to the marina. In the low light of the evening, he could make out the men under the dock lights as they turned onto pier three and disappeared behind a large boat docked in the corner slip. He would wait just outside the marina to see whether either man returned.

A tracking screen to the right of the Nevada drone pilot sounded a beep to indicate that the GPS Mitchell had hidden aboard the boat was on the move.

*

The boat's motors came to life as Ibrahim turned each key, and he motioned to Atash to cast off the bowline. Ibrahim kept a sharp eye out as he slowly motored the boat from the slip into the harbor. The handgun still hung in the sash that he wore over his shoulder, providing a sense of security. Several men standing on the pier next to their fishing boat waved at the men in the small boat, but only Atash waved back. Ibrahim kept scanning the docks for armed men, expecting a police boat to stop his forward progress. But none came, and he motored out past the no-wake zone, slowly adding power and bringing the boat up to speed.

The Dubai evening was like most in the summer months in the Middle East, hot and humid with calm winds. A high, thin layer of clouds was blocking out the few stars that could normally be seen against the bright lights of the city. The Gulf's waters were smooth, and as the boat built up speed, Ibrahim's tension eased. He looked back at the dark harbor, the city lights reflecting off the ripples in the water left by his boat's wake. He saw nothing out of the ordinary and smiled, feeling like a free man, knowing he had escaped. They would never seek him in Iran, which lay less than five hours ahead. He was in no real hurry, and he kept a close look out for patrol boats and the fast pleasure boats that cruised the area. The small navigation unit on board showed a straight line across the Gulf and displayed their arrival at the small harbor close to sunrise. The fuel gauge showed a full tank, and the engine instruments were running in their green arcs. Atash walked forward to the bow, helping to scan for other boats, as the boat moved toward the line marking the start of international waters.

*

The Grim Reaper—tail number 155, operating as code name Sea Dog—had been on station now for two hours, having replaced the previous drone aircraft for refueling. The crew watched in Nevada as the GPS tracking device slowly moved across the map on the colored monitor that was mounted between the airmen operating the drone.

In the dark evening sky, Sea Dog's infrared camera picked up a small craft eight miles from the Dubai coast on heading three-five-five at thirty-two knots. The GPS tracking overlay confirmed that it was their target. After several minutes, the camera picked up the distinct image of two body heat signatures, as well as that of the boat's motors. The target was continuing north. If the small boat continued on its current course, it would soon be at the center of the Persian Gulf at this longitude, away from prying eyes. They were only waiting for clearance from the White House to take out the target.

Several commercial barges were in the shipping lanes that traversed the Gulf, passing the Strait of Hormuz through the Gulf of Oman and out to the Arabian Sea. Most of them were oil tankers coming out of Basra, now that Iraqi oil was flowing once again. If the target were cleared for a strike, they would have to avoid any traffic in the area. But the crew was confident that there would be little or no evidence of the boat left, just a bright flash on the horizon from any nearby ship's vantage point.

After a moment, the CIA agent on duty's phone rang. He answered, and then hung up after only a moment.

"Target cleared for strike," he announced to the Sea Dog crew.

"Sentinel copies."

"Pilot copies." Sea Dog began a descent to fifteen thousand feet in preparation of the planned strike.

All three operatives followed the target, watching the heat signatures of the two men in the middle of a boat outline as they raced across the sea and the Grim Reaper, unheard and unseen, pursued it from high overhead.

"Target nearing position," announced the Sentinel.

They armed the weapons and completed the checklist. "What's the distance to closest commercial traffic?" asked the agent.

"One tanker at eighteen miles, traveling twenty-two knots."

"Clear to engage," directed the agent.

"Pilot copies. Sentinel, lock onto target."

"Sentinel copies, target locked."

"Roger. Launch auto track."

"Established."

"Laser."

"Laser selected."

"Arm laser."

"Laser armed."

"Fire laser."

"Lasing. Target in range. Three, two, one, rifle."

There was a pause, and the crew's adrenaline spiked.

"Three, two, one, impact."

The infrared screen exploded with a bright, intense light.

*

Mark Mitchell stood along the waterfront next to the marina and watched a small, bright flash on the dark, smooth horizon of the Persian Gulf reflect off of the high, thin clouds. He took a drag from his cigarette, crushed out the butt with his shoe, and smiled as he exhaled the smoke. His cell phone rang.

"Yeah," he said, answering.

"Completed," was the response.

Mark hung up the phone and walked toward the street to hail a taxi. He had one more task.

HOME

The slush fund, Mark Mitchell liked to call it. Petty cash. Emergency money that enabled him to achieve the results expected from a CIA operative with his expertise. Today, the result he wanted was to give Jafar and his son the chance to get back home, away from the hell that they had both just been through.

Mark knew that the odds of a fair outcome for Jafar in the Dubai justice system would be slim. He had admitted to planting the explosives on board the Raine Airways airplane, which would ensure that he spent time in prison, regardless of his son's kidnapping. But the real perpetrators of the bomb plots were now either eliminated or in custody. So why was there a need to detain Jafar and Agib any further, Mark wondered?

His taxi ride to the police station where Jafar sat in custody took less time than it did to hail a cab at this time at night. He made a call to Detective Josh Barad while en route, explaining his plan.

"I want the CIA to take custody of Jafar and Agib," he

explained.

Barad, asleep at home when he got the call, was at the station waiting when Mark walked in. Both men knew that this was the best chance to send the two back to their home country.

They both quickly persuaded the State's prosecuting attorney—anxious to be rid of his latest foreign prisoner—that releasing Jafar to the Americans was in everyone's best interest.

Still housed at the police station, Jafar had been made as comfortable as possible while Agib was residing at the Dubai Youth Hostel, compliments of Mark and the CIA. Mark walked unescorted to Jafar's cell. The cell area was clean and looked new, but had the jailhouse smell, and Mark hoped not be too long. Jails gave him the creeps.

"Good morning, Jafar," Mark said in Pashto through the yellow bars of his cell.

"Good morning," Jafar replied, not rising from his bunk.

"I have an important question to ask you."

"Even more questions?" Jafar said. "I have told you all I know."

"What will you do if and when you are released from here?" Mark asked.

There was a long moment of silence. Mark waited, and Jafar cleared his throat. Speaking, his voice cracked with emotion.

"I came to this country to build a better life for my son, to work and earn an honest living, to earn enough money to ensure Agib's education. Now, thanks to some mad men, I am sure to rot in prison and Agib is sure to fall to the likes of the Taliban." He turned and looked at Mark. "How can you ask me this when you know they will never release me?"

"Would you return to Loralai?" Mark asked.

"I would like nothing more than to return with my son to

our home," he replied, staring up at the gray ceiling.

Mark smiled. "I think I can make that happen."

Jafar sat up on the edge of his bunk. Slowly, he turned toward Mark.

*

Scott and Greg arrived back into Anchorage, their last flight leg in from Hong Kong after two weeks of flying to far off places around the globe. They walked into a hero's welcome at Raine Airways' Flight Operations. The office was full of people, including John Fenton and his entire staff, all of them offering handshakes and congratulations to the two heroes. Jenny Christine was there with a big hug. The party had her handwriting all over it, Scott knew. Many of Scott and Greg's closest friends were there, and everyone wanted to hear the story of the terrorist and pilot's act of heroism. Scott's takedown of the terrorist had made the front page of most American newspapers, and he was suddenly Anchorage's hometown hero. He played down his role as best as he could, thanking Greg and the agents on board for their work and leaving himself out of the story.

It was a party, but it was still the middle of a workday for most, and the group soon disbanded. Scott and a few friends left the airport, gathering at The Bradley House, their local watering hole, already filled with pilots and business folks alike in for an early evening libation. Even here, Scott was the celebrity. He settled for a single beer, thanked Greg for the great flying, and headed home to get Bair and check on his house.

He was looking forward to the next day. Maggie was arriving in the morning to pick up where their vacation had left off so many days ago.

*

Margaret and her NTSB team had completed their on-site analysis and all the investigators and scientists had departed the crash site, returning to Washington to finalize their findings. Her final report would be presented to David and the UAE government for their official review and release. She had her doubts that the true facts of the accident would ever be officially released, and that *on-board fire with undetermined cause* would be the final answer from the Dubai authorities. No blame toward any Arabs—even a terrorist like Anwar al-Awlaki—would ever be put in public print.

Margaret left those issues in Washington and departed for Anchorage, where several weeks of vacation with Scott were waiting. She sat in the third row of first class on the Alaska Airlines flight from Chicago with under an hour to go. Time now to forget about the stress, the heat and the sand of the past weeks, and leave it all behind her for the next three weeks in the cool weather. David had faded from her mind somewhat, but she knew she would be in distant contact with him in the future, and the crash of Flight 6 was far from over, the final outcome had yet to be written. She counted ten men that had lost their lives over this latest senseless act perpetrated by insane Muslim extremists. The number could have been so much higher. If Flight 6 had impacted into the large apartment complexes that lay all around the accident site, hundreds of innocent people would have died. Countless lives had already suffered due to the loss of Flight 6: wives, children, even the families of the terrorists that had been eliminated. The thought made her head ache. Instead, she tried to focus on the *People* magazine she had in her hands. The jet had already started its descent into Anchorage, where Scott would be waiting.

*

Jafar's emotions were mixed with joy and disbelief as he and Agib walked toward their first class seats aboard the United Emirates B-777. The American agent, Mitchell, had personally driven them to the Dubai airport, escorting them as far as the security checkpoint.

"Thank you," Mitchell had said sincerely, "for your help in eliminating the terrorists." It made Jafar feel proud, with a new hope for his future after all he and his son had been through. Mitchell left them both with a handshake and an envelope.

The kind people at the hostel had given Agib a new backpack for his trip home, complete with snacks, magazines, and a new iPod equipped with games and a headset. The stewardess politely helped them to their seats, offering water and juice. First class was a new experience for them both.

How things had turned around, Jafar thought, as he looked out the plane's window at the tugs passing below him, pulling dollies of luggage. The stewardess returned with their juice. Agib's full attention was in his iPod, and he did not notice as his father thanked her and took a sip of the cool drink.

Jafar felt inside his small pack for the envelope that Mark had given him before saying goodbye. It was a plain brown pouch, sealed closely with a red string wrapped around a small peg. He unwrapped the line and opened the flap. Tipping its contents out, he was startled to find a banded stack of US one hundred dollar bills. His heart raced from what he saw, and he quickly stashed the bills back into the envelope, looking around to see if anyone had seen them. Agib was still intent on his game and paid no attention. Jafar slid the stack back out. His mind was spinning. He thumbed the cash—there were somewhere around two hundred bills—and then placed the envelope into his pocket.

His palms were sweating, and he felt hot even as the cool

air from an overhead vent blew on his face. It was far more money than he had ever seen at one time. With this money, and with what he had saved while working in Dubai, he would have enough for Agib's schooling and a home of their dreams. His hands were shaking and he closed his eyes, hiding his tears of joy.

*

It was early August in Alaska, and summer was in full swing, with many days of salmon fishing left in the season. Scott was planning his attack in detail. The Alaska All Over tour, he had told Maggie. There were some Alaska towns that neither of them had visited on the agenda, and he hoped to finish filling his freezer with fish over the next week or two before heading off to Chicago for all the fine dining the Windy City had to offer, a visit to Maggie's relatives, sailing, and more.

As he pondered the fun ahead, the reality of the past weeks entered his thoughts and seemed to overwhelm him. Don and Mike had been lost so far from their home, and now their families had to carry on without them. *Was it a bomb that brought down Flight 6? Were terrorists to blame for their deaths?* He thought about the briefings he had received from Agent Johnson explaining the drone operations that had put a stop to the terrorist cell sending the bombs. *At least we took out the sons of bitches that started all this. Still, ten people lost their lives over this Muslim bullshit, and two of them didn't deserve it.* The thought made him angry. He stood up from his desk and walked over to Bair, giving him a hug.

After a while, he sat up. "Time to get Maggie, buddy. Want to ride along?" Bair's response was instant and affirmative, and they both headed for the truck.

Flight 6

*

Mark Mitchell's C-130 touched down in Sana'a. The latest intel had heavy AQAP activity in and around the city of Radda. The demise of Anwar al-Awlaki and his henchmen had left an immediate power vacuum, and Mark knew revenge would be on the minds of the latest terrorists that assumed control. Once again, he would be returning to the never-ending battle against radical extremists.

He had been hoping for a few days off in Hawaii, but that would have to wait.

ABOUT THE AUTHOR

David Henry is a pilot and 747 Captain for a major airline. He spends much of his time flying around the globe and flight instructing. He has been flying since the age of sixteen.

He is a Purdue University Graduate with extensive writing experience, authoring numerous trade articles and pilot training manuals. It was the Loss of Flight 6 in Dubai, 2010 that sparked his interest in moving from technical writing to that of fiction and suspense.

Blue ocean sailing is one his favorite past times. He lives in Anchorage Alaska with most of his family, where he spends his free time writing, boating and fishing for salmon.

www.ingramcontent.com/pod-product-compliance
Lightning Source LLC
Chambersburg PA
CBHW072204170626
46813CB00003B/784